Between Greek Balconies

OTHER TITLES BY FRANCESCA CATLOW

Little Blue Door Series:

The Little Blue Door

Behind The Olive Trees

Chasing Greek Dreams

Found in Corfu

Other Fiction:

The Last Christmas Promise

Another Greek Summer

Greek Secret

Under a Greek Sky

Reminders of Greece

Between Greek Balconies

Francesca Catlow

LAKE UNION
PUBLISHING

Published by Lake Union Publishing, Seattle

www.apub.com

EU Product Safety Contact:
Amazon Media EU S.à r.l.
38, avenue John F. Kennedy, L-1855 Luxembourg
amazonpublishing-gpsr@amazon.com

ISBN-13: 9781662538599
eISBN: 9781662538582

Cover design by Emma Rogers
Cover image: © wallerichmercie © Pixel-Shot © Wilm Ihlenfeld © yalcins © Altug Galip / Shutterstock; © Roman Sigaev / Adobe

Printed in the United States of America

This book is for my mum and dad. Thank you for sharing beautiful places with us. If you hadn't, I'd have nowhere to set my books!! Love you both more than words. xx

Chapter 1

> Hiya, Auntie Alisha. I can see you're there. How is it? As good as the pictures? I hope so. I'm low-key jealous but mostly missing you already. Let me know everything and try to relax! Love you.

It's nice to hear Odina dropping me a voice note. Her upbeat tones always bring me joy, even if it is dreadful to be told to *relax*. If only there were a button one could press to achieve such a goal.

I don't know about the house itself, but Mandraki is better than my memories and certainly more vivid and dreamy than any photograph could ever project.

This street, which is just a normal street here, is lined with white-rendered houses, others with exposed stone – presumably volcanic – or painted peach or lemon. The one to my side has windows edged in a pale lime.

I wonder if there's an agreement on the island that paints should only reflect clouds or the soft pastel colours of fruit.

My Saint Laurent bag slips down my shoulder for the umpteenth time, trying to escape me. I can't blame it. I shift my weight in an attempt to keep it with me.

It's stuffed to the brim with my laptop and books. It's the reason I've been sweating since arriving in Kos last night and all the way across on the ferry today. That, and the surprising warmth of September on this tiny Greek island.

Contrary to Odina's suspicions, I haven't *actually* arrived at my new home in Mandraki, Nisyros yet. I'm probably only a few doors down, though.

I had hundreds of similar '*have fun*' and '*relax*' messages from friends and colleagues before I got on the plane. Each was written as though this is just another holiday or fun trip abroad, not a forced sabbatical.

I drop the weight of my handbag on to my suitcase as I scan the street, not knowing how much further it'll be until my new home is upon me.

Trust Odina to take it one step further and be tracking my every move on her phone, only to message when I'm moments away from seeing my new digs for the very first time. She's a self-confessed online stalker. I only let her track me so I could track her in turn. Now she's seventeen, she won't let Augustin or his wife, Nancy, track her anymore.

It's an unspoken rule that I can't tell them where she is, but Odina also trusts me to keep an eye on her. I'm grateful for all of their trust. As the middle child between Augustin and Toby, I somehow became the mother hen, being the only girl. Sexism at its finest, but we all settle to our roles at times.

I lick the salt from my upper lip before I begin again.

My suitcase rattles along the uneven stones for a moment more until I recognise a set of dark wooden doors shaped in an arch, each with two small windows. I've only seen it in photos, but I've spent the last month studying those images well enough to know these doors are mine.

Inhaling a steady breath, I fill my lungs with the thick, clean air of island life. I might be from my own island, but this is nothing like my home in Kensington. Here, the air is fresh and lightly salted with a hint of mint, perhaps from one of the balconies overhead.

Pink and peach flowers trail down between the wooden bars of the balcony above, weaving their unruly vines out of their pots.

My balcony. It must be mine.

All the other doors along this street are various shades of blue, from bright cobalt to a rich shade like the Greek flag. Mine stands out as older, and traditional; although I have every urge to paint it blue right away, there's something regal about the difference. It's almost like a small church door.

There's a lone black moped resting in the shade not far from me, with a cat, equally obsidian in colour, lounging across the seat. Other than that, no vehicles are to be seen and I'm alone in the street.

The moped is next door, outside the worst-kept door in the row. The bright blue is flaking away to reveal the green of a former life.

I slip the heavy key into the door, and for the first time ever, I feel like I live on a planet empty of human life. The key clicks to the backdrop of chirping birds and the hum of electricity wires, but nothing more.

I push the doors open with a Halloween-esque creak, and two stone steps lead me down into the first of the living areas. I lug my suitcase inelegantly down each step.

Inside my new home is the stale smell of neglect, with a touch of mildew.

I agreed the previous owners could leave some furniture, knowing it would be sensible to have something to arrive to before buying new or having things shipped over from England.

That's the thing about having money, you don't need to think about things too much.

I slide off my oversized bag from my shoulder, carefully leaving it a short way from the front door, and begin to voice-note Odina in return.

Hello, Odina. Yes, I'm here now.

I hit pause on the note and slip my feet out of my Birkenstocks to silence them on the cool tiles before continuing. It's hard to know how to describe it all to her. The white walls still hold the faint lines of photo frames that have been removed, like the shapes left by bodies lined with chalk on trashy TV crime series.

I move from one small stone room to the next with my phone hovering not too far from my face, waiting for me to continue.

She's going to want me to be upbeat about it, as though this is all my decision, as though this is where I thought I would be at this time in my life, swanning off to Greece to try something new, even though we all know that couldn't be further from the truth.

I snatch a breath and try to continue.

> I'm now inside my new home. It's lovely and cool inside compared to the baking heat in the sun. There's a stone chimney breast and log burner ready for the onset of winter. It's all lovely. There's a quaint wooden bench they left behind for me in this room too, so I have somewhere to sit, and . . .

I trail off and hit pause on the recording again as I enter the kitchen. There're sea-foam-coloured wooden units, just how I imagined when I wanted to live on the island as a child. I just wish the circumstances were somewhat different.

I thought I would be coming here to celebrate my successes, perhaps buying a holiday home, not wishing to dissolve from the acid burns of my failures and trying to figure out if I'll ever be able to act as a barrister again, the only job I ever wanted to do, or whether I'll be able to carve out a new life and a new passion.

It never mattered to me how difficult it was: the long hours, the occasional death threats and the never-ending streams of emails and deadlines. My job was important.

I close my eyes tightly shut and lean my back against the stone archway that joins one room to the next. My stomach squeezes like fabric being wrung out and I can feel the pressure in my chest of a panic attack throbbing and swelling.

No. I have to find air again and finish this message to Odina or run the risk of her calling me. I can't have her worrying about me, that's not her job.

I take a moment to push out two shaky breaths and quickly continue with a lump locked in my throat that seems to have been there for the past few months. I don't want my voice to break and give my emotions away. This has never been a problem before. I've always been able to lock it away and get on with what needed to be done.

> . . . and, I miss you too. You'll have to come and visit in October half term. It's only a matter of weeks away. I love you. Say hi to your mum and dad for me.

My body quakes a little, but I'm relieved to make it to the end and to have figured out something normal to say.

Now, if only I could figure out a new normal for my life. Right now, that seems like an impossible dream.

Chapter 2

This is a world away from my sweeping apartment with foot traffic and cars down below. The sound of other people living their lives has become a comfort to me.

Peeling myself off the wall after a little too long trying to calm down, I take to the stairs to discover the bedrooms and second living area. Only one room should have a bed, for now at least. That was all agreed before purchase.

A swathe of organza floats across the open door of the first of two balconies. The other is in the master bedroom.

Behind the organza, the balcony is stuffed with plants. There's a large pot brimming with mint and another with leaves that almost sparkle in the light as it trails between the dark wooden bars of the parapet.

This is the balcony that has a safety indication, which is why it has plants on it, to prevent it being used. The whole place could do with having a little money spent on it, but I'm not going to do that, not unless I decide to stay past six months.

All the doors have been left ajar. The bathroom is to the left of the small rectangular living space, and the bedrooms are to the right.

I'm desperate to see my new bedroom in the flesh. I don't mind. Space isn't everything, I wanted this place because it was the only one available with a slice of a view.

The bed is a decent size, perhaps larger than a standard double, with a solid wood frame. Another piece of fine organza hangs across this balcony door, but no light streams in as the shutters are closed. The room smells of wood and the pausing of time.

I draw back the organza, tug open the door and push open the shutters with a creak. The warmth of the late-morning sun dances on my face, drenching me in vitamin D. The glowing white of the buildings reflects and gleams. It's enough to bring me back from the brink and settle my nerves. Which is exactly why I'm here.

The balcony is a wooden structure that juts from the building, with a single metal chair. The floor is marked with a few rings where pots once held plants but only one has been left on this balcony, as though it were forgotten when the rest all moved home to the other one. It's been abandoned on the thick top of the parapet.

Maybe it wouldn't fit with the other plants. Looking across to my left, there was no obvious space left on my other balcony.

Behind the crispy dead plant in the blue ceramic pot is the reason I purchased this specific house. A sliver of a view out to sea and across to the island of Kos. The sky is clear and pale, making the sea look dark and mysterious from back here.

This is what I need. The sight and sound of the sea to calm me after everything that happened at work. It's taken me a couple of weeks to not just verbally agree with my peers, but to internally agree that I *do* need time away. That having a panic attack in a judge's chambers is perhaps a sign that I am not able to handle everything that happened back in July.

Here, at least, I'm fulfilling a lifelong dream of living on the volcanic Greek island of Nisyros, and I can figure out what happens next with my life . . . one way or the other. But accepting this concept took time, and up until now I've been going through the motions.

A cough splits the air, making me spin around so quickly I knock the plant pot to its final death in the street.

It's lucky it's quiet here. In London, that might've killed someone.

The man sitting on the balcony to the right of mine leans forward in his chair to inspect the damage below us and I do much the same. The blue pot has shattered beyond repair and dirt has scattered from the epicentre like a spiderweb.

'*Kalimera*,' he says in a gruff voice as he lifts one dark eyebrow at me.

My new neighbour's wearing a loose-fitting cotton shirt that looks like it's never seen an iron. It would be hard to say whether he is against daily shaving or has made a poor attempt at designer stubble.

Either way, it all oddly suits him.

He has devastatingly dark eyes, full lips and a touch of silver creeping in at his temples. He no doubt has a wife somewhere who appreciates his good looks, so I probably shouldn't.

We are so close, my balcony is almost kissing the one attached to his house.

'*Kalimera*.' My tone has never sounded so meek. I'm used to filling courtrooms with my voice without even thinking about it, and here I am squeaking at a hello.

'*Tha thélate éna tsigáro?*'

My Greek is extremely limited, and although I know I'll pick it up quickly, I haven't had a chance to start yet. I was good at languages at school and I can speak Latin, of course.

His deep eyes must have read the lack of understanding, though, as he nods slightly and says something else.

He raises a cigarette to his lips and the packet towards me.

I'm almost tempted to say yes to his offer.

Up until a month ago I hadn't had a cigarette in fourteen years, three months and six days. I choked over the one I had a month ago, just wishing it would numb the tingling of my nervous system. It didn't work.

I only started smoking at university to deal with the pressure I felt I was under, and perhaps in slight rebellion against my father and his preaching from what he would see at work as a doctor.

'*Óchi, efcharistó.*' I wave and shake my head to make sure my *no* is understood.

He cups his hands around the cigarette and lights it, taking in a deep drag. Smoke billows up around his face.

The man looks up and meets my eyes.

'I'm Alisha, your new neighbour,' I say slowly. My Greek has pretty much reached its limit, outside of knowing a few fruits and vegetables.

He squints at me. His blank expression tells me everything: he doesn't speak English. Nor should he have to, I'm the immigrant here, showing up and buying the place next door.

'Alisha.' I tap my chest to make it clear.

'Helios,' he indicates in return.

The formality is quickly over and I'm left staring at a handsome stranger who I can't communicate with.

'Well, I do hope you have a nice day. *Antío*.'

Helios nods.

I shuffle back off the balcony and away from the gorgeous man with bad habits.

I slump down on to the hard creaky bed in front of me and for the briefest moment I close my eyes and see Helios with his pouting lips wrapped around his cigarette.

It's the first time I've closed my eyes and managed to think of someone other than Karine.

Chapter 3

After cleaning soil, a dead plant and shards of blue plant pot off the street with a carrier bag and my bare hands, I was gifted exactly two hours of relaxation time. Since then, other gifts have been trickling in.

First it was Iris, with a tray of homemade moussaka and a fritter of some kind called a pythia that's made of chickpeas.

Iris told me about a book club. All the books are in Greek but she's pretty sure many are translated from English so I could probably still read along with everyone else.

Then came Theo and Daphne, who are perhaps the same age as my parents and speak very little English. They were very smiley and gave me my second tray of moussaka and some lemons from their garden. Or that's what I think was said.

Now Calliope is here, with very near-perfect English, better than my Greek anyway, telling me about her mother's jewellery shop in town.

She brought me a piece of pumice, too, knowing that many of the other women would bring food to welcome me to their corner of Mandraki town, and she thought I might very well be overwhelmed with it all. But she has promised to bring me food another day.

'Will you have more furniture to sit with?' Calliope leans on the kitchen counter with the confidence of someone who doesn't owe anyone anything.

I like that.

I like a woman who knows her mind and doesn't stand like her very being is an apology. It's my hobby to call women out who say sorry too much when they've done absolutely nothing wrong. Even though I often catch myself partaking in the same frustrating practice.

Calliope has no requirement for make-up. Her wild brown curls are just about contained by a claw clip and she's in jeans and a navy T-shirt with the sleeves pinned up with safety pins. It wouldn't matter what she wore, she's quirky and stunning. Not beautiful, but interesting, with a dusting of freckles and eyes as sharp as any cat.

'Yes, my assistant is arranging a delivery of things to arrive in the coming days.'

'And what it is that you do before you move to our island?'

'I was a barrister, specialising in human rights. Particularly women's rights.'

My mind momentarily slips back to Harriette, Francine and Yori. The other barristers in my chambers. The ones, along with the judge, who called for the first-aider when I had a panic attack and thought I was having an allergic reaction.

'That's a big job. Why did you leave?'

'That's a complicated question. I'm not sure whether I *have* left, exactly. I'm here to . . .' I pause a little longer than I mean to as I try to formulate something I should've worked out by now. I'm also unsure how much I want to share with a woman I've only just met. '. . . I'm here to gain focus, find peace and make a decision about my future, I suppose. I want to try new things.'

I could go on. As a barrister, I can always go on and talk up any side of any debate.

I could continue to tell her I was sick to the depths of my bowels with sexism and the ability of people to wear each other down faster than a hurricane sweeping across an open field. Or the truth that I was advised to take some time off. Banished away to figure out if I can handle my job anymore.

Burnt out.

I hate that term, but there it is, that was what they told me when I arrived in hospital unable to catch my breath. There was no allergic reaction to something unknown, it was a simple panic attack. Something I had never experienced before.

I was burnt out like a discarded car. Even though I knew exactly the moment that I was set light to, it's too late. I'm a shell now, and either I can fix myself and become who I was, or I find a new job. A new role in life. Something else to whittle away time while earning a living.

I've been a fool, from the moment I was last on this island right up to forever, and now I'm here to *change.*

'It is hard to carry on with a job when you don't know how you feel about it. I can understand this very well.' Calliope studies me with a squint, as though she's trying to take a peek at my soul. 'I should be going, but if you need help when the furniture arrives, then you tell me. I will bring strong men to move things.'

'Like Helios next door?'

'You're here one minutes and you know his name? I am impressed. Very impressed.' She wags a finger at me and smiles behind it. 'But no, I bring some men who smile with me.' Her slender eyebrows very slightly flick up and there's the hint of an eye-roll before she peels herself away from the counter.

One of the skills important to a barrister is that of reading people as well as textbooks. I'd hedge a guess that Calliope isn't struck by my neighbour all that much.

'It was nice meeting you. Feel free to pop in anytime,' I say, and actually mean it.

'And you come to me very soon for a good strong coffee. The house with the big pots outside the door, yes? Big red pots. It's easy to find me.'

'Thank you.'

I walk just behind her towards the front door, closing it when she leaves.

Quiet descends once more between the white walls of my new home.

My phone beeps from the kitchen counter, where I've left it on charge. I head towards it to find another voice note from Odina.

> Just because you are having the most enviable brat-summer doesn't mean we don't get it. I still think you should do what I said and send a note or something to Karine. It can't hurt and it might help, you never know. I know you don't want to talk about it, but what happened is clearly at the heart of what's going on. If you deal with . . . *that*, then maybe it'll help you figure stuff out. Mum says I should basically leave you alone, by the way. Or 'leave you be' is actually what she said. Anyways . . . who needs a couch when you have the beach? Go sit and relax in the sand. Love you, queen.

I do my best to sidestep my first thought of *What on earth is a 'brat-summer'?* but it's tricky to avoid the question rolling around my head. I'm used to Odina sounding like she's insulting me while promising me it's complimentary, so I'll go ahead and assume it's meant in a positive way and google it later.

I don't remember being so upside down when I was seventeen. But then to the average thirty-eight-year-old, maybe I was.

I pull back the tinfoil on the first moussaka, the one from Iris. It smells divine, like fresh garlic and oregano have been lovingly blended together.

My stomach groans at the idea of it.

I've not really eaten much all day. I've been skipping breakfast since university. Back then, I was opting for expensive coffee to spend my money on.

Now I'm suddenly starved.

I pull on the nearest drop handle and tug the drawer open to reveal a stale smell of old wood but no cutlery. Automatically, I reach for the next and the handle pulls right off, leaving the drawer closed and me with what looks like a small door knocker in my hand.

Discarding it to the worktop, I begin trying each drawer, only to find more of the same.

'Hey, Siri, how do you say *Do you have a spoon I can borrow?* in Greek.'

I can't translate into Greek pops up on the screen.

Closing my eyes, I slowly draw air into my lungs and calmly release it.

'Fine,' I say to myself, or perhaps my phone.

Perhaps the people the other side of me speak English and will kindly help out their new neighbour.

I march out of my house and into the warmth of the sun and the smell of freshly cooked pitta emanating from an unknown source. Turning left, I put on my best smile and take a step up to the house attached to mine.

Rapping on a door is an art form. Too hard and an aggressive impression is made; too soft, and no one hears it.

I do my best to keep the taps light-hearted in rhythm, but loud enough to be caught even by someone a few generations above mine.

After waiting the socially acceptable fifteen seconds, I knock again and wait another thirty counts.

Nothing.

I try the door opposite, but apparently everyone is out enjoying their day except for me.

When I was in Nisyros with my mum and pop all of thirty years ago, I remember telling them I wanted to knock on all the beautiful blue doors.

I close my eyes, tilt my chin to the heat of the September sun and shake my head. This isn't what I meant, and I've changed a little bit in that time. I guess I should remember the old adage of be careful what you wish for.

Bringing my chin back level, I stare at Helios's uncared-for door. Not the sort I imagined myself knocking on back then.

I wonder whether he has a family hiding in there with him. Something about Calliope's reaction to him tells me he doesn't. His moped is still outside, so the chances are he is my only hope for cutlery.

It's time to play charades with the dishevelled-yet-handsome Greek next door.

Chapter 4

When presenting myself at Helios's home, I don't quite manage my well-rehearsed decades-old knock. It comes off a little sharper than usual, more aggressive.

I step back and begin to count to fifteen.

At the end of the count, I wait a moment more before stepping forwards and raising my fist . . . just as the door swings open, releasing the most intoxicating scent of freshly cooked pitta.

That's where the smell was coming from.

Helios raises both eyebrows as his eyes land on my balled fist, hovering in mid-air to hit a door that's no longer there. I quickly lower it, flick my dark hair off my shoulder, lift my face into a smile and try to collect my thoughts, and my Greek.

'*Kalispera* . . . again. *Signómi*, sorry, do you have a fork or a spoon, perhaps? That I could borrow?' I do that irritatingly British thing of speaking slowly and loudly, as though this is the magic sprinkle for people to understand our mother tongue.

I understand his repetition of the word *signómi*, but that's about all. I'm not actually sorry, I just don't have another Greek word to soften my uninvited arrival at his home.

'Erm, I don't have cutlery.'

As I begin miming eating with a knife and fork, Helios slides his weight on to the wall and scrubs his fingers along the stubble of his chin.

Heat rises up from my toes all the way to my cheeks.

Generally, I'm not one to feel embarrassed. I was brought up knowing how to conduct myself with confidence and to value myself. It takes guts to argue for what you believe in within a court and to never back down even when mistakes are made, but there's something about the way this man is looking at me that leaves me feeling a tickle of something uncomfortable.

My arms flop down by my sides. I'm not going to stand here and continue making an utter fool of myself when he would clearly never win at a game of charades.

'Not to worry.' I begin stepping back, resigned to the fact I'm about to find out what it's like to eat layers of lamb, aubergine and bechamel sauce with my fingers.

He says something in Greek then disappears inside his house, leaving the door ajar. I'm not really sure if I'm meant to follow him, wait on his step or just leave. I take the opportunity to be nosy and peek into his home.

Like mine, it has two steps down into the living room. He has simple tastes with a house full of functional items, all except for a sideboard stuffed with photos. It's across a side wall, so I can't see what's inside the frames, but there's got to be at least twenty photos, including one or two larger frames at the back.

I step back out towards the street. That way, if he does ever return, I'm not caught with my nose in his door.

Only a moment or two later, he reappears with a knife, fork and spoon.

'*Efcharistó polý.*' I put my hands together in gratitude before moving to take them.

There's a moment as our hands come together and fumble as we nearly drop the spoon.

Our eyes meet in a laugh, and I could swear it's not just me who lingered on it. There's a moment, a beat, before eventually Helios steps back and lowers his eyes.

Everything in my chest tightens, so much so I have a brief fear that there will be a panic attack around the corner, but this tension is different. It's looking into the dark chasm of his eyes while wrapped in the smell of pitta that's putting me off balance.

Helios's face stays in a gentle smile as he shrugs and says something else I don't understand. His eyes meet mine again and I can feel the warmth of the smile still lingering on me before he nods and closes the door.

My heart is skipping as I turn on my heels and study the decorative handles of the cutlery he's handed me. It's more elaborate than I'd have imagined based on the simplicity of his home. There's more to him; I could feel it in his touch and the look in his eyes.

He might not give the famous Greek welcome, but I'm more than happy with a neighbour who keeps themselves to themselves yet will lend me things when needed. In fact, that is the *best* type of neighbour to have.

The bonus, of course, is how easy on the eyes he happens to be. There's no harm in having someone nice to look at now and then.

Walking the few paces back home and down into my entrance room, I close the heavy wooden door behind me, grab my laptop case resting against the wall and carry on through to the kitchen. Placing down the cutlery on the counter, I slip my laptop from the case and open it to watch something online while I eat, only to remember there's no internet yet and I don't really want to use all my data on being mindless.

Scooping up the now almost cold moussaka and my recently donated spoon, I slide down the cabinet to the floor, ready to shovel it straight into my mouth.

As my spoon slices through the cheesy topping, two hard knocks beat down on my front door, making my heart jump up to my head.

I had hoped I was done with today's quota of the meet-and-greet.

I clamber back up and replace the moussaka, carefully covering it up again so it looks untouched before jogging towards the door.

Taking a breath, I swing it open and smile broadly . . . at absolutely no one.

The muscles in my face crumple as I'm faced with the row of whitewashed houses opposite and nothing more. I stick my head out and look down the road, but unless it was a cat, it was a knock and run.

As I slowly retreat back down my step, the reflection of the sun on foil catches my eye. A small silver parcel on the doorstep shimmering and hoping to be noticed. I pick it up to find it's warm. The smell gives away the contents before I even open it.

Pitta.

It must be a gift from Helios.

It feels as though my lips have been hooked by a wire and someone else is tugging them up little by little into a smile.

This time when I sit on the floor, I bring my laptop with me and peel back the foil of the pitta to take a taste of the soft white bread.

It was kind of everyone to offer me food when I had none with me.

Karine did that for me once.

It's not quite the same. I'd left my purse in a taxi and she got me coffee and a cake. My chest tightens at the memory.

Maybe Odina's right. An email couldn't hurt.

As I thoughtfully chew on my bread, my fingers move slowly over the keys.

06.09.2025

RE: Forgive me

Dear Karine

I know this is pointless, but I still had to send this email wishing you could forgive me. I let you down. We both know I let you down. I will never be able to forgive myself, so why would you? I can only hope for some sort of redemption.

I'm in Nisyros now. I remember our shared love of the Greek islands fondly. There's an intriguing man who lives next door. He left me some fresh pitta on my doorstep. I'm not sure why I'm telling you that. Perhaps in the distant hope that we can all believe in good people again? Perhaps that it's nice to be around people who have no idea who I am or what I've done. That have no idea how broken I am.

Thinking of you always.

Alisha x

Chapter 5

I woke up to the slight vibration of the heavy wooden bed beneath me. It took me a moment to register that it was the power of Mother Nature nudging me out of slumber with a mild earthquake to remind me *today is the day.*

That, or she's telling me to get up and sort out the remaining boxes of last week's delivery of random things I clearly thought I couldn't live without for six months of island life.

I did my best to keep it simple. I already had my large suitcase filled with clothes that I brought with me, so my delivery included all the things I couldn't fit in the case. Like a small dining-room table, chairs, lamps and anything else my assistant, Gigi, thought I might need. She knows my taste, and has done a good job. She's been invaluable throughout everything, a friend as well as a colleague. I share her with one other barrister in our chambers. Or I did.

I can make a coffee just like I used to back in London, as they also brought my coffee machine, thank goodness.

Since being forced to take a sabbatical, I've regressed to my early teens and started sleeping in until past eight in the morning.

Usually, I'd be up with the lark, sometimes going for a brisk walk or a jog, other times getting straight to work, depending on what was needed.

Now there's not much to wake up for. No one waiting to talk to me about their clients and the details of cases, no meetings, no coffees or dinners with friends or family.

Although, I have been given enough free food to last another day at least from kind neighbours welcoming me to the street. I do wonder, judging by the portion sizes, whether some assumed it would be more than just me living here alone. Not that I'm complaining.

I thud down the wooden staircase a little quicker than I have over the past few days and set the coffee machine to grind the beans and steam the milk, in my usual routine. Then I sit down on one of my new kitchen chairs, resting my elbows on the highly polished wood of the new square table, the way I have every late morning for the past week.

Today is the day I start something new.

The criterion is relatively simple. It needs to be something relaxing and something that I could earn a living from. Perhaps not the money I'm used to, but as I've barely spent the money I've earned over the years, other than buying my home in London and now in Nisyros, I could concede a considerable pay drop and still have a comfortable life from sensible investments made.

This change should be quite easy for me. All through my academic career I excelled, never having a grade slip below an A, even in the subjects I didn't care for.

I'm determined to make this a fun endeavour, and at the end of the six months I'll know whether I'm able to return to my old life in London or whether I've found a new one here in Nisyros.

Pushing back the chair, I stand and knot my fingers together, bringing my arms over my head into a stretch until my back clicks to realign myself.

Pulling one of the four mugs I had delivered from a high kitchen cupboard, I finish making my coffee and head back upstairs, cup in hand, to fetch my laptop.

I'd been staring at it last night, wondering whether to send Karine another email. Odina thinks it's a good thing, sort of therapeutic, and even if nothing positive comes from it, it can't hurt to write it all down.

I think she's right. She's always been insightful for someone so young. There was a lightness that came with sending Karine an email. A strange mixture of releasing my thoughts and, perhaps, hope.

Picking the silver rectangle off my dresser, I open the balcony door and the shutters to sit on the lone chair with the laptop. I enjoy looking at my sliver of sea from here, between the houses and bright-blue balconies.

It's not much, but I love it.

I do my best to check Helios isn't sitting on his balcony without obviously turning to stare. All seems to be clear. The sun is rising over the houses in that direction, so I would be loath to squint over at him just to say good morning and feel like I should retreat indoors for want of things to say.

Leaving my coffee cup on the edge of the balcony, I open up my laptop and start a note. Today is going to be the beginning of being proactive. The first list should be things I want to try, then things I must do.

I note that I'd like to try my hand at painting and crafts, but first I think I'll write a book. I've always said it was something I thought might be fun. Mum and my younger brother, Toby, always make writing look so very easy. Odina too. I might not have their poetic way with words, but I'm sure I could craft a story that's literary, insightful and meaningful, even if it doesn't have their flair – that surely comes in the redrafting anyway. So today, I might start with that.

But first are the *to-do*s. A walk to clear my mind ready to write, food shopping, and I must pop in and see Calliope, but before all of that, I must give back Helios's cutlery.

I look at the top right-hand corner of the screen. It's Thursday the 25th and over two weeks have elapsed since my arrival on the island. That's too long to hold on to someone else's cutlery, particularly when mine arrived days ago.

Thursday. I must remember to call Pop later this morning too. He ended up ringing me last week as I'd forgotten again.

Since Mum passed away two years ago from cancer, I ring him once a week on a Thursday, and if for any reason I need to change the time or day I always let him know. Apart from last week, as I slept all afternoon until he called me instead.

He had retired early at sixty-two so he and Mum could travel and spend time with Odina. They looked after her once a week through the summer break when she was small.

He went back to work in the private sector two days a week after Mum passed away. He was amazing through her cancer treatment, becoming her doctor as well as her husband, looking after her until there was nothing left but skin and bones.

It broke him. It broke us all.

When I see him now, he looks more like a man of eighty-five than a man in his early seventies. He does his best to fill his time and avoid looking into the void she's left. That's what he said to me once after a few too many whiskies and streams of tears.

She's embedded in everything he owns. He can neither part with things nor look at anything without wanting to scream that life is unfair. He told me that too. The pain has remained deep and raw.

I can't imagine being so consumed by love as to feel such a deep loss as he describes. Other than the love I hold for my family, of course, but never with a chosen person who I've decided I *must* have in my life or everything around me would break.

I tried to persuade myself I *did* feel like that, ten or more years ago now. I soon realised I was trying much too hard for it to be *real.*

It's since then I realised I was happy enough on my own. I didn't need to try to fall into the clichés of modern life.

I don't want to have to constantly think of someone else. Some people find that selfish, but I think it's quite the contrary. I would defend anyone's right to freedom of choice and their right to live a free life, even their right to dislike my choice, but most people haven't seen the things I've seen.

Most people read the AI-generated or edited news via their social media platforms, which has been tailored to their very own echo chamber of thoughts, so they often miss seeing the realities of the dark side of humanity there in front of them. If they do see it, they're seeing it only from the view they've chosen and their online presence, which has been honed over time.

Whereas I have been behind the scenes of those headline stories, and many that never get spoken of because they would shock the public so much they are hardly reported. Where once I perhaps did want a husband and a family, now it's my worst nightmare to bring life into this world, particularly a daughter, because I know I can't protect them from everything. It's hard enough with the love I have for Odina. So instead, I do my best to make the world a better place for others.

Or at least, that's what I *had* thought I was doing. It was my intention, my vocation.

Karine's face forms behind my eyes. Her dark hair chopped to frame her face, her boyish attire of crisp white oversized T-shirts tucked into tartan trousers and a matching blazer.

That was what she was wearing the day she walked away from me, slipped into a cab and left for good.

I move from notes to my email, suddenly unable to hold in other words I should've said to her. Tomorrow will be two and a half months since I last saw her.

25.09.2025

RE: Thinking of you

Dear Karine

I count you as an old friend, you know? I have many acquaintances, people to take cocktails with, people from university and work who I socialise with, but you have always been so *real*.

I remember the first time we were introduced. We were at a bar not far from the Houses of Parliament. It was your birthday, and I had been invited by Penny to come along for a drink after work. I can't even recall now how you two met?

I loved to hear you talk about your life, not just because of your luxurious French accent, but because you were so passionate about your role as an investigative journalist, and how you had just finished a two-year stint in the Congo collecting information on big oil companies and their long list of crimes against peace, humanity and the natural world.

I was barely starting out back then and I was in awe of you. Everything you had achieved to help others.

I snatch a breath as thoughts catch on the hooks of memories, threatening to travel to my eyes in the way of tears. I swallow it all back with a gulp of my rich coffee. The sun has been keeping it warm for me, and it hits hard on the back of my throat.

My hope is that time here will do more than keep my coffee warm. It'll thaw me too.

I type a quick sign-off and hit send without even reading it back or taking a moment to think about it too much. I usually read emails twice for consistency and flow. I shouldn't, it wastes so much time, but I always do.

It's too late now, it's sent.

I flick away from my emails and back to my list. It's clear the order they should be achieved: Walk, get food and visit Calliope and then write a book.

But before all of that, I need to drop the cutlery back to Helios.

Chapter 6

My heart flutters the way it would if I was about to give a closing statement in court, and I haven't a clue why.

I manage my light-hearted-but-firm knocks on Helios's door and begin to count the obligatory fifteen seconds. He answers in seven seconds.

He's wearing jeans and a well-worn navy polo shirt. He pushes glasses back from his face into his messy mop of hair and blinks at me like he can't quite make out what or who I am.

I'm glad I put on a little make-up and let down my hair.

'*Kalimera*,' I smile. '*Efcharistó polý* . . . again. For the erm . . .' I look down as a pure black kitten rubs around my ankles. 'The, erm, cutlery.' I hold them out for him to take.

He says something that I, again, don't understand.

I can't help but be distracted by the kitten softly standing on my bare toes in my sandals. For a small creature, it has a purr like a motorboat.

Helios goes to take the cutlery from me and his fingers almost take mine along with them because I still have my eyes glued to the sweet kitten strutting about between us. It's almost as bad as the last time.

'Sorry,' I laugh as I try to disentangle my hand from his.

'*Signómi*,' he mirrors me in Greek, and we share a moment's bashful smile all over again.

I could almost believe there was purpose to it, but perhaps he was looking at the kitten too, I can't be sure.

At least body language is often readable across cultures. There are, of course, exceptions and variations, but usually a shared smile is easily understood.

He breaks our eye contact first, taking one step back down into his house. He's quickly followed by the kitten, who hops down the steps and trots into the house like it belongs there.

Leaving the door to gape open, Helios begins ranting, not harshly, going by his tone, but more of a monologue as he gestures to the kitten with the silverware in his right hand.

'Isn't it yours? The kitten?'

He stops talking to the ball of fluff sniffing gently at his armchair and fixes his eyes on me. If I didn't know better, I would almost think he was irritated at the laugh in my tone, but he's probably trying to work out what I'm saying.

He answers me, or perhaps he doesn't, because all I can understand is no, *óchi*, and *mou*, my or mine. A sensible hunch is that the kitten isn't his.

I squat down at the top of the three steps into his living room and reach out my hand while making the mandatory kissing noises made by all cat lovers when trying to make a new furry friend.

The kitten turns to look at me with a tilt of its head before trotting over with the trust and naivety of a dodo. That's what it is to be young and impressionable, I suppose.

Taking the kitten carefully under its front legs, I tuck it into my arms in the same manner I would a baby before commencing the act of chin-tickling and cheek-rubbing.

I've wanted a pet for some time, but it would be cruel to keep them locked up indoors all day, and most days I wouldn't even get home in time to feed them at a sensible hour. However much I knew I'd love them, it wasn't a kind undertaking in London.

Helios places his handful of cutlery on the sideboard with all the photographs and comes back over to the door, fixing his eyes first on me, then on the kitten in my arms.

The ghost of a smile lurks in the corners of his mouth, desperately trying to hide in his stubble as he strokes the kitten and mutters something else in Greek. I'm not even sure whether he's talking to me or the kitten.

'Do you think she belongs to anyone? The cat.' I look from the kitten to him, hoping he'll magically understand me, only to roll my eyes at myself. I might as well zip my mouth shut for all the good opening it does me.

I continue to talk to Helios under the high-pitched guise of soppy talk to the kitten. 'It doesn't matter now, does it? Huh? Nope. I'll get there, won't I? Give me time to clear my mind and I'll get there. I'll speak Greek. Yes, I will. Yes, I will.' The kitten squirms and pushes its cheek against my fingers as I go from stroking to tickling.

I look at Helios to address him instead of baby-talking the kitten. 'It's not your cat. Whose cat is it? You can't help me, of course. I'll leave you be. Thank you again for the cutlery. It was most generous of you.'

Helios takes his hands off the kitten and says, '*Antío*.'

I repeat his goodbye as I step out of the shade and back into the sun, still holding my new-found friend.

I look down at the fine threads of black fur beginning to coat my white T-shirt. It's lucky I don't have to be anywhere important.

It's nice to have that freedom for the first time since childhood.

I carry the kitten a few paces away from the door before turning back. I catch Helios still looking at me, a smile lingering on his lips, before he quickly vanishes back inside his home.

If only he spoke English . . .

It's probably best that he doesn't because I'm sure I'd get myself in a lot of trouble with a scruffy sexy man like him.

Chapter 7

'I'm going to put you over here,' I say, placing down the kitten. 'But if you *are* another stray, then I might have to adopt you, because you're much too cute.'

She begins rubbing round my legs again before strutting towards my front door to flop down, as though the last five minutes have taken it right out of her.

'It looks like you might be adopting me,' I whisper as I take in how perfect she looks sitting on my doorstep. 'I wonder whether you are a girl. You're very pretty.'

'*Kalimera.*' A voice coming up beside me makes me jump enough that even the kitten jolts, puffing up its fur ever so slightly.

'Calliope, *kalimera.*' I press my hand to my chest to feel my heart racing beneath. 'I was going to come to see you later.'

'Then you come now, I make us coffee. Good Greek coffee.'

'Sounds lovely,' I agree. Even though I've often found Greek coffee a touch rich and sweet for my taste, I wouldn't want to be rude. 'Can I carry one of those bags for you?'

Calliope's arms are tense under the weight of whatever is in her plastic carrier bags.

'No, no, it is good to carry things around, and here, we are almost there already.' She nods towards the end of the street.

Taking a quick glance back towards my new front door, I see the kitten has curled up and already looks ready for a snooze in the shade.

'Do you know who that kitten belongs to?' I look from my door back to Calliope as she holds a strong pace down the street between the houses.

'Its mother?'

'I take it that means no one. It's a stray?'

'Yes, I think so. I don't think anyone on the street will be taking all the fleas into their homes today.'

I graze my hands over my T-shirt to brush off the fine layer of fur as I consider how many fleas could live on a kitten that size. If I want to keep her, I'll have to get to a vet and buy everything she needs.

As we reach the end of the road, where the street winds into another in a staggered crossroads of sorts, Calliope's house sits on the corner.

It's easy to pick it out. It sits back from the others, with the big red pots either side of her indigo front door. The pots are bursting with flowers, all the same British-postbox red as the pots they're in.

Her home is on the opposite side of the street to mine and that bit closer to the sea.

Without putting her bags down, she swings open her front door, which is of course not locked, and steps into her entrance hall. The layout is different to mine, along with the decor.

A decor I didn't expect.

It's very busy, something I'd anticipate from someone a generation above Calliope. Although I've yet to see an icon hanging from the wall like I remember seeing when I was here as a child, and in other traditional Greek village homes on my travels.

Calliope has ornaments and photographs everywhere. Her many knick-knacks include Greek evil eyes, small statues of mythical creatures and even a large painting hanging under her staircase of what I imagine must be Poseidon at war with someone or other.

It's not what I expected, and yet I'm not at all surprised by her collection of things.

'Poseidon created Nisyros in a great war. I will tell you about it some time. But, for now, you are here tomorrow, yes? I do a big party for you to welcome you to our corner of the island. Everyone is coming.'

'For *me*? A party for *me*?'

I follow her through to her kitchen, which isn't too dissimilar from my own. There are used mugs and breakfast bowls here and there that reflect a busy house. As soon as she drops the bags of food on to the kitchen table, she begins to tidy things away with the efficiency of someone who does this every day without thought.

'Yes, yes. You will come.'

This is not said like a question. This is a command, albeit a kind-hearted one.

'Well yes, thank you, that's very kind of you.'

'It's nothing,' she shrugs as she puts another cup into her dishwasher. 'Sit, sit.' Calliope points to one of the wooden stools around the table and I quickly do as she requests.

Calliope begins making the coffee with the *briki* on the stove as she chats away about food for the party. She begins to put away her shopping, which I now gather is almost exclusively for tomorrow night's do.

In no time I have a cup of hot, sweet Greek coffee in front of me and Calliope leaning against the kitchen cabinet quizzing me.

'Why here? Why this tiny island in all of Greece? In all the world?' Her eyes shrink to slits as they focus on me under her curly bangs.

'When I was a child we came here on holiday and I announced that one day I would live here, because I liked the doors and the cats.' I take a sip of my coffee as I consider just how odd this statement to be.

It's the truth, though, and when I was forced to leave my beloved London for a time, this was the only other place I'd ever shown an interest in living. So it was the first and only place that came to mind.

Calliope shakes her head with a distant look of disbelief.

'You are a strange lady. Most homes here owned by foreigners, they rent out or come on holiday. Most like the sea, volcano or food and traditions. You like the scavengers and doors.'

I shrug. 'I like all those things too. But when I was eight, I wanted to knock on the doors and keep all the cats. And what about you? I take it you've lived here all your life?'

'Yes, I am very boring. My family has always lived here. My husband's family moved here from Kos two generations ago because they did not approve of all the tourism. They thought it would be over quickly. They were right, of course.'

Calliope arches an eyebrow before burying her nose into her mug and I chuckle into mine.

She tells me about her life here, how she helps her mother with her shop in the summer when it's busy and how she used to help with all aspects, until one day she realised it wasn't what she wanted to do.

'It was easy to be helping my mother all the time, but when my sons all left the house, I start to feel . . .'

'Disillusioned?' It's an easy suggestion, it's how I've felt since everything with Karine.

'Yes, this is a very good word. I realised my whole life was lived for other people. I married young, had children straight away, help my mother with her love of jewellery. Then what is for me? I'm still working this out.'

'Maybe we can work it out together? I was thinking of writing a book. How hard can it really be? And if not, perhaps I could try my hand at painting, or perhaps jewellery-making?'

'I like this idea. You help me, I help you. I teach you jewellery. I think maybe I want to help people, maybe to get them moving. Maybe yoga or breathing and meditation. Maybe when people visit the island they want to look at the sunrise from the mountain and feel better as they meditate. There is a friend I went to school with, Dimitri. I was talking to him about the energy of the volcano before he goes to England. He can heal people and make them better with his hands.'

I keep my face blank. I'm well practised in nodding along and not giving away a single thought in my head.

It's an important skill for a barrister. It would be dreadful to give away anything that the opposition could use to their advantage when working a case.

Right now, I'm hiding my thoughts and queries as to the skills of this individual. My father is a *real* doctor, after all. I have faith in modern medicine and have heard all too many times the stories of people falling victim to charlatans claiming to heal things they can't.

'Is he a doctor? Dimitri?'

'Oh, no. He is a tour guide.'

I nod my head and do my best to stay open-minded, against my better judgement.

Calliope continues without a prompt, 'He heals with his hands and the energy of the volcano. You know Kos and Nisyros are the birthplace of modern medicine.'

It is true that even my father has always thought there is some very interesting energy around volcanoes. Perhaps that was why he dragged us around so many of them.

Pop . . . I can't forget to ring him again.

I twist my wrist. Ten twenty-five. I'm meant to call in five minutes.

'I think people would love to look out across the sea while doing yoga or meditation. If that's what you want to do, then you should. You should get qualified and set up some classes.'

'And you will help me? When I start a class, you come? Yes?'

'Of course.'

'And I will help you. I can teach you jewellery. You have to do the book on your own, but when you write it, I read it. It will help me with my English.'

I let out a long breath and study this woman before me. A woman I've only met twice yet has offered me as much help as people I've known for decades.

My organisation hat drops on to my head. The voice that gets me organising Gigi around the chambers when I need my assistant to find something in among boxes of files or something researched for a case.

'I'll get some chapters to you in a week, and you need to find out what qualifications you need and how to get them. Unless you've done that part already?'

'No, nothing. I've been living in dreams.'

'Well, I'll leave you to your morning, but we will reconvene soon. We are now accountable to each other. I'm also very interested to meet this Dimitri when he's back from England.' I stand up from my stool. 'Thank you for the drink. What time should I arrive tomorrow for the party?'

'When you are ready.' Calliope shrugs and places her cup on the counter so she can walk me out.

'*When I'm ready?*' I chime back at her.

'Yes, that is fine.'

I maintain my composure, but inside my stomach twists and my toes curl.

The idea of not being given a set time for an event is almost repulsive to me. I don't want to arrive too early or much too late. What if I'm ready at nine in the morning and it doesn't start until nine at night?

'I'm not used to such broad time frames. Could you give me a clue as to when you might be ready?'

She chuckles to herself as we reach her front door. 'Maybe, eight? When people start walking to my house, you will know they are also ready.'

'Perfect. I'll see you tomorrow at eight.'

Calliope locks eyes with me. Fine lines crease the corners of her eyes and a warm smile lifts her face.

'You are a strange woman, Alisha, but I think we will be good friends.'

My phone starts to ring from the pocket of my chino shorts as I share a goodbye with my new friend.

I know it'll be Pop, beating me to the punchline. I pull it out and look at the screen.

It's not Pop's name there, it's my older brother, Augustin.

Augustin almost *never* calls me. Not unless there's a problem.

Chapter 8

'Hi, little sis. How's island life?' Augustin's cool tone does nothing to dampen my anxiety. He isn't one to call for the sake of small talk, even if he partakes in it.

'You are aware you also live on an island? It's just that Britain is bigger.'

'Ninth largest in the world.' His tone is much too upbeat.

'So I've been told.'

Instead of heading back home, I carry on down the winding roads in the general direction of the sea so I can get some shopping done.

'None of that answered my question. How's island life?'

'I'm sure Odina has been keeping you up to date. Things are going well here. I have furniture now and she's planning to come and visit me next month during half term.'

'That's actually why I'm calling.'

As I meander along between the cats and the blue doors, a chill runs along my spine. I pull myself tall, ready for a fight.

'Oh, really? I'm happy to pay for the ticket.'

My brother – the talented and renowned plastic surgeon who is always given the most difficult jobs working with children who have been badly burnt or disfigured, who could afford just about anything he likes and is always in high demand – is as tight as the head of a needle when he wants to be.

'It's not that. It's Odina. Something's happened.' Augustin snatches a breath, but the tiny pause is long enough for me to have her dead and buried.

My heart breaks and my feet falter underneath me, jerking me to a standstill as an older couple walking towards me nod and greet me with '*Kalimera*.'

I do my best to nod and smile, but it's tough.

'What do you mean? What's happened?' rushes from my lips.

'I don't know. She went to the cinema with some friends, and when she got home she locked herself in her room and wouldn't come out. Not even for dinner. On a *Sunday*. Nancy tried everything but there was no getting through to her. She thinks she's so grown-up but she's a kid. Seventeen is nothing. Has she said anything to you? She went off to college this morning without breakfast and frankly, she looked dreadful. She's been strange ever since.'

It has to be bad. Everyone loves Nancy's Sunday roast dinners. Which always seems strange to me, as she's American, and a Sunday roast, to me at least, is quintessentially British. Either way, not a person on this planet who has tried her Yorkshire puddings or her crispy roast potatoes could possibly deny how great they are. I remember once Odina announcing that if she were on death row, or something similar, and was asked what she'd like as her last meal, it would be one of her mother's roast dinners.

'She hasn't said anything to me. Although she hasn't messaged me much this week. Do you want me to call her?'

'No, she'll know we've asked you to.' Augustin clips his words the way he likely does with a patient who needs to be told something when they're not listening. He's very well spoken, and that's coming from *me*.

'So what do you need from me?'

'Keep us in the loop. I know you would never break her trust or go behind her back. We know that, of course, but if we *need* to know something, if we need to do something . . . You're not just around the corner anymore . . .' A sigh breaks out of him and I can almost see him rubbing away at what's left of his thinning hair.

'You know I'll always put her first, and that includes telling you something if I think you need to know it.'

'Thanks, sis.' His tone is a little brighter, but it still holds the broken edges of a distraught parent. 'I'd better go, I've got a patient coming in soon. Nancy told me to send her love. Also, with this trip . . .'

I brace myself a second time, ready with the *I know she's still young, but she can be trusted and I'll be at the airport waiting for her* bit.

'Maybe she could come sooner? I was thinking just before the start of the break . . . maybe in three weeks? If she wants to?'

'Of course, I'd love to have her.'

'And you're happy to pay?'

My eyes roll up to the pale-blue sky overhead as I do my best to suppress a laugh.

'Of course.'

'Great. Once you arrange it with Odina, let me know.'

'Love you.'

'Love you, little sis.'

With that he's gone, leaving me with more anxiety, not less like I'm meant to be creating, and I'm late calling Pop again.

Chapter 9

I toy with the idea of messaging Odina and telling her openly about her father's call. Giving her the knowledge and the power can help her to feel safe with me, but I don't want to disrupt her relationship with her parents.

I think better of it. Instead, I skim to the app that will reveal her location and check where she is. She's at college now, exactly where she should be. There's nothing more I can do.

The thrumming of a moped calls along the winding street and I tuck in as best I can to the nearest house.

I look over my shoulder to catch the focused eyes of Helios on me as he bombs along the street on his moped with no helmet and only jeans and a T-shirt for protection.

He nods as he passes and I return it with the same simple gesture.

That man is truly wasted being single. I'd say he is a little older than me, perhaps in his mid-forties. He holds himself in such a way that could break hearts. He has that *I don't care* look about him that shouldn't be attractive but inexplicably is. If he didn't live next door, he would be perfect material to have a few nights of fun with.

That's something London was very good for.

For a long time I've had no time or interest in a relationship, but I could quite easily find someone to entertain me when I wanted or needed. I have a feeling that a lifestyle like that here might get a lot of people talking rather quickly, and I really can't deal with judgement on my life choices at the moment.

I'm a human, and even when I disagree with someone's choices I do my best not to cast the first stone, or any stones for that matter. Unless they are actively hurting others, of course.

Watching Helios and his bike weave seamlessly along the snicket does get me thinking: I would like something like that. A moped of some kind. Something to open up this island for me and help me to explore every corner of it. Perhaps it could inspire something for this book I'll write.

I want something that's mine. I find hiring someone else's vehicle too stressful. I don't want to accidently damage something that's someone else's. I've hired cars before and I've found it impossible to relax.

I quickly type out a message to Gigi to help me find a suitable moped to purchase, so I have a mode of transport. I've never actually ridden a moped before, but I can't imagine it's very difficult. Teenagers are allowed to ride them about, after all, and I can ride a bicycle. I'm sure it'll be fine.

As soon as the message is sent, I call my pop.

'Hi, Pop. I know I'm late calling, Augustin rang.'

'Problems with Odina? How *is* my beautiful granddaughter? I'm sure you're as qualified to answer as he is.'

Even Pop knows Augustin only calls me when he needs or wants something, usually relating to his darling daughter or a family get-together.

'There might be problems. She's not opening up and they think something has happened. They want her to come and visit me in three weeks' time.' A shot of excitement dances through me – although I have no desire for my own children, I've loved and adored Odina from birth and knowing I'll be seeing her soon is always a joy.

'She's a teenage girl. It doesn't seem five minutes ago you were that age and your mother was pulling her hair out every Friday night, wondering where you'd got to.'

'I wasn't *that* bad.'

I think back to being seventeen. I would stay out late sometimes on a Friday to hang out in fast-food places because they wouldn't kick us out as long as we put in orders now and then. It was perfect, I could sit and flirt in relative safety. In the end, though, it was the first time I had my heart broken. He wasn't a monster, but he was gorgeous and an insensitive eighteen-year-old.

My hormones had me by the neck and my main interest was boys. I found them fascinating on every level. I wanted to tame them, like they were lions, and I wanted to hold the chair and the whip to keep them in line.

Boys were the creatures my mother said could so easily hurt me, the ones to be cautious of, yet none of them ever had.

I look back and I was seeing sexism all around me; I just didn't cite it as such. I knew I wanted to save individuals being hurt by *big bad monsters*, I just thought they would be easier to pick out. Even then, I didn't see the wider picture of culture and systemic issues in society. The bad guys don't look like monsters and the good guys aren't always the ones perfectly turned out.

Heartbreak and boys may be causing similar issues for Odina.

This is exactly why I never want children. It's impossible to protect them. It hurts me when she is hurt, and she isn't my responsibility. I don't know how parents ever sleep.

'If your mother were here, I think she'd recite many instances that would contradict the idea of you being *not that bad*.'

'Probably.'

We both fall momentarily silent as thoughts of Mum rattle around us. Thinking of her as gone makes my chest feel like it might cave in. I hate the idea that I gave her added pain or worry.

'If I could go back and change it, I probably would.'

'Don't say that. There should never be regrets, only memories and experience that help you to grow and will help you with Odina should she need you.'

As always, Pop is there on the other end of the line with a soothing tone and solid advice.

Before Mum's death, it would be her on the line first, updating me about family and various adventures she and Pop had been on or were going on, before Pop would get on the line and have nothing left to tell me because she'd already said it all.

'You're right. I shouldn't regret things.'

The unsaid words are that I do.

I do have a heart and stomach filled with regrets. I regret the last time I saw Karine. It fills me up and consumes me to the point where I broke down at work. The one place I've always felt in control.

I can't ever imagine regret like this coming to an end. Which I guess is why I need to get on and write a book instead, because if I can't maintain a level of control at work, I can no longer be trusted to do my job.

'So what's it like there? Left the house yet?' Dad probes.

There in front of me is the sea. Loud and glorious, with rippling shades of blue pulsing towards the shore that lies somewhere out of sight below the sea wall.

I intentionally take a deep breath through my nose to enjoy the scent of cooking food and the pots of flowers in full bloom bringing colour to the streets outside various tavernas. I fill myself up with that instead of regret.

This was the right choice. I need this to clear me out, to find my own peace and purpose again.

'It's wonderful here. It hasn't changed much in the last thirty years. Well, it has and it hasn't. It's almost like I've never seen the colour blue before. The sky, the sea . . . It's *so* blue, it's not blue. Do you know what I mean?'

A low chuckle rumbles in my ear. 'You always did have a way with words.'

'I got your logic, not Mum's artistic flair. That's more Toby and Odina than me or Augustin.'

Mum used to write poems in our birthday cards. Toby soon joined in with her little tradition. He went on to study English at university and holds a master's degree in English literature and is a university lecturer in creative writing.

Helios's bike comes into view as I begin to walk along with the sea by my side. The wind plays with the loose tendrils of my hair as I look about for the man himself. I can't see him anywhere. Which is a shame – I'm almost beginning to enjoy our strange version of small talk that includes mime and coy looks.

'Have you made any friends, other than . . . Cassie?'

'You mean, Calliope. No, not really. Everyone is lovely but I need to start learning Greek.'

'It's unlike you not to have started yet.' He sounds puzzled.

I want to point out that none of this is like me, but he knows that deep down, so what would be the point?

'Well, Calliope is hosting a party in my honour tomorrow night, so maybe I'll find more people to mime at.'

'Sounds like fun. Sorry, Alisha, can you hear that? The doorbell's ringing. Did I tell you? I have a new neighbour. Her name is Brenda. I invited her over for a drink this morning and she's early. Remember what your mum said to you all on your first day of school, OK? Bye.'

'Will do. Bye, Pop.'

I take a moment to let the sea breeze whip my hair around my face as it gets up. I wish Mum was here to tell me the story all over again the way she would.

My first day of school is easy to remember. There aren't many memories from age four that are so easy to bring to mind, but that one has been relived so many times there's a special ridge for it in my brain ready for me to travel along it.

Mum walked me to school, hand in hand, while Pop took Augustin. Before we got to the gate, she lifted me up from under my arms and placed me securely on her hip.

Remember, she said, *we need water, food, air and people to live. Education is important, but people are more important. Without other people we'd all go mad.*

Tears nip at the corners of my eyes, knowing the only way I can hear her voice now is by watching the small number of videos I have. I didn't take enough videos. Phones attached to our hands with cameras there, waiting to be used, and yet most of my videos are of us all singing happy birthday to one or the other.

I turn away from the sea to head in the direction of one of the small supermarkets here in Mandraki.

Helios is there in front of me. He quickly looks away but I'm sure he was watching me. He looks up again, meeting my gaze. His full lips fold in on themselves and it's almost like he can sense my pain even from a distance.

He nods again, mounts his bike and rides away, leaving me alone.

Chapter 10

26.09.2025

RE: Wine

Dear Karine

I was pouring a glass of wine and it made me think of the last time I saw you. We shared a bottle of red. I remember you saying it had to be from Languedoc-Roussillon, as all your favourite wine is from that region in France. Your home region. Every time I close my eyes, I wish the rest of the night had gone differently. The regret will never fade or lift. How could it? I need you to know, I'm sorry. I'll write it every day if I have to.

I love the sound of wine being poured. You said that to me that night.

Always thinking of you,

Alisha

I hit send on the email and close my laptop.

It's the most I've written all day, even though I've spent most of it sitting outside a taverna looking out at sea and trying to write this book of mine.

It turns out that a blank screen and a head that's so full it may as well be empty are not conducive to writing a bestselling novel.

I need a premise, that's all. I would ask Toby but then he'll get too involved in it all, and this needs to come from me.

Perhaps I should switch and write non-fiction.

No. I know deep down that even though non-fiction would be akin to writing one of my all too easy essays or articles on women's rights, I don't think I can pull at those threads of me just yet. I think I need fiction to pull me along.

I scoop up my freshly poured glass of red and head towards the balcony so I can spy people heading towards Calliope's for this party – or not, as the case may be. It's only seven, but I've already washed, scrunched and blow-dried my hair into waves and narrowed down three maxi dresses to one sunshine-orange dress that grazes the floor.

It's been sitting in a wardrobe for three years without the occasion to wear it. I'm not completely sure tonight *is* the right occasion, everyone else might be in jeans, but it will be worn either way.

Life is short and my mum told me when she was dying to *wear the dress, drink the drink* and *kiss the boy*. So I am taking all of Mum's advice today. I'm wearing the dress, about to drink the drink and, as with her first day at school advice, investing in people.

I doubt I'll be kissing the boy, though, however cute he may be.

Pushing open the shutter doors to the balcony, I pull and tuck my dress with my free hand to keep it from wrinkling as I take my seat. The chair is primed to get the best view out to the sea in the distance. The sun is on its slow descent in the far distance, perfectly aligned to slip between the white houses of Nisyros as it goes.

October is rapidly on its way, but it's still warm here. The sea breeze can make it feel cooler in the evening. I've never spent a whole winter somewhere warmer than London. It's going to be a new experience. I hope it doesn't make London seem even colder next year when I return.

If I return.

My phone buzzes from the pocket of my dress.

Putting my glass on the wall of the balcony, I pull it out. There's a voice note from Odina.

> Guess what? I can totally come and visit! If you book the flights I can come for a whole week from the 13th of October! That's only three weeks away. I'm so happy. I've had such a rubbish week so far, but this is the best news. I thought I was *delulu* even thinking Dad would let me get on a plane alone, I can't believe that he's *actually* letting me come to see you all on my own. Looking forward to meeting that man with the yummy pitta too. I'll help you work out if he's suss or not. Love you!

Hearing Odina's voice always brings a smile to lift my face. I hit the button to record a reply.

> I'll book the flights now and send you all the confirmation. OK? Love you more than you know and can't wait to see you.

I begin the quick hunt for flights from London to Kos. I'll go across to meet her at the airport and travel back with her to Nisyros. Depending on the timing, we might need to stay over one night in Kos town or Kardamena.

As soon as it's all booked, I forward the confirmation to a group chat with Augustin, Nancy and Odina to share the good news. Within seconds, Odina is already sending back excited replies.

However lovely it is to have her there at the touch of a screen, I do wish she would spend more time off her phone and more time with her eyes on the world around her. But that's not my responsibility.

I take a deep sip of the wine and stand to look over the edge of my balcony to see if there is anyone milling about. There's only my semi-adopted kitten, Luna, waiting to be fed. I purchased cat food yesterday. I've never seen such a small cat eat so much so fast. I gave her some this morning too, only this morning she brought a friend along.

A scrape of a chair behind me makes me flinch slightly. I look over to see Helios disappearing into his home. Was he there the whole time? I rarely look in that direction, keeping my chair aimed towards the slice of sea in the distance.

I think back to Odina's voice note about working out whether he's *suss*. Thank goodness he doesn't speak English.

Voices approach below. I look along the street and see a small group of people coming along. They keep walking, and, from what I can tell, they head into Calliope's home. I swig the last of my wine and flick my wrist to check the time.

Quarter past eight. Perfect.

I guess it's now or never. The first celebration since the last time I saw Karine.

Chapter 11

'You know Daphne and Theo? Yes?' Calliope says as she indicates the couple who make one of the best moussakas I've ever eaten, even though it was consumed with a spoon straight from the foil tray it was cooked in.

'Yes, lovely to see you again. Thank you again for the moussaka, the minced lamb was beautiful, such a rich sauce.'

They nod and smile, but I feel confident I've used a few words outside of their English knowledge. I vow to open my language apps to learn more Greek tomorrow.

As more people pile into Calliope's house, I also get to meet her husband, Nikos, and one of her sons. They're all about the same height and athletic in build.

More people than I would've thought possible to fit in her house arrive in waves. They file in and welcome me with varying degrees of English.

'So is anyone else coming to this party I should know about?' I say to Calliope over the chatter and the traditional Greek music that is emanating from an invisible source.

'Everyone is welcome here, but hopefully not too many more.' She raises an eyebrow at the number of people milling around her upstairs lounge and out on to her sweeping balcony. It's entirely different to mine and has space enough for a party of its own.

'No Helios then?' I try to sound casual, but I was sort of hoping to use Calliope as a translator to find out even the most simple things about him.

'*Helios?* He did not even come to his own party. I sometimes wonder if he is Greek at all,' Calliope laughs, then goes into a flood of Greek as she grabs the wrist of a passing guest, whose name might start with a T. I can't be sure. 'Sorry, sorry. Where were we?'

'Helios.'

'Oh, yes, yes. He is a polite man but not a social man. He spends most of his time in the house or swimming in the sea. Nothing else. No guests, no family to visit. You are the social one of him and you.' She lets out a laugh, to herself more than to me. 'Your glass is empty. I will get the bottle.'

Calliope passes me endless local treats to try, so much so that I'm glad I wore a flowing dress to hide how much I'm eating. She also keeps my glass no less than half full and it's hard to know how much I've had as time passes. Some people only stay a short while, and others stay and sing and dance even in the smaller rooms of Calliope and Nikos's deceptively large house.

I muddle along with people in broken Greek-lish and games of charades like the ones I've had with Helios. That is, until my head feels a little swimmy.

With a warmth of wine coursing through me, I have an overwhelming need for space and air.

I weave past laughing faces and gossiping mouths to head to Calliope's balcony. It's more of a maisonette really, sweeping along with stairs at the back.

A man with broad shoulders stands with his back to me, smoking and looking out towards the still, inky sea reflecting the moon across its surface. He's hunched over the balcony wall, with his forearms taking his weight.

I walk up to him with purpose, trying to figure out whether this is someone I've been introduced to. From the back, in the dark, I can't be sure.

I lean my hip on the wall to look the man in the face and can't quite believe that I do indeed recognise him.

'Helios?'

Helios peels himself off the wall and pulls himself to his full height. He isn't the tallest man, but he's a good few inches taller than me.

'Alisha.' He nods at me.

My mouth is suddenly awfully dry as my mother's voice whispers *kiss the boy* just as he takes a drag of his cigarette, making it flare into a deep-orange glow.

'Calliope told me you wouldn't be here. Not to worry, erm . . . could I possibly have a cigarette? But only one, don't allow me any more than that. I gave up, you see. It's a dreadful habit, I know, but it's stressful with all the people and the dance of not understanding . . .'

Helios squints at me, his eyebrows lowering.

'Yes, that. That look that I've been getting all night. I'm so used to being eloquent and understood and . . . confident.'

I shake my head and begin acting out the possibility of him giving me a cigarette as he puts his out on an ashtray in the centre of a table not far from the balcony wall.

After a moment, he understands and pulls the packet from his back pocket, offering one to me. I hold his wrist, the one of the hand holding the packet, to steady myself as I pull one out. The night air is offering a crisp edge that's enough to bring goose bumps to my skin and a shiver that ripples down my spine.

I put the cigarette to my lips. Automatically, Helios leans in to cup it with his hands and I do the same as we try to shelter the lighter. He rubs his thumb along it to spark it into life and he's doing the same to the fire in me. He then lights another one for himself.

As I fill my lungs with poison, I close my eyes and feel my muscles relaxing. Nicotine calms my nerves and warms my blood in a way I loathe myself for.

'Thank you, *efcharistó*,' I say through a cloud of smoke.

'*Parakaló*.'

I lean my elbows on the balcony wall and Helios joins me there, so close I can feel the warmth of him next to my shoulder.

'Words are funny, aren't they? We all need them to understand each other yet no one really understands anyone else. All those languages and all those words and there really isn't much point. So many people don't listen anyway. I think we're probably better off with our basic sign language. I wonder what it would be like if we could read minds.' I look over at the man quietly listening to me rattle on without any understanding.

The moonlight catches on his cheekbones and his Cupid's bow in the dark. Despite his messy hair and general disregard for traditional beauty standards, he's really rather beautiful.

'It wouldn't matter, would it?' I continue. 'You'd be thinking in Greek so I still wouldn't understand a word.'

Smoke billows around us before being caught on the breeze and whisked away. I took one puff and I've stopped. This isn't who I want to be. Even tipsy, confused and overwhelmed, I know this isn't who I am. Instead, I let the cigarette burn away between my fingers and hope Helios won't notice.

It's oddly peaceful out here, with most people laughing down in the depths of the house now we're edging into tomorrow.

I twist to lean my back against the wall, wrapping my left arm around my middle, propping my right elbow on top of it. My wrist flops as though my cigarette weighs a lot more than it does.

I think back to my pop telling me I need to listen to my mum. I wonder what she'd say about it all. She'd be telling me to put out this *death stick*, as she liked to call them.

It's OK, Mum, I'm not really *smoking it.*

'You know, before she died, my mum told me to *drink the drink, wear the dress* . . . but don't worry, I won't be *kissing the boy* . . . Bit of a waste, though, with lips like *that*.'

My eyes trail over him as he turns to face me. It's not only his lips that are wasted in his isolation. He puts the cigarette to the corner of his mouth and furrows his eyebrows.

'That's one lucky cigarette you've got there. It's also lucky you don't understand me, isn't it?'

Peeling myself off the wall and away from Helios, I put my death stick out in the ashtray on the table behind us.

I glance back towards him and wish I could read his mind, but I'm glad he can't read mine, or my lips.

'*Kaliníhta*, Helios.'

I have to walk away before I let my body do more of the talking.

Chapter 12

Today is a big day. Gigi has organised for a moped to arrive from Kos on the ferry, ready for me to explore the island. It's my last-ditch attempt to write a book before trying my hand at something else.

I wait patiently under a tree in Mandraki's port, looking out across the undulating turquoise sea. Dappled light falls like golden autumn leaves on the ground and spiderwebs catch from place to place and glitter like strings of minute fairy lights.

As October has edged in, more local people have been sporting trousers and jeans. I'm still finding it too hot for the trousers I brought with me. There have been a few more clouds gathering overhead now and then, although so far I've only seen two days of rain.

The ferry edges closer and closer to me as I sip on my sweet coffee. I'm getting quite used to the Greek way now. I still like my latte in the morning sugar free, but there's a comfort around the care taken with a Greek coffee that I'm starting to enjoy.

As I put money in a shot glass to pay my bill, the captain of the ferry manoeuvres the vehicle effortlessly into the harbour for people to disembark.

My body tingles with excitement to start this new phase of adventure and distraction. Up to now, the furthest I've been is down to the beaches, many littered with volcanic pebbles, and up to the monastery to have a walk around. I'd like to get back to the heart of the island, like I did all those years ago. Back to the volcanic craters.

If this trip had a bit more planning, I'd have asked Pop to get out old photos from when I was last here. As it is, I only have my memory to remind me what it was like. It was our first volcano, and I was positively fascinated and repulsed, mostly by the smell, in equal measure.

With all the foot passengers safely on solid ground, an older gentleman walks a shiny red moped off the ferry. It looks to be in very good condition, with silver rims and a black leather seat.

Our eyes meet and he gives me a big grin, concertinaing his leathery skin as he displays a mouth with one or two teeth missing.

He talks slowly, in very broken English, and my Greek has only progressed to pleasantries and ordering food and drinks. It's a start, but it isn't ready for this sort of exchange.

We muddle our way through payments and papers before he needs to hop back on the ferry and return to Kos. There isn't time for him to show me the basics, so I'm left holding a moped without the slightest clue how to ride the thing.

Glancing around, I begin to feel rather silly, clutching the keys and too nervous to start the thing up. I've never felt more like a cliché woman in my life, which I know is ridiculous because surely Augustin or Toby would be exactly the same.

We took trains and taxis everywhere in London, and only passed our driving tests because my mother said it was a simple but important qualification to have. One I was glad I'd achieved and did end up using more than I thought I might. But now, holding the weight of a moped, I feel rather foolish to think I could simply hop on and know what to do.

In this open space, with people milling about who have just arrived from the boat, some about to get a coach to the volcano and others starting their walk into the depths of Mandraki's winding streets, I don't want to hop on and just *see* if I know how to start her up or ride her . . . what if I ride straight into someone?

No.

This has to be a private affair.

I don't want to hurt myself or anyone else.

I begin to walk the bike towards home, pushing the weight of it up the incline before quickly veering off the main sea road and between the rows of rendered buildings all blindingly white, trying to grab my attention with their pretty doors and pebble-decorated doorsteps. I can't let myself be distracted by them in the way I'd normally study them. I don't usually walk this way home, and with the weight of the bike seeming to increase tenfold with any incline, I don't want to drop the thing into someone's house or taverna.

As I reach an empty square, the floor beautifully decorated with stones that form the shapes of tridents and dolphins, I take a pause to catch my breath. Sweat has gathered above my lips and in my hairline, making me curse my decision not to pull it up and out of my way. I had thought I'd be donning a helmet, and a ponytail would be a pain.

As it is, a helmet wasn't provided or even required as I escort my bike to my house.

The sound of steady footsteps carries up behind me from between the houses. I do my best to look composed, ready to greet the passer-by before continuing my arduous walk home.

As the footsteps almost reach me, I flick my head to get the hair from my face and look at them in one single swoop.

'*Kali*—' I falter as I see Helios is the passer-by. '. . . *mera*,' I finish, and do my best to smile. This is exactly the problem with living on a tiny island in a small town. This would never happen in London.

We haven't spoken since Calliope's house party, although we have often kept each other in quiet company on our balconies without so much as an acknowledgement. Sometimes we're both reading side by side, like we're members of a very odd book club.

Since the party, my glass of wine after dinner, watching the sun set, has become my nightly ritual. Something I look forward to. I hear him leave, closing his shutters at the same time each night, back to the depths of his house.

'*Kalimera*,' Helios echoes without even attempting to hide the eyeballing of my bike. His eyes are wide and glittering in the sun before he pulls back what I think could've been, and probably was, the beginnings of amusement at my predicament.

I do the same back to him, only at his bag of shopping to mirror his motion. I've no interest in the shopping bag, but it means I can take in his jeans, which fit perfectly on his buttocks, without making it too obvious.

Getting the hint that I don't really need someone to stare at me, he does his usual nod and begins to move on towards home. I wait a moment to let him get ahead before beginning my slow ascent.

He's the other side of the square when he falters and turns back to look at me. I pause in pushing and feign interest in the speed dial of my new purchase. When I look up, he's still staring at me.

Helios gently shakes his head, looks up to the clouds gathering above and then marches towards me. I glance over my shoulder to see if someone's behind me, but there's no one. I can hear people talking a few streets along, that natural hum of life in a small town, but no one in close proximity.

Helios is heading for *me*.

He begins to chatter at me in Greek. Juggling his shopping, he stabs at the bike with his index finger, clearly asking me something about it.

Eventually, he pulls out his keys from his front pocket and jangles them at me. The penny drops and I take out the keys from the pocket of my shorts.

Taking them off me, he passes me his shopping and relieves me of the bike. Putting the key in, the motor bursts into life, making Helios look even more confused. Perhaps he thought I was pushing it because it was broken. He must think I'm completely bonkers.

He steps back a touch, one hand still holding the handlebars, the other sweeping over the seat, indicating that I should sit and ride the thing.

'No, no. Thank you.' I shake my head and my free hand before taking a step away.

I really don't fancy toppling over sideways with the gorgeous Greek standing over me thinking what a foolish Englishwoman I am. I know I'll be able to figure this out on my own, and soon I'll be as competent as anyone.

Just not today.

Still holding the handlebars, he reaches for me and pulls me in, chatting away in Greek.

'No, I don't know how to ride it yet. Stop.' I step back, irritated he thinks he has the right to pull me around and boss me about.

He takes a moment to study my face, and I do the same to him. His dark eyes are slightly sunken and rimmed with a shadow that I'm sure matches my own. My nights are often marred with fruitless attempts at a full eight hours. Not always, but often.

Of course, none of this takes away from the way he looks at me and the appealing way he has been made. If I believed in a God, I'd think he or she spent a little extra time carving out Helios. A little extra time painting in the lighter flecks of hazel in his dark eyes to make them look like they're reflecting the sun in such a heavenly way.

It's such a pain having sexual urges at times.

What it must be to shut off that part and live happily without need of the opposite sex for anything at all. I've done the best I can to carve out a life of my own. I'm happy in my calm routines, but I'd also be happy enough to make space occasionally for someone like Helios to keep me warm, even in the heat of summer.

Helios's tongue edges tentatively around his lips as he squints at me. He's almost always squinting at me, like that will help him figure me out. I wonder if I'm doing the same to him.

Stepping across me, he kicks one leg up and mounts the moped before putting his hand out to take back his shopping. I do as he wants and pass it over in a daze. He revs the engine, making her growl instead of purr. At least now I know she seems to work all right.

Our eyes lock for a moment; there's something about the lift of his eyebrow, as though he is waiting for something, while he looks at me with the confidence of a man without any responsibility. When I don't respond, he flicks his head down towards the part of the leather seat still available behind him.

He wants me to hop on the back.

For a split second, my mouth moves to reject his proposal, and my feet automatically take another step away. A small group of people appear from one of the alleyways that converge on this particular square in town. As the clouds part, the sun glaring down on me, I look up and think about pushing this thing up the incline. The heat even now begins to burn into my skin like the sun is shooting down tiny knives.

Without wanting to make a fuss of standing about in the way of life passing us by, I follow suit, throw my leg over the vehicle and, without too much thought, put my arms around his waist before he pulls off on the short ride home.

He smells of fresh pitta again. Fresh pitta and fresh morning dew.

I do my best not to melt into him. I'm sticky and hot, and being so close to him isn't helping that. I attempt to hold myself at a respectable distance, as much as is humanly possible where a moped is concerned, and I press my hips against him.

We set off over the bumpy stones of the square, which rattle and vibrate right through me before shaking our bodies together. I bite my lips and try to think of anything other than what's under Helios's clothes. Luckily, it isn't too far until we make it to the smoother surface of grey and white stone slabs.

We scoot past cats and people sitting outside their house on a bench, past the play area for children and the outdoor gym for adults and the melange of greens from trees poking up here and there.

In early October, it could still be summer, with life still growing in pots and trees still green and as fresh as spring.

It's a matter of moments before Helios pulls up outside our homes and edges the bike in front of his own on the street, kicking out the stand.

I'm quick to peel myself away from him, not wanting to give the wrong impression, and thank him for his kindness.

He shrugs before placing his shopping bag down on the floor.

Twisting and pulling the key from the ignition, he waves it at me slightly before putting it back in and turning it. He then breaks down everything I need to know, while narrating slowly in Greek, as though the pace is the issue.

Luckily, the age-old language – body language – is enough for me to grasp all the basic workings of the moped, which, as I had originally assumed, are reasonably simple.

When he is done with his lesson, he switches off the engine and hands me back the key.

He grants me one of his legendary nods and the lift of the right side of his mouth into a half-smile, while all I have in gratitude is '*Efcharistó*.'

For all his nonchalant looks and his scruffy appearance, there's clearly a kind man underneath.

As Helios closes his door behind him, Luna appears, rubbing herself around my bare ankles. I pick her up like a baby, just the way she loves, and begin to tickle her belly.

'I think I need to say more than thanks to him. I'm just not sure how yet.'

◆ ◆ ◆

Pouring myself another evening glass of wine – my second when including the small glass with dinner – the idea catches to pour a glass for Helios and pass it to him over the balcony in acknowledgement of his kindness today.

It's only a small gesture. From the corner of my eye, I've seen him drink red before.

'Maybe it's a silly idea,' I voice to Luna, who's curled up under the kitchen table on the seat of a chair.

As if knowing I was talking softly to her, she gets up and stretches before trotting over to me, nudging against my legs.

'I think you're right, Luna. There's no harm in offering someone a glass of wine.'

Opening the cupboard, I pull out another of my four wine glasses. They all look like small fish bowls, for a single baby fish perhaps.

Before reaching for the wine bottle, I pick up my phone and quickly translate *this is for you* into Greek. I listen to the words spoken by a synthetic voice three or four times before I pour out a second glass of wine and head for the stairs. With each step, the wood groans at me and I begin to doubt myself.

I never used to have any self-doubt. After everything with Karine, and the panic attack in the judge's chambers over the silliest little thing . . . it's hard to shake the feeling of self-loathing at times.

My heart sinks and my chest feels tight as I reach the top of the steps and head towards my bedroom balcony. I use my elbows to get outside, pushing down handles and shoving at the wooden shutters until I'm free.

I look across to my right, something I always avoid doing so as to leave Helios with his privacy. His eyes are on me, cloaked behind the smoke from a cigarette as its billows up and over his face and into the sky to join the clouds.

I clear my throat as though I'm about to make a speech before stepping to the edge of my balcony and leaning on the wall, my arm stretching towards him.

'This is for you, for teaching me how to use my own moped. *Aftá eínai gia sás*,' I add, which I can only hope translated correctly.

Calmly, he rests his cigarette in a silver ashtray and dusts his hands over his navy T-shirt before standing and reaching over the gap between our balconies to take the glass.

'*Efcharistó polý, yámas*.' He takes the glass from me and raises it.

'*Yámas*,' I say as I raise mine to him.

We both sip and comfortably hold each other's silence. Or at least, I'm perfectly happy in it.

I've had him there over my shoulder for a few weeks now. It's become comforting having him there. Consistent. Even if we don't have anything much to say.

Chapter 13

'What do you have for me today? Did your trip to Stefanos Crater help? I love it there. It is ugly-pretty, yes?' Calliope studies me from my kitchen table as she does her best not to turn her nose up at my coffee.

I can read her well enough now to know she hates it, but she doesn't want to hurt my feelings. She likes a traditional coffee, not one from my machine. She does her best to hide her response behind her mass of slightly frizzy hair.

'Do you want me to make you something else?'

'No, no. This is good. Fine.' She covers the mug with her hand but as she looks down at it the twitch of her nose makes her freckles dance and tells an entirely different story. 'Stop with this distraction. Bring me the book you write.' She taps her nail down on the table in three quick successions.

'Then *you* get me the business plan we discussed.'

'I have it, but only in Greek.' She twists to face the chair next to her and rummage around in her floppy cotton shoulder bag. 'Here.' She passes me the paper with handwritten notes in Greek. I can read the letters, as I know how to make the correct sounds for Greek, but I would have no idea what I'm saying.

'I think I want to do meditation and breathing for the start. Yoga is longer to get the certificates. But it is for wellness, and I would make a proper Greek lunch. A healthy lunch.'

'Sounds really good. I'm ready to start when you are.'

Calliope takes the paper back from me and looks over it with a deep exhale.

I turn to my own handwritten sheet. The most I've managed to write so far. I pass it over to her. She carefully lays it out on the table and studies it intently.

It's impossible to stop myself from chewing my way through my lip as I watch her from my spot leaning against the counter.

'It is . . . err . . .' Calliope's hesitation is enough to ignite all my fears.

'It's dreadful.'

'No, no. It is not what I expect, this is all. Who is talking?'

'I thought maybe I could write from the perspective of the volcano.' As I say it out loud, I know it's as ridiculous as I feared.

'A lot different, *nai.* I don't read many English books yet. Are they all like this one? In Greek, we don't write this way. It is normally . . . people.'

'Well, no, actually . . .' I cover my face with my hands. 'Urgh! That's it. I'm done. I'm not a writer. I can't do it. I've never been the creative one, but I thought with all A-star English results this wouldn't be *that* hard. Time to try something else. When can we start jewellery-making?'

'Don't be so hard to yourself! I like the description: People ride their motorbikes over my scaly yellow bumps up to my—'

'Please stop.' I tear the paper off the table and scrunch it up into a ball, tossing it into the corner of my kitchen counter.

I may have to leave it there as I never want to touch it again. *What was I thinking?*

'We will make jewellery soon. Everyone can put beads in a row. Why not write about you? Your life must be interesting?'

'No. It's too personal. I don't think I'm ready to talk about . . . reality.'

I thought I could do almost anything. I don't remember ever failing at anything I put my mind to. Not until this. Toby and Mum always made it look so easy to put words on paper and make them seem beautiful.

'If you keep your pretty face like this you will get ugly wrinkles, I know.' Calliope screws up her face, much like my discarded paper, to display as many wrinkles as she can muster.

It's enough to make laughter spill out of me, of us both.

'Actually, I don't find wrinkles ugly at all. I think ageing is a privilege.'

The first person to pass through my mind is my mum, followed by a painful stream of those I've lost through time. I'd love to have seen the laughter lines grow around their eyes with each passing day.

Calliope taps the table with her finger. 'You are right.'

After taking another strained sip of coffee, she tilts her head. 'And what about Helios?'

'What about him?'

'He is very handsome. Maybe you write a romance?' Calliope tips her mug to hide the twisted smile on her lips, only to think better of drinking any and lowering it back down.

'We don't even speak the same language.'

'I know. But he came to the party. Mr Next-door who never goes anywhere. He came to the party for *you*. He didn't come to his welcome, but he comes to party for you? Strange, *nai*?'

'I don't think it means anything.'

'Everything means something. You have to look to see, Alisha. Now I will go. Why not try to paint? Everyone can paint. Children paint. Then soon we do jewellery together.'

Calliope cups my cheek with her surprisingly rough fingers before she heads towards my front door.

I guess I'll be trying my hand at painting next. I'm not sure how much I can earn as a painter, but at least it might be therapeutic.

As I say goodbye and close the door, I do my best to push her comments about Helios to one side. That, and the idea that everything means something. I suppose it does, but it doesn't always mean the same thing to everyone.

Chapter 14

I carry my laptop under my right arm and my wine glass in my left hand while doing my usual dance to open the balcony doors with full hands. I look over to greet Helios with a smile, but he isn't there, which is highly unusual.

Each day since getting my moped I have had an adventure, including the trip to Stephanos Crater that ended in a disastrous first two pages of a book no one would ever want to read, then I eat out as I'm a terrible cook. *But* I'm always drawn home for my quiet glass of wine next to Helios, on our separate balconies.

We usually acknowledge each other now, with a nod and a muted smile. He also has a glass of red with him each night, and I wait to hear him leave before heading off to bed myself.

In fact, this is the first time he hasn't been there waiting for me since our nightly routine began.

Our routine is probably all in my head. I've spent too much time acting like a teenager harbouring a crush and playing out ideas that couldn't possibly be true, wondering whether he's looking over at me, and whether he always sat on his balcony at this time in the evening before my arrival.

Much like the well-known island of Santorini, Nisyros is photogenic. It's different, but the blues and whites are similar.

Without my quiet companion by my side, I lean and look across the row of balconies along the street in a way I wouldn't when I'm not alone. Each looks strangely fragile from the side. Like they should *all* have safety warnings on them, but they don't. People hang their washing, read their books, live their lives around them. Particularly those like me who have no garden to speak of.

They're special little wooden spots of joy and practical living.

Shadows are being cast on them by low-hanging clouds now, though. So low I feel I could almost stretch and reach the grey-tinged puffballs.

It's been a gloomy day overall and tomorrow promises rain.

It's typical that now, with Odina arriving so soon, the weather seems to be on a downward spiral.

At least we can hunker down, watch something on my laptop and eat chocolate until we pop. She's now at an age where she thinks I should be handing her glasses of wine with it too, but I'm still not entirely comfortable with that. I suppose she'll be eighteen in no time, and I'll have to start treating her like the adult she's becoming.

Placing my glass next to me on the floor, I open my laptop to update Karine on my life. It's become an obsession I can't move on from, even though I know she'll never reply.

11.10.2025

RE: I wish you were here

Dear Karine

I always check to see if there is an email from you even though I know there won't be.

> I used to enjoy our correspondence. Even though it was often few and far between, it was always an exciting moment to open an email from you and hear about your latest adventure.

The sound of Helios's shutter swinging open and smacking against the balcony wall makes me jump. I twist to look over to him for our evening exchange, but he doesn't look back at me. Instead, he leans his forearms on the wall facing the houses opposite, and hangs his head under the cover of the clouds and the setting sun.

I watch him for a moment, not wanting to intrude, but he seems far from himself. Exhaling hard, he stands upright to fish out his cigarettes and then lights one behind a cupped hand. His shoulders are tense and hunched. Even the way he drags back the smoke looks like a punishment.

Not wishing to invade his privacy further, I slide down low in my chair and look back to my laptop to continue with the email.

> The man next door, Helios, has arrived home. He doesn't seem at all himself.
>
> After everything that happened with you, I wonder whether I should say or do something? The problem there is, I don't even speak Greek.

I glance back towards Helios. He's sitting now, his head hanging low. My heart races as fear begins to strangle me. The beginnings of that sensation rise up. What if he needs me? How can I help him if I can't even ask him whether he actually needs help?

My chest begins to constrict as I do my best, with trembling fingers, to focus on the email.

I don't want this moment to be another one I regret. I wish I could ask for your advice and you would give it to me. I wish I could go back to that night and change everything.

A tear slips down my cheek as I begin to hold my breath to stop myself becoming overwhelmed with the desire to snatch smaller and smaller breaths. My body forces me to keep it in and to attempt to calm down, but everything about Helios's body language is triggering me and I can't let it go.

Forever thinking of you,

Alisha

I hit send, close my laptop and try to steady myself and recall the Greek I learnt on my app. I've done *How are you*, I know I have. Τι something, Τι, Τι something.

My head begins to pound in time with my heart as I try my best to steady my body from shaking and take sensibly paced breaths.

Helios's balcony door slams shut.

I stand on trembling legs and look across. He's gone. I'm too late.

I can't let this happen all over again. I can't let another person down when they might need me.

I jump up, making spots appear in front of my eyes as I stumble through my bedroom past all my pointlessly beautiful new furniture and down the stairs. I keep going until I'm at Helios's door, the last throes of the blood-red sunset trickling down the street.

I knock on the door, hardly able to do my usual system. Even counting to fifteen feels laborious.

Nothing, but I know he's in.

I knock again and the door swings open.

'*Ti kánete?*' I blurt out the words, as though they were waiting to be said the whole time. They just needed to see him before they could be recalled.

Helios looks stunned. He's stripped down to only his jeans, usually something I would stop to admire, but all I need is an answer. There's a tinge of red to his cheeks and his eyes look puffy, perhaps from crying. I need to know he's all right.

'Are you OK?' I repeat in English, more aggressively than intended.

'*Nai.*' Yes. He's OK.

'*Ti kánete?*' he bleats back at me.

'*Nai.* Yes. No. I will be.' I grip his door frame as my knees quake underneath me.

Helios's warm hands grip my shoulders as he whispers to me in Greek. My head is spinning and the white spots keep darting in front of my eyes.

He encourages me to come forwards. I don't make it into his home, not really. Instead, I take a seat on his top step. My feet are the only things inside.

'I'm so sorry, Helios. I came over to check on you and now you're looking after me. I was worried about you. That's all.' I try to softly sniff back the tears, but they won't stop running down my cheeks. 'As long as you're OK, I'll go. Are you sure?'

I move to stand but he tugs at my hand, forcing me to remain seated.

For the longest moment, we look at each other. His face has softened but there's still that quizzical look of not understanding in his eye.

'*Efcharistó polý*, Alisha.' Helios squeezes my hand as he rubs his thumb along my knuckles. '*Efcharistó.*'

I know that coming here and checking on him was the right thing to do.

Chapter 15

'What do you mean, there's no ferry today?' I stare back at Calliope, forgetting the old adage of *don't shoot the messenger* and wanting instead to argue with her and demand that she's wrong.

'I know you are going to Kos to meet your niece, but the storm . . .' She shrugs as she stands in my living room, dripping on my floor. 'I thought I must tell you right as I hear.'

I heard the rain start in the night, but I didn't expect *this*.

Everything has been planned for weeks. I was to go across to Kos on the midday crossing and we were going to stay together in a hotel overnight before coming back here to Nisyros. But now she's already on the plane and I won't make it there to meet her. She'll be all alone.

Lightning fires through the heavens like a knife carving up the sky, ripping apart my plans.

I squeeze my eyes tightly shut wishing this to change, knowing I can't do a thing to make it better.

'What the hell am I going to do?' I mutter to myself more than to Calliope.

'There is nothing, she will be fine. You call her when she lands and get her a taxi to the hotel you were going to stay at and then,' she shrugs, 'you get her tomorrow. The storm will be gone for tomorrow. Today, not so much. I have to get to my mother now, she is waiting for me. Be safe, yes? Let me know if you want me. Just call.'

'Thanks, Calliope.' She pushes open her umbrella before stepping into the downpour.

Shielding my eyes, I try to look down the street, but the rain is springing back up and making a mist before running down the paving slabs.

Calliope hugs the sides of the buildings for shelter, but it doesn't seem to make a jot of difference. Her wide-leg jeans are already dark to the knees and the back of her coat looks like a water slide.

Why today? Of all the days the rain wouldn't make a difference to anyone, why does there have to be such a storm *today*? Particularly one such as this, one bad enough to make the sea toss and turn and boats give up altogether.

My fists curl into rocks at my sides and my heart pounds in my chest like a prisoner trying to spring loose.

'Why today?' I say to Luna and Cloud, Luna's new companion. They've come in to shelter from the weather.

I look at my watch. One hour until I was meant to get the boat and two hours until she was meant to land.

Now I have two hours to figure out what to do.

◆ ◆ ◆

After phone calls with Nancy and then Augustin too, they have agreed that it's best Odina gets a taxi to stay in the nearby hotel I'd already booked, just as Calliope suggested. I think they were trying to reassure me more than I was trying to reassure *them*.

They know that in my job I've seen every worst-case scenario known to womankind and they play out in my head when it comes to Odina.

I do my best to tell myself it's fine as the minutes claw their way slowly past me.

This is all my fault. If anything happens to her, it's on me.

These are safe islands, filled with good people.

But it only takes one. I know that all too well.

It only takes one evil mind to snatch someone away.

I shake my head and try my best to regain my composure. I'm no good to anyone if I spiral and have another panic attack.

As the time comes for her plane to land, I check my phone again and again only to realise there's no signal, either on my phone or my Wi-Fi.

I charge up the stairs, through my bedroom, throw open the balcony doors and step outside. Our building has a decorative lip at the top of it, offering a small amount of dry space for me to hold my phone just outside of the doors.

Augustin and Nancy agreed that I should be the one to call Odina and tell her what to do, as I know the area and neither of them has ever even been to Kos, let alone Nisyros.

'Please, please, please,' I beg my phone as the *no signal* logo persists. 'Come on,' I screech to the thunderous navy sky.

Doing something I know is ridiculously dangerous, I dart around turning things over until I find my umbrella. It's still at the bottom of my suitcase, completely unused since I was in London.

I pull it out, rush back to the balcony, cross my fingers I don't get struck by lightning and open it out. The lightning seems mostly to be contained to firing into the sea, at least for now, as though the sea is the sky's whipping boy.

I hold my phone up high underneath the umbrella, searching desperately for signal. A bar appears and I hit the call button then put it on speakerphone. It pauses for the longest moment as it tries to make the call, only to fail.

'No, no, no!' I shake my phone, wishing it had a neck I could squeeze. 'Don't do this. I can't leave her on her own.'

Lightning flashes to my left and after only two counts thunder rumbles down our street, shaking the houses. It's enough to make me feel dizzy and stupid. I'm no good to anyone dead.

Stepping back, I shake out the umbrella and discard it.

Tears roll over my cheeks as the smell of fresh rain on warm paving – petrichor – fills my lungs.

'Why today?'

I edge out and hold my phone straight upwards, trying to keep it sheltered under the lip of the building. I'm pretty sure the phone is water-resistant, but the rain is so dense it reminds me of standing under a waterfall in the Brecon Beacons. I can't imagine my phone would last long in this and I have to hope lightning won't pick me as the next best place to smack.

The single bar comes back. I hit call and begin my silent prayer to any god that might be listening, but probably isn't.

It begins to ring between crackles, then Odina's voice sounds on the end of the line.

'Auntie Alisha, I've just landed but the weather is—'

'Odina? Odina? Can you hear me? Odina?'

I swear under my breath and it's all I can do not to throw my phone at the house opposite mine.

I try to call again but I just get those infuriating beeps to indicate the call isn't even attempting to connect.

I take the phone indoors and move around with it high over my head, stepping on my bed with wet feet, not caring about the white sheets.

A hammering drums on my door to rival the thunder raging outside of my balcony.

Even though I was doing my best to stay sheltered, I've still managed to get wet, and I have to be careful making my way down the stairs and across my tiled floor.

I climb the two steps to pull open my front door to a man with his back to me, holding a thin black waterproof jacket over his head.

He turns to face me and briefly pauses before saying, 'Can I come in?'

My mouth drops open and heat fills my body, enough to make me wonder whether my skin will steam off the rain.

Helios speaks perfect English.

Chapter 16

'Can I come in? I know, I speak English. It's a shock, but I think I can help you.'

I stare at Helios as he stands on my doorstep being pummelled by rain so violently that it bounces off him and down the steps into my home.

It's impossible to move or respond.

I stand stock still, not really knowing how to react. My brain slips back to all the things I've said in the honest belief he couldn't understand me. One particular moment slides into view from somewhere in my peripherals . . . what did I say to him? Something about his cigarette being lucky because it was between his lips? I wish I could remember the exact words. They didn't matter until now.

'*Help me?*' I repeat. I don't make a habit of inviting fraudsters into my home.

He steps forward and automatically I politely step back, cursing my upbringing.

'Odina, she's your niece, right? Is she stuck over in Kos?'

'You speak English,' I bleat, as though he is the one who didn't know.

'I'll explain that another time. There's not much signal with the storm, I could hear you from my balcony. I know the owner of a tugboat, he owes me a favour. I have a satellite phone, I can contact him with it.'

I really want to interrogate him further on his magic linguistic skills, but I refrain, instead focusing on why he has now decided to talk to me.

'To get her to me, or me to her?'

'Her to you. He works for a towing service. They have people stationed in various places. If he hasn't already been called out, maybe he could help. He has teenage daughters, he will understand.'

This isn't as reassuring as it could be, coming from a man who has hidden his true identity under my nose like he's a Clark Kent wannabe now announcing he's Superman.

Questions fill me up, some about him, but most about how on earth this would work.

I step back, pressing my fingers in my ears to block out the hammering of the rain to give me a chance to think. I do this in the office sometimes when I need to make a quick decision, sometimes even in court if I can get away with it, but usually it's quiet enough there.

All the options race past my eyes like one of my pros and cons lists.

She could come here, but even on a tugboat it incurs the risk of being on the water in the storm.

I could ask the tugboat to come here to collect me and go back, but they might not agree or be out saving those in real danger.

If Helios has a satellite phone, he could at the very least get a message to her for me.

'Could you contact someone on the mainland to give her a message? Perhaps get her a taxi to the hotel I've booked?'

'Sure. Or I can call her?'

'You can try but she has spam filters and strict instructions to never answer unknown numbers.'

Another layer of panic rises up as I remember once needed to contact her, my own battery dead, using a friend's phone only for her not to answer.

Helios sucks in through his teeth as he turns and steps back out into the rain. 'You might want a coat,' he says as he looks back at me before disappearing towards his house.

I don't even consider a coat, I follow him straight into the downpour.

Chapter 17

I stand soaked through to my bra and knickers from the three seconds I was nipping from my home to Helios's.

This was a bad day to wear a white T-shirt, but I'm far past caring. I cross my arms over my chest and shiver while I make a puddle on his terracotta-tiled floor.

After being ordered to *stay here* by Helios as he disappeared upstairs, I've had no choice but to wait. I keep holding my phone in the air, but there's still no signal to be found.

There's no luck, no signal. Nothing.

Like the thunder outside, Helios's feet rumble down his wooden stairs.

'Here, catch.' He throws me a towel. It almost hits me in the face, but my hand gets to it just in time.

I'm already bubbling over with what could best be described as volcanic irritation, so it takes a lot not to do more than scowl at him.

I'd like to verbally pull him apart, but he's my only hope at help so I bite it back.

He's now shirtless, with a beige towel around his neck that matches the one he's thrown at me. I turn around, pull off my sopping T-shirt and wrap the towel over myself like I've just got out of a swimming pool instead of out from the rain.

As a woman all about equality, I have no qualms about bras, breastfeeding or nipples in general. I find the Victorian notion of embarrassment about such things to be childish at best, but I know that's not a notion held by all and I wouldn't choose to make anyone feel uncomfortable in their own home.

Helios isn't even looking at me, he's pacing in self-made puddles as he tinkers with his phone, which is more like a black-and-red brick with an aerial than a modern phone. Which is what I expected, although I didn't expect my next-door neighbour to have one hidden under his bed.

I didn't expect him to speak perfect English either. Although his accent isn't perfect, it's pretty good. There's only a touch of his native Greek. I assume it's native, but now I can't be sure at all.

He gets someone on the phone and begins talking away to them in Greek. This makes him stand still in his puddle on the floor, much like me.

I glance back at my phone. Still no signal. Odina must've landed over thirty minutes ago now. At least hearing her voice means she landed safely, that's something. She's a smart kid who was just on a flight right through the bad weather, so she'll know exactly why I'm not there, or at least, probably will. And will probably have worked out why there's no signal either.

Unless she thinks something has happened to me, and she has signal and I don't and she's worrying. If she is, and she has signal, being on the larger island, then logically she'll call Nancy or Augustin. I'm sure that Nancy would've made her promise to text or call on arrival anyway, so maybe she already knows I can't get to her and what to do . . .

Other than I was meant to organise this and they don't even know the details of the hotel.

'Alisha, my friend can get his wife to help. Your niece is called Odina . . .' He pauses for me to fill the gap.

'Harding,' I confirm.

'And what does she look like? His wife might go to the airport and look for her, they don't live far from it.'

'Well, she has dark-ish, golden-ish skin with long silky black hair. Her mum is half American Indian and Augustin, my brother, he's quite dark too. Sometimes she has her hair loose, sometimes a ponytail. She has black-brown eyes, medium height, slim. Wait—' I look at my phone and go back to a message she sent me early this morning before she got on the plane. A selfie she also posted on her social media stories. 'She's wearing a lilac crop top with a denim jacket over and jeans with rips, look.'

Helios takes the phone from me and begins his own description in Greek to the person on the other end of the call.

'What hotel have you booked?'

I take back my phone and find the screenshot of the booking, passing it back so he can read it out.

A moment later, Helios ends the call.

'Can we try Odina? Just in case?' I pass him my phone with her number there on the screen.

Looking from my phone to his, he types it all out, but as I expected, there's no answer. I can't know whether the call was marked as spam, or whether she simply stuck to her rule of not answering an unknown number.

I'm the same, never answering numbers I don't know on my personal mobile phone, we all are. It's a family trait.

'He will let me know what happens, but they'll find her and make sure she is fed and taken to her hotel. They'll keep her safe and happy. This has happened before, with the signal being lost on many of the networks. Some are better than others, but it's a small island. You may have noticed the internet isn't great either. Coffee while you wait? Or do you want to go home? I can come and get you when I know more?' Helios drops his towel on the floor and begins shuffling it around with his foot to soak up the puddles, displaying his toned, but not overtly ripped, body. Firm without screaming *I love the gym*.

This would usually be a delightful distraction, while I'd also be careful not to stare or make someone uncomfortable in my admiration. Not right now, though. Now he might as well be wearing a thick jumper. I am used to the opposition using bells and whistles to try to win a case against me. When I want to, I can ignore the most elaborate of distractions. Even cliché handsome men, silky looking with olive skin.

'Helios, could you please explain to me exactly why you've been hiding the fact you speak English, and why it took an emergency to reveal this fact?' I step towards him with purpose.

He pushes his fingers through his thick wet hair and takes a deep breath before blowing it out in a huff.

'I could, but I'd rather not.'

'I think I'm owed an explanation.'

'Yes, *you* would.' He folds his arms across his chest, likely in an attempt to tip me over the edge with his thick biceps, but I'm not so easy to make swoon.

'And what exactly does *that* mean? Are you saying it surprises you that I'd wish to know why you've been making me play mime games over the past month? Do you somehow believe that another person might not wish to have an explanation as to your behaviour? Or is this not the first time you have played this game with women? Am I meant to have an equal reaction to someone else?'

I stand tall, moving towards him again while firmly gripping the towel clinging to my body and the other with the knuckle of my finger pointing at him, curled to keep from looking threatening, but still maintaining some element of force.

'Wow. You're quite impressive at pressing a point aren't you? How about you go and get dressed, put a coat on this time and maybe use that umbrella of yours to get back to me. I'll get dressed too. I'll have a drink and some cake ready when you get back. But don't expect as many answers as questions. If it wasn't for you needing help, you'd have lived next door the full six months and never known I spoke anything but Greek.'

My teeth clamp together as he turns away like his word is gospel and I should do as the man demands.

'I'm not a child. I don't have to do as you say.'

He stops and turns back to me. 'Of course you don't. You're a grown woman. But the fact you didn't leave when you had the chance suggests to me that you want to be here waiting for this call, and you are the one who wants to ask *me* questions. I'm going to get dry. You can stand there and shiver if you wish, but I'm going to get dressed.'

I keep my breathing steady even though I'd like to take a deep soothing breath to calm myself, but that would reveal how much he's got underneath my skin. It's not only the underlying humiliation, but his entire attitude.

Chapter 18

My hair looks almost black from the water soaking it. Sleek and glossy, like the slippery flesh of an eel. I yank a brush through it and peel off my clothes, throwing them in the shower to deal with later.

My heart pounds in my chest as hard as my feet stomp from room to room.

I've seen deception of every type from people you would least expect, so why has this hooked me so badly? Why am I *so* surprised?

My naked body jolts to a stop in the middle of my bedroom and I cover my face with my hands as thoughts crash down in my mind.

What if I've just delivered Odina to some sex-trafficking opportunists? I can't believe I've put her life in someone else's hands. She might've waited there, called her parents. At least in the airport there's security, people that will keep her safe.

My chest rises and falls and panic creeps over my skin like cats' claws until they reach my throat and dig in so deeply I can't breathe. My lungs feel punctured and only a handful of times in my life have I felt this same pain, this same helpless agony and deathly inability to breathe. All of which have been since what happened with Karine.

I drop down to my knees and on to the borrowed towel I brought back with me from Helios's.

I need to calm myself and find air.

Removing my hands from my face, I bunch the corners of the towel between my fingers and concentrate on the idea of taking an overdue breath. It's shaky and small, but I catch one.

It takes time and concentration not to make it worse or to fall into a pit of fear and anger all over again, but I need to pull it together so I can get back to Helios and not leave his side until I'm completely sure Odina is safe. I need to hear her voice for myself.

If she isn't, if he has lined this up, then I will move more than heaven and earth to find her and to put him in prison for eternity.

If I'm not there keeping an eye on him, he could leave at any moment, and then I would have no clue where she could be or any bargaining chip to find her.

Steeling myself for a fight, I stand on legs that move like thin branches in the wind. But I do stand, and I begin to dress myself so I'm ready for anything.

◆ ◆ ◆

I arrive at Helios's house under my umbrella in trainers, black jeans, a blazer and another white T-shirt. The difference is, this is one that Odina got me for a past birthday, and it reads *I Support Women's Rights, And Wrongs* in golden writing. Most of my clothes are plain and understated. I try to be stylish but without giving away too much personality. This is something different, something I love because it was from her.

I feel ready. I'm still not sure what for, but I guess I'm ready for anything. As ready as anyone can be for *anything*.

The rhythmic tapping of the rain on my umbrella feels like it may never end.

I do my best to achieve my usual three knocks on Helios's door, but I'm also balancing a bottle of red.

Helios calls, 'Come in,' instead of actually opening the door

Stepping down into his home, I shake out my umbrella with one hand and clutch the bottle with the other. I know there is a very high chance that everything is in my head, all the crazy negative stuff, but what if it's not? At least if I bring my own wine, I can make sure I'm not drugged to prevent me from keeping my eyes on Helios.

I'm overthinking, I'm sure, but I'm also not ready to instantly trust a man who is willing to lie for over a month.

If my mum were alive to see this, she'd be rolling her eyes at me and demanding I give everyone the benefit of the doubt. Telling me to find the truth and to listen to his story.

Helios isn't in the entrance, which, like mine, also serves as a social space.

Each house I've been in has its own unique quirks, but some follow a similar format and retain certain traditional styles.

While Helios is out of the room, I move quickly to his sideboard of photos to see what information I might be able to gather there. I'm a quick study, with a memory for faces and facts.

Most of the photos are family shots. All are in black and white, so it's hard to tell if they're old or just printed that way for styling. I would guess by the fashions, the latter.

A boy and a girl feature heavily in them. The boy could be Helios, with the same intense deep-set, slightly turned-down eyes. It could be him and a sister growing up together. Maybe a cousin, but more likely a sister. In the centre there's a posed photo of the boy and girl that's very slightly larger than the others. It looks like it could be a school photo, but with the black-and-white image, and without a uniform, it's hard to tell whether or not that's the case.

The sound of the stairs creaking makes me dash back across the room. In my haste, I slip on the wet floor, my feet disappearing behind me like I've had a rug pulled from under me, and I land with a slap on my hands and knees on the tiles.

The muscles in my face screw up like I've eaten a lemon and I'm momentarily paralysed from the pain. My chest contracts like I could cry, but it's the swirling concoction of not knowing what's going on with Odina, together with the screaming in my knees and hands, that pushes me to this pitiful edge again.

'What are you doing down there?' Helios sounds confused as he enters the room.

I don't answer right away, gritting my teeth.

'I slipped in a puddle.'

Helios says something in Greek and moves quickly towards me.

Not wanting to get more than my knees wet, or to have too much help getting up, I push my weight back towards my heels and start to straighten my legs ready to take a step out of this embarrassment, only for my hand to slip again, landing me back on my knees.

'Woah, woah, be careful.' Helios wraps his fingers over my hips from behind to steady me.

Humiliation burns hot behind my eyes as he grips me.

'Please, let go,' I snarl.

'Sorry, I was trying to help.'

My knees ache but my pride hurts more as I play a solitary game of Twister on the tiles.

'Here.' Helios puts his hand out.

I hesitantly accept it, because I can't play this game of slip-and-slide a moment longer.

He roughly pulls me up and towards him, as though I'm a lot lighter than he first expected, and I end up inches from him with both of my hands gripping his.

I can feel his heat all over me, permeating my clothes.

'Thank you.' My voice is no more than a whisper. We're so close, it doesn't need to be louder.

My blood skips along my veins – audibly so as it passes my eardrums, as though it has hands and joyfully taps on them to make a dizzying banging in my head.

I slip my fingers away from the comfort of his and carefully step back. He watches me dust my hands over my knees. I'm glad my jeans are black and don't show how wet the knees are.

Straightening my spine and sweeping my caramel-brown hair off my shoulder, I turn back to Helios. 'Any news of Odina?'

'Not yet. Are you hungry? I can make a feta and tomato omelette before cake?'

I'd suggest sending a text message from his phone, but it would also probably fall through the cracks of spam being an unknown number. If this carries on, it might be worth trying, just in case.

All my plans have turned to dust. The ones of dinner at a taverna in Kos with Odina and treating her to whatever she wanted. It's all blown away. The realisation that I haven't eaten all day, worrying too much about what's going on, hits me and my stomach growls to give me away.

'That would be very kind, thank you. I also brought wine . . .' I trail off as I look around for it before spotting it on the sideboard. 'Oh, there it is.'

I must've absent-mindedly placed it there when I was studying his photos.

Helios looks from the sideboard to where my umbrella had made a trail of water for me to slip in.

'What did you say you were doing when you fell over?' He picks up the bottle of wine and tilts his head at me.

'I was running away from being nosy.' I keep my eyes on the photos instead of his intense stare. 'You were a cute kid.' I nod towards them.

His head snaps towards the pictures and his face shifts into a frown.

'Oh, thanks.'

Without so much as another word, he takes the bottle of wine behind a curtain leading into another part of the house, and I follow on behind him, wondering what other mysteries I might uncover in the depths of his home.

Chapter 19

I look at my phone for the hundredth time to see if there's signal. Nothing. There's no kitchen table like at my house or Calliope's. There is a single tall stool, which Helios indicates I should sit at.

'Do you think they will call or message? Your friend's wife?'

'Call. You will hear it.' Helios pulls out two mismatched glasses, pops the cork and glugs the wine into them before handing me mine. The sound brings my mind back to Karine, but I do my best to pull it away and back to the here and now.

I've been gifted the yellowy-brown smoked glass that looks like it's from the seventies, and he has the smaller blue one that I've seen him use many times from the corner of my eye across the balcony.

'So, Helios, the time is nigh. You need to tell me why you've been withholding your ability to understand me all this time, or my suspicions of you will only increase, thus making me a nuisance until I uncover the mystery of "a most notable coward, an infinite and endless liar, an hourly promise-breaker, the owner of no one good quality".'

'Oh, really. Well, perhaps I'll counter with "Away, you three-inch fool", and we'll be done with it.'

My glass is at my lips, but I don't take a sip. This man doesn't just speak English, he knows its depths all the way to Shakespeare. This isn't English he's learnt from slinging shots behind a bar.

'Well, I do suppose the "best portion of a good man's life" is "his little, nameless, unremembered acts of kindness and love". Wouldn't you agree?'

It's not exactly how Wordsworth intended the words to be placed, but I wait to see whether Helios catches them before I take a sip of wine.

'I don't know. I wouldn't like to disagree with Wordsworth, even if he *is* dead.' Helios clears his throat. 'Do you only read works by men named William?'

I shake my head. 'No.'

'Would you like to quote someone else to test my grasp on the English language?'

Helios turns away from me, takes a frying pan from the cupboard and places it on the hob.

He clearly has an excellent grasp not only on the language but its literature. I've been well and truly duped.

'What I would like to know is *why* you've hidden it from me. I'd also like to know how concerned I should be in trusting a liar with the whereabouts of my niece.'

I rarely lay all my cards on the table, but frankly, I feel as though it won't change a thing. I'm still stuck here with a knot inside me and itchy feet that, if they could, would run me all the way to Odina. If only the sea wasn't so black and turbulent today.

Helios takes a bowl out of a cupboard and turns to face me. His eyes seem darker than before. They've become more intense and serious. Suddenly, they're nothing like that boy he once was.

'I would never do anything to put her in danger. I trust my friend and his wife. You can trust they will help her and look out for her. I swear on my life.'

'I'd very much like to believe that, but as I still can't begin to understand your deception, it's hard to believe you.'

'Surely "there is no charm equal to tenderness of heart", so you may allow me my secrets and trust that my act of kindness is enough. I didn't want to share anything with you.'

'I'm serious. Quoting Jane Austen only leaves me with further concerns about your true identity. How can one be so knowledgeable and hide it so well? Are you a spy?'

Helios scrunches up his face just enough to look like a moody teen before he exhales and says, 'Of course I'm not. Who would I spy on here? The cats? I didn't want you to talk to me. OK? I could see you popping over asking for more favours than just cutlery.' He turns and walks into his larder, where I have a utility room. He quickly returns with six eggs balancing in his hands.

'You'd have me believe that it was just to avoid helping me, and yet now you're helping me anyway?' I take a sip of wine.

'I'm helping a young woman stranded alone on an island she doesn't know.'

'I'm hardly stranded.'

'Not you, Odina.'

Of course that's what he meant. I was too wrapped up in the language deception to realise his meaning.

'So it's specifically *me* you don't want to help or talk to? Or just me you're spying on?'

'No. I don't really want to get to know anyone. I have a busy job, and it takes up all of my time. There's nothing more to it than that. And I'm not spying, I can just hear your voice notes and calls on my balcony. You have a loud voice. That is not my fault.'

His back is to me as he lines up the eggs to crack, keeping them from rolling off the counter with a wooden spoon.

I don't believe him.

I can tell from the curve of his shoulders, even from the back, that something is off.

'I'm not that loud.'

His head sways and there's a shake to his movements that suggests a silent laugh.

I narrow my eyes on him with the twist of irritation. 'What do you do that's so important?'

'I did not say it was important.'

'Fine. *Busy*.'

'I'm a translator. I speak, and translate from, German and French but mostly English. I've always enjoyed books and when I was young, I realised I had an aptitude and interest for languages. I studied English literature at Reading University for a time.'

That explains why his English is so good – not only does he speak it, he studied it in its place of origin.

'That's ridiculous. You have a job that connects people of various languages and yet want to keep the people in front of you as far away as possible. Hiding behind imaginary language barriers. Couldn't you have just said, like any normal person, that you spoke English but you're not very social?'

'I tried to avoid Calliope and her parties, but all that did was offend her. I'm not here to offend anyone. I just want to get to spend my time getting on with my work. That's all.'

Helios doesn't look at me again. He moves fluidly round the cosy kitchen, crumbling feta and slicing tomatoes, until the omelette is ready.

I want to point out that he *did* choose to come to one of Calliope's parties, but I don't want to remind him of the things I said while we were on her balcony.

I follow him up the stairs and to his living-dining room that looks out on to his balcony. There's a rectangular table covered in a plastic cloth with an olive branch border. There are four wooden chairs with thin mint-coloured cushions tied to the back in bows. A very yellow icon of the Virgin Mary looking forlorn heads the table on the wall opposite the doors to the balcony.

'Take a seat.' Helios puts down the food for us to sit across from one another. I take my place at the first seat, and he moves around the table to sit opposite.

'Thank you for making this. I can't deny that you're a very strange man, but you've demonstrated some kindness today.'

Guilt rattles behind my ribs. I wonder whether Odina has eaten, and if so, what? Has she got enough money with her? She thought she'd be with me the whole time, I can't imagine she brought very much when she knows I wouldn't let her pay for anything.

'I feel bad eating, not knowing if she's OK.'

'Don't worry. Anna, that's the wife of my friend, would never let her go hungry. She'll be lucky if she escapes not feeling ill from eating too much.'

'Noted.'

I can't believe I didn't ask for her name sooner. I've been in too much of a panic, it's so unlike me to not think clearly. I sneak another look at my phone and hope for signal, but there's still nothing.

'The storm is meant to pass in the next hour or so. These things aren't very easy to predict, of course, but hopefully some signal will be restored then. We should hear from Atlas before then anyway.'

I cut off a corner of the omelette and pop it in my mouth. Even this small morsel is delicious and bursting with fresh flavours. I watched him making it with hawk eyes, making sure both were identical and nothing untoward was done to either of them. All he did was mix eggs with feta and tomatoes, a few miscellaneous herbs and salt. It's perfectly seasoned and yummy like no omelette I've had before.

'Is it all right?'

'Delicious, thank you.'

I cut off a bigger slice, this time to fill the ache of hunger that started to scream when the pan was filling the air with the scent of warm olive oil.

Glancing up at Helios, with his solid chest and shoulders, messy hair and handsome face, is enough for a cold sweat to rise up from my toes all the way over my skin.

'I still can't believe how you've let me carry on. *And* kept a straight face while understanding everything I've said . . .'

Helios smirks into his omelette.

'It's OK, you were drunk. You're not the first drunk woman to hit on me. Although it has been a *very* long time.'

The cold sweat burns off my cheeks in an instant and flips to a flame-grilled heat.

'I wasn't hitting on you, I was simply complimenting you.'

'In an overtly sexual way.' Helios lays down his knife and fork on the side of his plate and then grabs eye contact with me without so much as a hint as to his inner thoughts. He is blank again, just as he has always been. Fooling me into the belief of his obtuse facade. Perhaps he *should* become a spy, as he says he isn't one. Or even a barrister, like me.

I match his eye contact with the confidence I've had to nurture over the years of coming up against men in my job who don't care what I think or how good I am at arguing a point, they'd cut me down just for being born if they could. Without self-belief, I would've withered long ago.

'Perhaps. I apologise if I offended you with the tone of my compliments. It was not my intent. And in my defence, as you both know and constructed, I thought you couldn't understand a word of it. I didn't mean to objectify you like that. Not outwardly, anyway.' I also put down my cutlery. 'How did that make you feel?'

Helios battles with his face as a smirk fights its way to the surface.

'Fine. I felt fine about it.'

'Good. I'll do my best to keep my sexuality in check in the future.'

Helios's tongue moves over his bottom lip, perhaps unconsciously, as his eyes narrow on mine. 'It irritates me that I'm intrigued by you,' he says. 'What did you say you do for work?'

'I didn't.'

Helios chuckles before turning back to his plate of food.

I can't wait to tell Odina all this.

I can't wait to know she's safe.

The lights flicker and the whole room is plunged into the darkness of the storm, only for the strike of lightning to blindingly light it up for a second before it falls dark again.

'That can't be good,' I declare, laying down my fork again.

Chapter 20

Time passes in flickering lights and the shadows of candlelight. Helios does his best to reassure me when he thinks I might need it. He's also given me two slices of a homemade orange and walnut cake he says is made with his *yiayià*'s secret recipe. It's delicious and sticky but still not enough to keep me from feeling on edge.

Time passes and the storm begins to ease, but my signal is still out and the lights are still off. Another hour and a half has passed without any hope of news.

Helios suggested we sit with the balcony doors open to make sure we're most likely to get signal. With the clouds bruising the sky and evening drawing in, there's not much light to be seen outside.

Outwardly, I probably seem calm, swirling wine in my glass between my hands. Inwardly, I'm dizzy from spinning in endless circles of worry. The only thing holding me together is knowing Odina landed, because I heard her voice. That, and the hope she will have called her parents.

My phone, along with the satellite phone and Helios's mobile phone, are resting on a separate chair opposite us, in front of the balcony. We face them like it's three friends we're conversing with. The five of us quietly wait for the outside world to come flooding back in.

Mostly we have sat quietly, which I'm happy with. But, much like this beautiful volcanic island, I can still feel a prickly heat bubbling away under the surface at the humiliation I've endured because of his selfish lack of honesty.

'So really, what *do* you do? Or what did you do before moving here?' he begins from the shadows at my elbow. It's day and it could almost be night.

I look down at the whirlpool of wine in my glass.

'I was a barrister. I *am* a barrister,' I correct myself. 'I'm on sabbatical. I'm surprised no one told you the gossip. I'm sure it's always interesting when someone new arrives.'

'I'm sure it is, but I was still the new guy on this street until you moved in. And I told you, I keep myself to myself.'

'All those languages you speak and not a soul to talk to.' I shake my head at the irony of it. 'And where did you move from?'

'Greece. And I still live in Greece.'

I press my lips together and twist my neck so he can take in my expression of loathing in the flickering candlelight.

'I'll go ahead and assume you lived on Kos before moving here, or maybe you were from there, because you have a friend with a tugboat over in Kos, and no friends to speak of here. But you do, for some unknown reason, have a satellite phone to contact him with. Which I can't imagine is particularly ordinary, unless of course you're often out at sea?'

He falls silent, protecting everything about him deep inside behind the wall of his skull.

'Why did you stop being a barrister?'

'I didn't stop. I'm on sabbatical, of which six months are to be spent here. Why are you antisocial?'

'Why aren't you married?'

'Why aren't *you*?'

'Who says I'm not?'

'Who says *I'm* not?'

I raise my eyebrows, and he lowers his.

He won't open up to me if I don't open up to him. That much I know.

Without some sort of trust, there's only distance, and I'd rather mend the bridge than live next door to someone I can't even sit next to on the balcony.

'I *was* married, once,' I begin. 'We're still friends. If I'm honest, that's all we ever were. We'd known each other forever, he asked me out and then he was living with me and before I knew it I was picking out a dress. We were married for less than two years before I told him that although I loved him, I wasn't *in* love with him. Besides, he wanted children and I don't. I think he thought he could change my mind once he put a ring on my finger, but that's something I'll never shift on. It was all suitably amicable.'

'Why don't you want children?' Helios leans in closer to me, resting his forearms on his knees, clutching the stem of his wine glass.

'Because I can't handle the responsibility in this modern world. I know too much. I've seen too much. Particularly if I had a daughter. I find it hard enough having a niece to worry about, but that wasn't my choice and I can't help but love her. Women can't wear any item of clothing without someone on the planet saying it's wrong. They can't grow their hair or cut their hair, because someone will say it's wrong. We get sexually assaulted and then we get blamed for it. It's hard to ever feel safe. Even a seemingly good-natured neighbour could be lying to you.' I give him a sidelong glance and continue. 'Having a child is to live with the constant hope that other people will be kind and will treat them with respect. If I had a child of my own, I know it would consume me and push me into a pit of fear.'

Helios's head hangs low and he nods at my every word.

'I think you're right. I think having children *is* all-consuming when you love them. No matter how much you love them, they'll always end up getting hurt. We all do, one way or another.'

'Exactly. I don't think I could handle that responsibility. I don't want to live like that.'

It's nice to feel heard on the matter at least. So many people argue against my thoughts instead of accepting them as my own. If I'd picked a different job, maybe I would think differently and maybe I *would* want children. But that's not who I am. Not now.

'And why here for your sabbatical?'

'Long story.'

Helios chuckles as he tilts his head. 'We have time.'

'For someone who is antisocial, you're rather chatty.'

His face doesn't change. He waits patiently for me to talk, because, as he said . . . we have time.

'At the tender age of eight years old, my fate was decided. My pop had it in his head that we were to spend a summer visiting volcanic islands across the globe. He often had these micro-obsessions, and my mum always indulged him. My older brother, Augustin – Odina's dad – was to join us later in our summer adventure, on another island, but at the start it was just the three of us. Toby, my younger brother wasn't born yet, not for another eight months . . . Anyway, Pop was particularly interested in Nisyros, as Kos is the home of modern medicine and my pop is a doctor.'

I can still see us all sitting at the taverna by the sea. It's still there. I've sat in the very spot where this all began.

Nisyros caught my attention too, not just Pop's, but for a completely different reason. Winding streets lined with kittens, shining blue doors that begged to be knocked and a sea so blue that it was no longer just blue, it was a moving blanket of sapphires muddled with pale emeralds and handfuls of diamonds. Each home was bright white as pure as clouds, and the quiet streets meant my feet echoed as I ran along them. For me, it was a heaven like no other place I'd ever been.

'On our first night, we had dinner in a small taverna that overlooked the lazy waves breaking against the rocks below us. I remember confidently announcing that Nisyros was the place I would very much like to live when I grew up.'

'Why is that?'

'It's beautiful, with good food and cats.'

'Ah, fair enough.' Helios leans back in his seat with a distant smile on his face.

'My father asked me that exact question. *Why is that?* Head tilted, his blue eyes looking dull behind his spectacles. I gave him the same answer I gave you, while eating all the fresh pitta and tzatziki. Fresh pitta is still a favourite of mine even now. My mother approved of my reasoning, but I think Pop thought it was a bit strange.'

We fall silent for a moment as we stare at the screens, waiting for someone to call out to us from Kos.

I fall into that night when I was a child. It was the same night I set in motion the process of becoming a barrister. I just didn't know it.

I was reading a pocket book of facts about volcanoes and didn't want to put it down.

Usually, I wasn't allowed to read at the table. *I'll allow it, sunshine,* Mum had said, her lips curled into a soft smile. I miss that smile so much.

Mum always called me 'sunshine' because she said it was the colour of my hair and the colour of my soul. My hair became dark with age, but she said my soul still shone.

I didn't need to be told twice. I buried my hand in my cotton bag hanging over the back of my chair, pulled out the book and skimmed over the words until I found the place where I'd been told to put it away.

That summer, my pop had taken a month away from his role as a surgeon because we were to move house for him to start work at a different hospital in London. My mother was working in a drug rehabilitation centre but had decided to leave the role and wait for something to come up nearer to our new home.

Not that she ever did, as she soon found out she was pregnant with Toby. My older brother, Augustin, was already eighteen at the time and studying to become a doctor just like our father. I'm pretty sure I was the only planned child among us.

I don't remember being particularly interested in why these decisions were being made, only that my life was changing and I wasn't thrilled with making new friends in a completely different school far from the home I'd always known in Birmingham.

It wasn't long before my parents had finished their first bottle of wine and they all but forgot I was there. I was enjoying the sound of the waves gently breaking below us on the sea wall and the warm evening worked like a massage to relax my parents further.

As I listened to them talk, my eyes flicked over the words *pyroclastic flow has an average speed of 60mph but can reach speeds of*. . . over and over again as my mum lowered her voice to continue a story. She was trying, and failing, to convey her story in a way I couldn't understand on the off-chance I was listening.

Little did she know I listened to everything.

Many people are flawed to their core. Her wine sloshed in her glass as she spoke. She spoke of a friend working with . . . victims. Mum must've mimed the word before *victims* because I didn't catch it at the time. It was many years later that I worked out that gap and filled it.

'What are you thinking? If you chew your lip any harder you'll make a hole in it.' Helios pulls me out of my reminiscing.

'I was thinking about the first time I came to Nisyros. It was also the moment that set in motion me becoming a barrister.'

'Wow, how old did you say you were?'

'Eight.'

'Eight? I think I wanted to be a superhero at eight. You were very practical.'

'No, it wasn't like that. My parents were talking about this friend who was working with women who had been sexually abused, but she wanted to work with the perpetrators as a study for prevention. My mother was so angered that there was no funding and no justice. I remember being so confused. When you're a child, you think everything is simple. The bad people get caught and go to prison. I always remember my mum saying to my dad that no one seemed to care. That the law isn't there to protect them..I kept thinking, *who are these people and why don't they feel safe in their own homes?* I'd always felt safe in my home. I suppose I was quite an innocent child really. Naive to a lot of the negative traits of humanity. In the end, I asked why these people weren't even safe in their own homes. After chastising me for being nosy, she explained that some people like to hurt people. Their brains are wired incorrectly, and they do bad things, even to their own children.'

I still remember every detail of that night. The world carried on buzzing around us, the air was full of sounds and scents from the waves to the food and the salt in the sea. Yet nothing was louder or more overwhelming than my urge to ask more questions. Outrage coursed through me like the hot lava described in my pocket book.

Mum informing me there was no one there to help women in need who I didn't know, who I would never know, was enough to make everything inside me split and curdle.

'A fire had been lit that burned as I looked out towards the stars that night, knowing it was my duty to help people, to save women and girls from the bad people out there, even though I wasn't completely sure at the time what those people were up to. I knew if my parents thought it was bad, it must be bad.'

That fire under my lungs stayed with me.

I solidified it and engrained it like tattoos on my bones. It went so deep that even in my sure-footed childish mind, I could never have comprehended how one seemingly simple decision would change everything.

I studied law, I was called to the bar, and I took on cases no one else wanted, the ones that were hard to win but which my gut told me I should fight for.

I've spent my working life so far fighting for a better place to live for all, and it was a fight I truly believed I could win, even if it was just for the individuals I served.

It's only now I see why I didn't deserve to be taken seriously at eight when I stated I would help them, as though I could save everyone.

I was a foolish child and this year, I finally grew up.

'I think you're a very impressive woman, Alisha.'

The lights flicker back on, making us both sit up a little straighter in our chairs.

I mentally cross my fingers that they'll stay that way for more than a moment.

My phone beeps, then three times more. I all but throw my wine on the floor to get to it.

Chapter 21

A string of messages come through from Odina. Many are voice notes that won't download properly or play, but some are texts saying things like, *The line cut out, are you ok? I guess it's the storm, not you hanging up on me lol* and *I'm here safe.*

I can't be sure they came through in the correct order. Is she at the hotel safely? Or had she just landed when she sent *I'm here safe*? By picking my phone up the signal drops out again, but at least it's something, and so far the lights are holding up too.

Carefully placing the phone back on the chair, I edge away, hoping the voice notes might eventually download so I can listen to them.

'Why hasn't Atlas called back?' I whisper, to myself more than to Helios.

'Do you want me to call him and find out what he knows?'

Tears sting at the back of my eyes. She's almost an adult, but she's not. She's probably fine, but what if she's not?

'Could you?'

'Sure. Even *I'm* starting to wonder why Atlas hasn't called back.'

'Please don't say that.'

Helios picks the satellite phone off the chair and steps outside. There's been a break in the rain for a while, but it's still thick with clouds and the balcony has had a good wash over the past few hours.

He pushes buttons without checking the number or any hesitation. Maybe this is why he has the phone, to contact his friend when he's at sea. Perhaps they're in regular contact this way.

A small drip smacks to the ground at seemingly random intervals out on the balcony.

After forever passes, Helios comes to life, speaking loudly in Greek and pressing his fingers into his free ear. The conversation isn't long-lived.

'What was said?'

'He's been called out to help tow someone at sea. That's where he is now and why he hadn't called back. He had to leave when his wife was leaving to find Odina. She was taking their two girls with her. I'm sure she's back at her hotel by now. She probably didn't want to call my satellite phone – it can be pretty expensive.'

I squat down in front of my phone, trying to leave it balancing in place while looking to see if any of the voice messages have uploaded.

I should've told them to spare no expense. I'd pay anything to know Odina was safe. At least I know Anna was on her way to the airport to find her.

After quite some time more, one bar of signal shows on my phone and I can't help but wonder why I've thrown myself back into the frustrations of the early 2000s when people knew exactly what you were up to if you were walking about with an outstretched arm and on tiptoe, waving a mini brick about. I can't remember the last time I didn't have signal and needed it so badly. This isn't a problem I've suffered while living in London.

One of the voice messages eventually loads.

Hey, I called Mum. She said that you're stuck over on Nisyros and that you were going to organise a taxi for me that would take me to the hotel? If you get this, I've already got my suitcase, so I'll wait at the front of the airport for the taxi. Love you.

I can hear the edge of tension in her voice. The discomfort at being alone but the confidence of someone who is usually independent.

In my job, I might be advised by solicitors, but the reason I'm good at what I do is that I actually care about people. I listen to them to know what's going on underneath their words.

'I wish I knew whether they've found her yet.'

Without moving the phone from its position, I press the screen to make a simple call. It takes time thinking about the idea but then it starts to ring.

'Auntie Alisha, you've got signal! Yay!' Odina's voice crackles from the speakerphone.

'Quickly, are you safe? Where are you?'

'I'm at the hotel.'

The knot in my chest relents and I thank the stars for keeping her safe.

'This lady called Anna helped me,' Odina continues. 'She said she knows your neighbour, Helios. Is that the pitta bread man?'

Heat rises in my cheeks. I push my hair behind my ear to turn my cheek away from Helios.

'Yes. He's right here with me, in fact. He's been very helpful. It turns out he speaks English. More importantly, tell the hotel to put any food you want on my bill. They have my card details, OK? Order anything you like. Not alcohol.'

'Do you think they'd give me alcohol?'

'*Not* alcohol.'

'Fine, fine. I'm not bothered anyway. I'm going to order desserts and watch a film. Do you think you'll be able to get me tomorrow?'

'I'll find a way, even if the ferry isn't running. Anna's husband has a tugboat – worst case, I'll pay him to get me sometime between now and then and bring me over to you. The weather is supposed to improve, though, so hopefully it won't come to that. So Helios assures me, anyway. Look, from now on, send texts, OK? The voice notes aren't loading. We're going to have to go old school.'

'OK. I need to charge my phone now anyway.'

'Be safe and be good. Love you, Odina.'

'Love you, Auntie Alisha.'

With that, I pick up my phone and there's nothing that could pull the smile from my face.

She sounded relaxed and happy, that's all I needed to know. She can lock the door and be safe until I get her.

'Thank you for everything today.' I stand up, clutching my phone in one hand and placing my half-empty wine glass on the dining table with the other.

'You're very welcome. But . . . pitta bread man?'

My lips vibrate in a splutter of laughter. 'It was you who left pitta on my doorstep on my first day, wasn't it?'

A smile creeps over his face. 'It was. And now I know it's your favourite thing. So apparently I made the right choice with that day's act of kindness.'

'You did. And with today's.'

We share a peaceful look before I make my way towards Helios's stairs and the front door.

I scoop up my umbrella and turn back to him. 'So . . .' I hold my hand up to count things out for him. 'One, you've done the one thing I hate. Two, I've humiliated myself in front of you. And three, I'm acutely aware that you never wanted me to know you could understand me in the first place. On this basis, would you like us to go back to nods and silent balcony dates?'

'*Dates?*' Helios tilts his head as he runs his fingers through his soft-looking hair.

'I didn't mean *dates* like that. I just meant us ignoring the other's fundamental existence while knowing that it's there.'

He pushes up his shirtsleeves before folding his arms, and all those thoughts and comments on his looks come creeping over me again. Now I've relaxed about today's situation, it's easy to notice his appeal again.

'Probably,' he says.

I turn to leave, knowing it'll be impossible to feel the same about sitting next to him now, but that I'll have to try all the same because he helped me when I needed someone the most.

'One question, before you go.'

'Yes?' I pause on his step.

'What did I do that you hate?'

I make a little noise in the back of my throat that's the ghost of a laugh. 'Without you, I would still be a mess. You saved her when I couldn't. You saved me when I couldn't save myself.'

Chapter 22

'Leaving pitta bread on your doorstep: beige flag. Lying about understanding English: red flag. Getting me help: green flag. That man is *all* the flags. He's almost a rainbow. How can he be *all* the flags?' Odina lifts my fluffy brown throw up over her legs, snuggling into the armchair in my upstairs sitting room.

The storm may have passed, but the October rain has left a chill in the air and a threat overhead that's kept us indoors.

'Good question.'

Odina pulls out a fruit sweet from a bag I'd left on her bed. I'd made a whole welcome pack for her, including a volcanic stone bracelet that I commissioned from Calliope to be dyed teal and pink, sweets, chocolate, some earrings I got in one of the gift shops near the sea and a few other bits too.

I would've made a bracelet for her myself, but Calliope has been busy helping her mother lately with shop administration, so she hasn't had time to show me how.

'What does he look like?' She watches my face as she unwraps the sweet and pops it in her mouth before grabbing another one out of the bag and throwing it to me.

It's orange, my favourite. I really do have the best niece.

I keep my expression as neutral as water and go ahead with a description like I've been mugged and he's the perpetrator.

'He's about five foot eleven, black hair with some grey starting at the temples. He's usually got a grazing of stubble on his face, sometimes more, and his posture isn't perfect but he *is* trim, and he often looks a little bit like an unmade bed. He also has exceptionally dark, slightly hooded eyes that turn down just a titch.'

'So . . . cute?' Odina tilts her head and suppresses a giggle.

'Yeah, very cute.'

I put the sweet in my mouth and toy with the idea of confessing the full story of what I said to him when I didn't know he could understand me. But for now, that stays locked away, ready to give me palpitations and sweaty palms every time I remember it.

'Cute older guys.' Odina exhales and shakes her head. 'They're the worst.'

Her eyeline lowers as she begins to unwrap another sweet.

'What makes you say that?' I try to sound casual as I cross my legs, pulling my feet up underneath me like it's a yoga class.

Perhaps this is why she hasn't been *right* at home. Some cute older guy. The question is, how much older and just how cute. Cute enough to get her in trouble she can't undo?

I have to remain in my calm yoga pose so as not to scare her off.

'Nothing. Just that they're the worst.' She lifts her face into an unnatural smile before changing the subject. 'Maybe he's so used to everyone fancying him, he just didn't want another woman falling over herself to talk to him.'

'God, I hope not. How arrogant. Anyway, he's not *that* cute.' I recall his features, masculine but unthreatening, not exactly model but enough to make you look again and want to keep looking just to check he really *is* that cute. Damn. 'I'm just glad the ferry was running today and we didn't have to call in another favour from someone who hides their true identity.'

'Do you think he's a superhero?' Odina throws me another orange sweet, making sure we've well and truly pulled away from her statement. I'll find a way to bring her back to it eventually.

'No.'

'Witness protection?'

I give this one a long humming noise before ending it with a 'No'.

'Why not?'

'I just don't.' I get up, pace to the balcony window and look out at the gloomy sky. The forecast says we should soon have some sun, and I can't wait to show Odina a little more of Nisyros. 'I've seen enough people who have been in witness protection in my time, and I just don't think he's one of them.'

'When can I meet him?'

'Do you want me to see if he's out on the balcony, smoking like a chimney?'

'Of course.' She pulls off the throw, dumps the sweets on the floor and jumps to attention, swooping her long black hair over her shoulder like she wants to make a good impression. She even looks down at her off-the-shoulder T-shirt and cropped leggings as though she's unsure whether she's presentable, even though she always looks perfectly put together.

Rolling my eyes, I lead on to my bedroom and open the doors and the shutters to outside. I know instantly we're in luck because I can smell Helios's earthy tobacco filling the air as the wind chops from this way to that in the wake of yesterday's storm.

Odina's fingers wrap around my arm and I can hear a little excited squeak building in her throat. All she wants is for me to settle down and have kids so she can look after them. She's told me that, and I've told her no.

'Helios, sorry to interrupt and break our vow of silence, but this is Odina. She wanted to thank you for coming forward and helping her yesterday.'

'Hi, Helios, nice to meet you.' Odina steps forward on to the balcony and grips the side.

Helios removes the cigarette from his mouth and quickly stubs it out in the silver ashtray before standing to address her.

'It's nice to meet you, Odina. I'm glad to see you've arrived safely in Nisyros. May the rest of your trip only be eventful in a good way.'

'Thanks.' She smiles with straight white teeth and the beauty of her mother.

'You're welcome.'

'I know you like your privacy' – I twist my mouth into a knowing smile, which he reciprocates – 'so we won't keep you, but I would like to ask for an address for Anna, so I can have flowers sent to her, if that's possible?'

'I will thank her for you. I'll send her flowers, it's fine.'

I fold my arms and my weight slips over to one hip in a stance of defiance at the idea.

'Why can't I send my own flowers?'

'I don't think I should give her address out to someone she doesn't know.' Helios tries to shrug it off, but I'm already offended.

'It was all right for this woman to pick up my only-just-seventeen-year-old niece, but it's not all right for me to have her address?'

Helios's cheeks graze rouge as he chews his lip.

'Flowers aren't an emergency,' he counters.

Odina clears her throat, putting a pause on our verbal see-saw between the balconies.

'Actually, it doesn't matter. Anna gave me her number, in case I needed her. I can message and ask her.'

Tension runs the line of Helios's jaw, before he attempts a smile.

'There, you don't even need me to ask,' he shrugs.

'Apparently not,' I confirm. 'Anyway, thank you again for your help.'

He nods, as he does, and we retreat back into the house. It's warm outside and humid from the rain, but I shut it all outside with the cloud over Helios's head.

'Red flag,' Odina says, widening her eyes to twice their normal size.

We both erupt into giggles.

Chapter 23

'Do you know what it looks like to me?' Odina says out of the blue as she looks down and across the mouth of the volcano.

'What?'

'That crust sort of stuff on top of clotted cream.'

'Maybe.' I tilt my head to consider this idea, and I guess she's sort of right. I shield my eyes from the sun and look down across Stefanos Crater.

'The people look like ants walking about on the clotted cream from up here,' she adds, before looking back at the sign in front of us that's all about the eruptions here in Nisyros. 'Are you still writing to Karine?'

I'm quite sure Odina is no longer reading the details on the sign about eruptions or looking at the photos of time gone by. I think she's already read it but didn't want to look at me when she asked that question.

I take a deep lungful of the sulphur-laced air and wish I hadn't as I try not to gag or choke.

'Yes.' I exhale hard on the word, almost hissing it out.

'Is it helping?' Odina snatches a look at me, studying my profile as I keep my eyes on the creamy yellow lines and splodges all around the mouth and centre of the volcano.

It has a thin layer that seals it shut until the next time it erupts. It strikes me that we're all a little like this – holding back our emotions behind a thin crust, hoping they'll stay put and not burn too hot in our chests. Sadly, my crust seems a little broken lately and those emotions can erupt into panic attacks with very little warning.

That's something I have to try to keep away from Odina. No matter how confident she may seem, she's still only young.

Odina's question rolls around my mind. *Is it helping?*

'It's hard to say. I can't go back and not write to her. It hurts not to have any emails in return. There's no back and forth. It's just me shouting into the ether with no response. I find that difficult, not to get emails hearing what she's up to . . . But overall, yes. I think the *getting things off my chest* part is helpful. It seems to spread the weight of what happened.'

'It must be hard.'

'It is, but that's life, isn't it? Hard things happen and we have to deal with them.'

This could be my opportunity to get something, *anything*, out of Odina about why she's been distant at home. I can't push her – I've wanted to since she arrived, but now that the sun is out and we're moving around in this humid weather, it's somehow easier to talk about difficult subjects, without having to stare the other one down.

I try to find an open question that might lead her to a place where we can talk. I do this all the time in court, try to make people lose themselves in the wrong question while bringing them carefully into telling me what I need to hear. It doesn't sit right to do this with my family. It would just be a question, though, I don't want to be *questioning* . . . even if I only have good intentions for her.

'What about you? Any drama in your life?' I begin.

'I'd hardly call what happened with Karine *drama*.'

'No, that's not really what I meant.'

'You were trying to change the subject.' Odina twists to face me, her chin dipped and her lips slightly pouting, making her face look even more narrow than it already is.

'Maybe.'

'I get it. And yeah, I've had plenty of drama lately.' Odina exhales and begins to walk away from our vantage point and back towards the bike. 'It was nice coming up here this morning. I would say it's good to get some fresh air, but the air here smells anything but fresh.'

We share in a smile at the acrid smell. It's much worse in the centre of it all but the smell lingers for quite some way around it.

'It's nice though,' she continues. 'It's peaceful. I bet it gets packed in the summer.'

'Certainly.' I count three beats in my head, enough time to bring her back without jumping straight in. 'So, what's the drama? Anything you want to tell me about?'

'I don't know. Maybe.' Odina wraps her arms over her chest and tucks her hands under her armpits as we continue along the dusty ground of the volcano and back towards the car park.

'Boy trouble?'

'I don't know – are twenty-two-year-olds *boys*?'

My stomach tenses at this question. A five-year age gap is nothing at my age, but at seventeen it's a very different thing. I do my best to keep cool, the way I outwardly always do.

'Yes and no, unfortunately.'

'Yeah, *that*,' she sighs.

'So . . . who's the man-boy?'

'No one. Not anymore, anyway.'

'Who *was* he?'

'I can't do this here.' Odina kicks one of the many loose milky-grey stones a little too hard. It hurtles along into the tarmac car park and hits the tyre of my moped.

Her hands rush to her mouth. 'Oops, sorry!' She stifles a laugh.

'If you don't want to talk here, how about at the beach? Do you want to go and see the one with all the black pebbles? Or would you prefer a little sand?'

'Pebbles sound cool.'

'Come on then.'

'Can we get some lunch first, though? Can we go wherever has the biggest Greek salad?'

'I haven't gone round measuring them.' I do my best to laugh as I pass her helmet to her when we reach the moped.

I'm glad I've managed to explore the island before she arrived. I know exactly where to go. It means the distraction of my lurching stomach won't stop me finding my way.

I may know where to go for salad and beaches, but I don't know where our conversation will go when we get there. It's enough for my mind to spin in circles of anger at what this twenty-two-year-old may or may not have done to my niece.

Chapter 24

Odina kicks more stones, sometimes picking them up and plopping them into the sea, as we walk over the black pebbles, talking. The sea calmly drifting across the stones makes a satisfying sound, like a wind chime made of shells.

It's the perfect soothing backdrop to the ringing sound of anxiety in my ears.

Now our bellies are full of feta, olives, big fat tomatoes and lashings of thick olive oil, I can't wait any longer and begin my line of questioning. Over lunch she refused to say any more, claiming she wanted to think it through. Instead, she asked me about any problems I'd had with men and boys throughout my dating history.

It was like walking a tightrope, knowing what to say and how far to go without falling off into unknown territory.

'What's his name?' I begin.

It's a calculated question.

If I have a name, I have information that I could use to hunt him down if required. If I ask after, and it's something bad, the chances are she won't tell me. But if I ask it at the start, and sound relaxed about it, then I'll have some information in my pocket if needed.

'I'm not an idiot. I don't want you after him,' she laughs. Only it doesn't have that beautifully free, slightly wild ring it so often does. It sounds a little off-key for her.

'So you think I'll want to go after him?'

Odina picks up another stone and shrugs before throwing it into the sea, a little harder than the others.

'Maybe.'

'What happened?'

Even *I'm* finding it harder to maintain a casual and placid tone.

'I'll only tell you if you promise not to go off talking to Mum and Dad, and I only want to tell you because I still feel . . . *confused* by it all. Like I need to talk to someone about it who actually has experience with men. Not one of my friends who won't understand or might think I'm being silly or something. So take off that barrister wig of yours and just be my aunt for three seconds, OK?'

I mime taking off my wig and kicking it into the sea, then grin at her when I'm done.

'That was super cringe, in case you were unaware.'

'I was aware, but it made you smile so it was worth it.' I lick my lips to gather a second, because the next bit *won't* make her smile. 'You know that if it's a matter of safety—'

'Fine, I'll find someone else to speak to if you're already thinking about betraying me to my parents.'

Odina quickens her step as shiny pebbles roll away from her every stride.

I stop walking. 'When have I ever broken your trust?'

I'm not going to chase her for information. That wouldn't help at all.

The wind comes up from nowhere and catches her hair, making it whip off her shoulder. She turns, as though her hair pulled her to face me.

'Fine.' She takes a step back in my direction. 'We were sort of seeing each other. Not going out but . . . you know how it is. We never said *exclusive* or anything like that, but he was taking me out places.'

I don't respond, even though I feel she wants me to. My silence will keep her talking.

'Anyway,' she continues, as expected, 'I told Mum and Dad I was going to the cinema, and *we* went, alone. We'd been out a few times to get food and walk around and stuff, but yeah, not in a dark room alone. I think Mum and Dad thought I was going with some friends from college.'

'What makes you think they thought that?'

'Because that's what I told them . . .' She scrunches her shoulders up to her hoop earrings and stretches her mouth into a wide grimace.

There's no need to pass verbal judgement, she knows it was wrong. I press my lips together to show her my disapproval but stay quiet in the hope she'll carry on. So far, nothing she has said has done anything to assuage my apprehension about where this is going.

Odina drops down to sit on the stones, flopping her long skinny legs out in front of her.

'We were in the cinema, and like, you know, kissing and stuff, which was fine. We'd kissed loads before *blah blah blah,* but then, he kind of . . .' Odina shakes her head. 'This is so cringe.' Her lips tighten and she says the rest through a mouth that clearly wishes it were zipped shut, but isn't quite. 'He took my hand and placed it on his . . .'

'Penis?'

Odina lets out an exasperated exhale, as though the worst possible thing I could've said was the correct word.

'Yes,' she mutters. 'But, like, it was out. *In the cinema.*'

Her eyebrows are raised to the sky as she looks at me out of the corner of her eye like a wild horse.

'One second he's just squeezing my leg and we were kissing, then' – she looks away – 'he put my hand *there*, in front of people, and he put my hand *right* on it without warning. He didn't ask if I wanted to or anything. Like, I know we were in the cinema so it's hard to have a chat but . . . he put my hand *there*,' she repeats, 'in the cinema. It wasn't empty and I'm pretty sure there are cameras. Like, I just felt – embarrassed. I didn't want to be seen by someone I knew to endlessly be called a slut or something. Being caught in 4K like *that* . . .' She shakes her head at the idea.

'Sluts aren't real. It's an idea made up by men to control women.'

'I know, I know, but that doesn't help.'

'I know . . . I would ask you how all this made you feel, because that's all that matters, but quite clearly it upset you, otherwise you wouldn't even be telling me.'

'Yeah, but it's not like I didn't want to put my hand there. I just didn't want it to happen like *that*.'

'Is this the first time you've had . . . direct contact?'

'Do I have to answer that question?'

'No. To be honest, I'm not sure I want to know the answer.'

'Good.'

'Did you speak to him about it?'

'A little bit. He seemed hurt I'd pulled my hand away as quickly as I did. I think he was embarrassed too. He's said sorry, and I still really like him, but I feel confused about it.'

'He shouldn't have done what he did. It was sexual assault.'

'Technically, I know, but it was *my* hand on his . . . please don't say penis.'

'I don't need to now – you just said it for me.'

'Urgh. I know you deal with a million times worse than this, and it was a red flag' – her mouth twitches in a brief smile at all our previous conversations about Helios and flags – 'but he seems sorry. I've told him I've been busy for the past few weeks, and it hasn't put him off or anything. He wasn't, like, angry, and did say sorry. It's not like it was some random bloke who pulled it out and grabbed me, my hand was already . . . in the area.'

'It sounds like you're making a lot of excuses for him.'

'Yeah, maybe . . . Things had been going so well, though.'

'Does he know you're seventeen?'

Odina moves on the pebbles like they're suddenly sharp, wriggling and squirming.

'We met at this house party. He's one of my friend's brother's friends. Age never really came up. Plus my friend is eighteen, we met at netball. So he might think I'm her age.'

Odina doesn't look seventeen. She could easily pass for eighteen, or older. She's tall and has shape to her body, even with her skinny legs. There's a maturity about her face too, perhaps in the depths of her eyes or the oval shape of her face. I've no idea what it is, but I can understand why someone might assume she is older than her years. But that's no excuse for not checking beforehand. She's still clearly a young woman.

'You should be honest with him, but if you want my opinion, *this* is a lot of red flags. He exposed himself in public and made you perform a sexual act without consent. If it was up to me, he'd be up in court by now.'

'Don't you think that's a little extreme?'

'Maybe, or maybe he's a sexual predator in the making? Has he been intentionally hiding your relationship? How much have you spoken to him about how you feel about what happened? He said he was sorry, but is he saying that because it backfired?'

'I don't know. I think I need to talk to him more.'

'I think you should move on,' I say firmly.

'I mean, it wasn't as though I was clear about what I thought was and wasn't acceptable, and he wasn't rough with me or anything. It was just a shock and now I keep avoiding seeing him, but I really like him.'

'There will be plenty of other man-boys to really like. You're only seventeen.'

'You sound like Mum.'

'I'll take that as a compliment. Your mother is a highly intelligent and caring woman who loves you very much. The thing you have to ask is, why are you lying about him to your parents? And is it OK that he has made you so embarrassed and uncomfortable with his actions?'

'It's not his fault I'm seventeen and he *has* said sorry.'

'Odina, with all the things I've seen, were you hoping that by comparison I would find this somehow minor and reassure you that something like this could be overlooked? If so, you've got it all very wrong.'

'No, I just thought . . . I don't know what I thought. It's confusing. I really like him and I've always been such a good judge of character. Plus, I asked you to keep that barrister wig off your head.'

'It's amazing how good looks can easily persuade someone out of the notions of logic.'

'You think I'm so shallow he's just a pretty face and that means I'll put up with anything?'

'Of course not, but you're still a child—'

Odina pushes herself up from the pebbles, her face suddenly as hard as the stones under our feet.

'I'm tired, I think I'd like to go home for a nap. Seeing as I'm a child.'

After that, her jaw locks shut, and for the first time I've really messed up with her. We've never had an issue like this. I've undermined her feelings with my extensive knowledge of why she shouldn't trust a man like this.

I just hope I can gain her trust again.

Chapter 25

'How is Odina's holiday? Did you take her to Stefanos Crater this morning? She told me she wanted to go?' It's the most Helios has ever willingly said to me over the balcony.

'When were you two chatting?'

'Yesterday. I think you were in the shower, that's what she told me. We were only talking for five minutes, more or less.'

'Noted.'

'Did she have fun?'

'Erm . . . yeah. It was nice. Or . . . it was at the start. We had a slight . . .' I take a moment to consider my words. 'I don't want to call it an *argument*, there were no raised voices, but she shared something with me and didn't like my reaction.'

Helios stands up, walks to the side of his balcony and reaches a packet of cigarettes across for me to take one.

'I shouldn't. I went for years without smoking and if I start again now, I'll need to start a whole new count every time I have one.'

'I was the same. I didn't smoke for fourteen years.'

'What were you, twelve when you started smoking?'

'How old do you think I am? No, I was fifteen when I started and twenty-four when I quit.'

I quickly do the maths and now know he has to be older than thirty-eight, my age.

'When did you start again?'

'Couple of years back.'

Around forty, noted.

'What happened to make you want to start up again after all that time?'

I know what it was that pushed me over the edge and into picking up a cigarette again. The crushing weight and burden that pushed me to be broken enough that being healthy didn't seem to matter anymore. But at least I've done my best not to carry on. Odina would be so angry with me. My whole family would.

Helios turns away and pulls out a cigarette of his own, throwing the packet back on his balcony table then cupping his hands to light it. He takes a deep drag and holds it in for three counts before letting out the smallest amount.

'Life,' he says through a puff of smoke. 'What about you?'

I think of Karine and my career and panic attacks and feeling so very pointless . . .

'Also *life*.'

'And what about that niece of yours? Where is she now?' He looks in the direction of my bedroom.

'Napping.'

'What did you do to piss her off?'

'Boy trouble. I would never break her confidence about the details. But broadly, I don't like that she's making excuses for a guy five years older than her.'

'Five years is a lot at that age.'

'That's exactly what I said.'

'You didn't point out she's *too young*, did you?'

'Not in those words—'

'Rookie mistake.' Helios begins to tut playfully, but I don't find it all that amusing.

I tug on the hem of my blouse and grit my teeth as Helios continues.

'If you belittle her, she'll never listen. From thirteen, they think they're fully grown. We all do until we look back and realise, no, we weren't. You have to let them make their own mistakes and guide them towards sensible decisions. You must let them have freedom to be who they want to be and to spend time with who they want.'

'What do you know on the subject? You don't have a daughter.'

Helios's eyes home in on mine. 'Neither do *you*.'

He's right. It's the blind leading the blind at best.

'So if you had a daughter, you'd let her spend time with some older boy.'

'Depends on the boy.'

'Not this boy,' I mutter, and think about how humiliated and confused Odina must've felt.

The fact she wanted to talk about it says how much she needed advice, and all I did was project my worries about what that boy might turn into, instead of supporting her in the now.

'I don't know what happened, I can't comment. But what I do know is, we all make mistakes. *When he falls, he shall not be ruined*: Psalm 37:24.'

'Did you just quote the Bible at me?'

Helios shrugs, taking another drag of his cigarette.

'This is Greece – from birth, many of us go to the church every Sunday, like it or not. You had the same expression when I quoted Shakespeare, I'm not sure why you're so surprised I read books. I can even tell you which version of the Bible that quote is from. In another version it reads *Though he falls, he will not be overwhelmed.* But the first one made more sense with what I was trying to say.'

I can feel the muscles in my face desperately wanting to screw up, but I fight the urge.

Helios smirks at my expression. 'I know,' he says, 'it's the word of God through the eyes of men and translated by people like me, so don't trust every word. The editors over the years have been a few too many for my liking. I wonder how Shakespeare would feel about *Hamlet* being in seventy-five different languages. None will be the same as the English. I have read Angelos Vlahos's Greek version . . . I like the original.'

His honesty and pragmatism make my muscles relax and a smile tugs at my lips to join his.

'Well, thanks for your might-be-but-possibly-isn't-the-word-of-God-probably-someone-else-translating-it-badly inspirational quote and Shakespeare trivia. Remind me to take you to the next pub quiz. I'm not sure how it helps me much with Odina, though. I haven't met this man and quite frankly, I don't think I'd want to.'

'But it's not about you.'

He's right, of course. It's about Odina and how she feels, not my backlist of horror stories and fear.

I need to talk to her and make things right.

Chapter 26

'Where's Luna and Cloud? I haven't seen them all afternoon,' Odina says as she walks in the room.

'Probably out with their friends, and possibly older boyfriends.'

Odina rolls her eyes as she slumps down into the armchair.

'OK, that was a dreadful segue, but I wanted to say I'm sorry. You have always been a very good judge of character. The issue with the teenage and young adult mind is, it's still developing. It hasn't fully transformed yet into what it will be, so it's easier to make mistakes.'

'Wouldn't that be the same for him, then? He's not *that* much older.'

'Yes, but surely most people know it's inappropriate to expose their genitalia in a public place? Aside from that, I think you need to make a judgement call. Perhaps you're right, you should talk to him, in a public place' – I hold up a finger as my brain interrupts with this key factor – 'to discuss the issue face to face, like adults. If the same thing happened to me, and things had been previously going well, I'd want to talk to him about why he thought that was acceptable. He also needs to understand your age, too.' I lower my chin and narrow my eyes on her for emphasis.

Odina falls silent for a moment before coming back to me with a question. 'Have you had anything like this happen to you before?'

I cast my mind back over the many years of adulthood. There's nothing I've experienced that's the same, or too similar, but I am used to the sexism behind the scenes in my job. The boys' club, the touching of my bottom and pretending it was an accident. But none of that was from men I was seeing, or men I particularly trusted.

'I think we've all had times in the heat of the moment where consent would've been nice but it didn't happen, as it's perceived as something that can ruin a moment. There's a fine line and we all have different opinions on what is and isn't acceptable. If you've given someone consent to kiss you once, they're unlikely to stop in every romantic moment and ask if you'd like another kiss. We all have different lines that we don't want crossed, which is why it's so important to talk about these things with a partner *before* they happen.'

'Yeah, I probably should've spoken to him before.'

'Odina.' I exhale hard and press my hands to my face. 'We cannot always put the blame on ourselves.' My fingers drop and I point at the floor repeatedly for emphasis. 'This was not a standard situation you could discuss in advance. I don't know anyone who would write on a list, *things to do today, discuss with the man I'm seeing whether it is acceptable to get his dick out in public and put my hand on it.*'

The silly voice I put on for the imagined list makes Odina laugh and she unfurls a little bit on the armchair.

'What I mean to say is, if this is what he wants to do, it would be *his* responsibility to bring it up in advance. At most, you could have broached the general subject of not feeling comfortable with sexual behaviour in public. General boundaries. But this was his doing and something he should have broached if this was his intention.'

'I'll talk to him. I think it's the only way I can move on without having him stuck in my head. I haven't been able to concentrate on anything because I really like him and he keeps asking to see me and . . . I'll talk to him.'

'In public.'

'In public,' she repeats, rolling her eyes over a coy smile.

'Shall we go out to one of the tavernas for dinner and fill ourselves up on vine leaves and pitta bread with tzatziki, and one of those rich tomato stews, or some big thick lamb chops?'

'That sounds amazing. Can I go and look for Luna and Cloud before getting ready?'

'Sure. Even if they're not there, can you put their food out for them?'

'Yep.' Odina turns and leaves the room to trot down the stairs.

They're probably both curled up on the blanket I put there for them. They usually climb in the open window and sleep half the day.

I go to my bedroom to lay out some clothes. The afternoon has slipped away and evening is already here. It's already past eight, I'd normally be out on the balcony enjoying my glass of wine and emailing Karine.

However much I'd like the glass of wine, I'll wait and have it with dinner. I pick up my laptop and take it outside on to my balcony, to write while Odina is distracted.

Stepping outside into the cool evening as the stars begin to prick the sky, a glass of red wine is waiting for me on the edge of my balcony nearest to Helios. He is also on his balcony, with his glass of wine and a book.

I look over at him quizzically.

He nods at me. 'Thought you might need it.'

'Thanks.'

Picking up the glass, I slip down into my chair, leaving my laptop unopened on my knees.

Even when I was married to Russell, he never anticipated my needs or what I might like. He would ask if I wanted wine while pouring himself a glass, but I never came home to a meal or wine there waiting for me.

This is the first time I can recall where someone else has anticipated something I might want and gone ahead and done it for me. Someone who wasn't a paid assistant at work or a parent when I was small, anyway.

Wine has never tasted so rich and sweet as it does right now.

Chapter 27

Hi, Auntie Alisha! How's Helios? Say hi for me across the balcony. And to Calliope too, I'm actually wearing the bracelet she made today. I wanted to update you about . . . everything. So we went out last night, just to a chicken place, nothing fancy. I told him how I felt, and he said he totally misjudged the situation and he would never do that again or even intentionally do anything to anyone without consent. I could tell he was mortified. Then there was the age thing. He wasn't happy about me being seventeen but he said he does really like me, so we are going to stay friends and if something grows over time, then it does, no pressure. Now I think he might be perfect. Give Luna, Cloud and Soleil cuddles from me. Ciao.

It's nice to have the sound of Odina's voice filling up the empty rooms again.

I didn't realise how much I'd miss her when she left. I'm used to my own space, always happy to fill it how I like, but even with three cats now and counting, the space seems a little empty.

I've fallen into a comfortable routine. Going for a walk by the sea in the mornings, reading in the afternoons, having a coffee with Calliope once a week to discuss our plans for the future, then sitting silently next to my evening companion drinking my glass of wine, just the way we like it.

Even with this reassuring message from Odina, I still feel cautious about this man in her life. I've told her to at least tell her parents when she is going on a date, even if she excludes the age information. She agreed to that much at least.

It's out of my hands now. I've done all I can and I'm always at the end of the phone.

Heading downstairs to feed the cats, I make sure all of them get an extra bit of attention in place of Odina not being there to cuddle them all constantly. They're all very affectionate, each pushing around my ankles when they get the chance.

As soon as I step out of my front door, Helios's door closes.

'*Kalimera*,' I nod.

'*Kalimera*.'

We begin to walk silently in the same direction. I haven't outed him as able to speak English to Calliope, or any of the other things I've found out along the way.

My pulse seems to race with him near me. I could argue it's being in such close proximity to the lie, but it's not. His don't-give-a-crap confidence, while knowing he cares enough to be kind, mixed with that face of his . . . it's all too appealing, and no matter how hard I try to exhale it, it lingers along with his masculine scent and the delights of fresh pitta in the air.

My phone rings from my handbag.

It can't be Pop, I'm sure it's not Thursday again.

'Nancy?' I whisper to myself as I look at the screen. 'Hi, Nancy. Everything all right?'

'Alisha, hi!'

'How are you?'

'Yeah, good, thanks. Busy. I've been meaning to call ever since Odina got home but days turn to weeks, right?' Her soft south-west

USA accent is warm and gentle in my ear. 'Plus I had two big fundraisers. You'll be happy to know a lot of money was raised for a women's shelter.'

'I'm very glad to hear that.'

'I was wondering a couple of things. First, could I have the details for Helios. I'd like to thank him for helping Odina. And second, what flowers did you send Anna? I'm about to contact her but I want to send something too and don't want to double up.'

A shot of adrenaline smacks in my chest. I got Anna's number from Odina and then totally forgot to contact her. I scrunch up my eyes in irritation before letting it go.

'I can help with Helios, he's walking along right next to me. Would you like me to pass you over?'

Helios turns to look at me, his whole face riddled with concern. His pace slows to an almost standstill next to a winding lemon tree in front of a house with what looks like its own secret garden.

'Really? Yeah, sure, put him on.'

I pass the phone over to Helios. He holds it like it's something disgusting and mouths *who is it?* at me.

'It's Nancy, Odina's mum,' I whisper back.

He frowns and turns his back to me as he puts the phone to his ear.

It gives me a chance to study him. Something I haven't really done since finding out he speaks English and therefore knows I think he's attractive.

Helios raises an arm over his head and places his hand on the back of his neck, rocking a little as he listens to Nancy. He has good arms for someone who sits about translating books all day. I wonder if he has some weights tucked up in his house somewhere.

Helios turns back to me with a little more light in his dark eyes and a pinch of a smile on his face as he hands back the phone.

'All OK?' I enquire with Nancy.

'Yes, but he won't give me his address to send him something.'

'He lives directly next door to me. I'll sort something for him.'

'Thanks.'

'Of course.'

'Now, there's one more thing. What are you doing for Christmas?'

'I haven't thought that far ahead. It's only October. After what happened with Odina, I don't want to make plans that I can't fulfil. I'll need to think about it.'

'It's Halloween in three sleeps. That means it's almost November and that means basically Christmas. Now, Toby and his current girlfriend are coming to ours, and of course Pop, so it's just whether you'll be there too.'

'Is it OK if I think about it?'

'Sure thing, but please let me know in the next few days, OK? We'd love to have you. You know that.'

'I know.'

'Right, I've got to dash for a meeting with a caterer for another charity gala. Speak soon.'

'Bye.' I drop the phone back in my bag and take a moment to realise this isn't where I was walking to.

I've been naturally plodding along next to Helios without paying attention. I was meant to go to the supermarket, and I've ended up not far from the church. It's an old stone building that doesn't stand out particularly in the street. A yellow flag hangs limp again the wall and, unless you're paying close attention, it's easy to miss it, other than its stones against the many white-rendered buildings that encase it.

Young children wearing shirts and ties or dresses with pink puffy skirts skip along the streets with their parents and there's a few adults gathered outside the church door as we reach it.

'Is something going on today?' I scan the alleyway littered with women in heels with floaty skirts and men in crisp white shirts and ties. 'Is there a wedding?'

'No wedding. It's Greek Day, Oxi Day. I was going to go into the church but I'm very late for the service so I think I'll skip it.'

'Oh, of course it is.' Somewhere in the depths of my mind, I knew Oxi Day was in late October.

'I might just go and watch the parade.'

'A parade?' My mind races with the types of parade that might ensue, and I'd rather not miss such an interesting cultural event. This is exactly why I came here over anywhere else, to divert my brain from its current fixations and swim in the magic of another culture, an island that has fascinated me since I was a child. This is exactly what I need.

Plus, I purchased a canvas a few days ago and this might inspire me to paint on it. It's my next exciting endeavour that might be a job in the making.

'Don't get too excited. It's a small traditional ceremony with words from the church, a military display and the children from the schools wave flags. Come and have a look for yourself.'

'Are you sure?'

Helios looks at me with quizzical eyes. 'It's a public holiday. Everyone is welcome.'

A smile slips across his face, making dimples appear at the corners of his lips, before he begins to walk towards the sea.

I hadn't noticed before, I guess I was too busy with my call from Nancy, but Helios has made an effort for today. He's clean-shaven and has put on a smart long-sleeve shirt and clean blue jeans. He's even put some product in his hair so it doesn't look like he's been sleeping in a hedge, the way it so often does.

I feel underdressed in my knee-length culottes, blouse and Birkenstocks.

It's warm today, much nicer than when Odina was here. The sun has been reflecting on buildings again, making them as bright and clean as sea foam.

'You've shaved. You look nice.'

Helios rubs his smooth olive-gold skin. He's nicked his cheek in a couple of places, probably being out of practice with such a clean shave. It doesn't matter, he still looks frustratingly delightful.

'Thanks. I thought I should make an effort. When I looked at myself in the mirror this morning, it was a bit of a shock. Putting in an effort made me late.'

'It was worth it.' I smile up at him.

'You would say that.' He playfully purses his lips before looking away from me to avoid stepping on a toddler chasing a ginger-and-white kitten through the street.

As we reach the taverna at the town square, many of the seats under the parasols are taken and people chat and drink wine or beer as they wait for the ceremony to start.

At the far right, men in rows of perhaps five stand with heavy-duty guns resting in their hands like walking sticks. Black berets adorn their heads and they're all dripping in thick-looking camo clothes. I begin to sweat just looking at them.

It's getting on for lunch and my stomach grumbles from being in such close proximity to the taverna, knowing how good their pork gyros is.

'Lunch?' I indicate towards a space in the shade, right at the heart of the tightly packed round tables. 'I'm buying. Nancy wanted to give you something. You can have me instead.'

As soon as the words are out of my mouth, I hear them.

I look up to the ice-blue autumn sky and then over to Helios biting his lips and suppressing a laugh.

I point at him. 'Not like that.'

'I didn't say anything.'

'You didn't have to.'

I step towards the tables, pointing at the one I have my eye on before someone else snaps up the prime location. 'Are you coming to lunch or not?'

Helios looks at a few of the tables and sends a nod or two towards different people before squeezing behind me around the packed tables.

'*Nai*, sounds good.'

Chapter 28

'Why did Nancy *actually* call? Just to harass me?' Helios keeps his eyes fixed on his menu.

'No, to harass *me* about Christmas. And to thank you and Anna for looking after Odina.'

I don't even pick my menu up, knowing I'll have the gyros. Instead, I watch the space between the heads and shoulders of those at the tables in front of ours.

Small children run and dance around the square. Speakers on stands have been set up at each end and bowls of smoking incense swirl from them . . . No, not bowls on two-legged stands – it's a helmet propped up by two tall guns, much like the ones in the hands of the men to the right.

Smoke billows up from the helmets and my first impression shifts, the visual more poignant than when I glanced at them and thought they were just bowls of incense.

'Wine?' Helios says, barely audible behind his menu and the chatter of the gathering crowd.

He peers round his menu, giving me a look I can't quite figure out. He catches his bottom lip between his teeth before looking away again.

I think he's hoping for a yes.

I rarely have a glass with lunch, sticking to my medicinal small glass of an evening, but then I rarely get to have someone so good to look at across from me, so I might as well enjoy the moment.

'Happily.'

'Did you ever send Anna flowers?'

'No. If I'm honest, I totally forgot. I'll leave it up to Nancy now. It is her daughter, after all.'

Helios's head bobs up and down. 'Good, good.'

He's a strange but beautiful creature.

I get the impression he thought Nancy calling Anna was better than me doing it. I'm not sure what's so bad about me. Although Nancy does have a wonderful way about her. It's why she's so good at getting people to give so much money to charities.

All the charities hire her for events and to liaise with the rich and famous because they know they'll make more money with her on their side. That's how we met, because of her charitable work. Then I introduced her to Augustin.

The waiter dances between the tables, trying not to hit his bottom on anyone before reaching us and taking our order. Helios seems impressed when I attempt to order my food in Greek.

He orders a carafe of wine to share, instead of two small glasses, and I don't protest.

'Why did you end up here?' Helios says as he leans back in his seat and out of the shade of the parasol.

The sun makes him squint at me like he's about to start an interrogation.

'I have to tell you, Helios, that doesn't sound very welcoming.'

A smile spreads across his face, making those little dimples at the side of his mouth appear.

'Sorry.' He suppresses a laugh. 'But for me, I moved one island along. Nisyros is part of Kos. It's the peak of a volcano that has roots all the way stretching back to my home, but you . . .'

'I told you already, I came here on holiday when I was a girl and announced I'd live here one day. So here I am. That's all.'

'I don't think that's all. What are you running from?' He leans towards me and back into the shade, but the intense squint stays on his face.

'Why are you always projecting?'

We fall silent as glasses and a carafe are placed down on our table. The waiter says *yámas* before twisting between tables to take the next order.

It came out too harsh, I know it did. But I truly feel that's what's happening. He questions me to cover up his own secrets, I'm sure of it.

As though someone has pressed the unfreeze button, we both move at the same time to the carafe, his hand landing on top of mine.

Heat from more than the sun permeates the whole moment as light flicks through Helios's eyes and lands on me. His face softens before I snatch my hand away.

His warm touch remains on my fingers as he pours the wine.

'I apologise, I was rude. Equally, I don't think it matters why I'm here. Only that I'm here. I am an immigrant, albeit only in the short term. Is that what bothers you? That I'm not Greek?'

I have to change the subject back to something neutral before I fall down the spiral staircase that is his dark irises and tangle myself up in the knot of his touch.

'Everyone should be an immigrant at least once in their life. It's the only way to find out other countries are laughing at your own and we are all just people. That's what I found when I studied in England and travelled through other parts of Europe in my twenties.'

'Couldn't agree more.' I raise my glass to the notion. 'And I'm not running. I'm healing. It's different and I don't want to talk about it.'

A soft smile rests on Helios's mouth as we clink our glasses together.

'Are you going then, or not?' Helios replaces his glass of wine on the table.

'Where?'

'England? For Christmas? Unless Nancy is in fact in America?'

'No, she's in England, she's lived there forever.' I take another sip as I consider his question. 'I don't know. What are you doing for Christmas?'

'I fell into that one, didn't I?'

I shrug and take another sip of the wine as it begins to settle itself on my palate. 'You rather did, yes.'

'I'll be here.'

'I think I'll be here too. Not here,' – I tap my finger on the white tablecloth of the taverna – 'but at home. If the weather's bad and I can't get over to Kos, let alone England, it would be such a pain. Besides . . .'

I trail off, wishing I hadn't started that particular thought. The one about not being ready to be around people with expressions of pity and questions about returning to work. At least here I've managed to stave off having a panic attack for some weeks now, but I worry being back at home before I'm strong enough might take me back a step, however much I miss everyone.

'Besides . . . ?' he trails right after me.

'I'm just not ready to be around my family all at once. I love them dearly, but I decided to take time away, and I think I need to do just that. Christmas included.'

'I can't imagine having this big family that wants to be with you and not wanting to be with them.'

'I didn't say I don't want to be with them, it's just hard, that's all. And what about you? No family at all?'

'Not any for Christmas.'

Three men in black robes form a triangle in the centre of the square and under the glare of the midday sun everyone stands, making it more difficult to see. The speakers fill the air with religious sentiment, followed by a melodic solo male voice singing.

One of the men, with a decorated white epitrachelion adorning his neck, crosses himself. A lot of what's going on is obscured by the row of people in front of me, but I still find the whole thing fascinating.

Helios leans his face closer to mine over the table. 'We all need something to believe in.'

I enjoy the pomp and ceremony of most religions. There's something about the traditions of the past being played out over the centuries that feels like walking through the ages.

'*Do* we all need something to believe in?'

'People of faith live longer. It doesn't matter what they believe in, only that they have faith and belief. It could be believing the universe has energy, or fate. But having faith and sharing it seems to have a correlation to longevity. But then, so does being a gardener.' He shrugs, keeping his eyes on the ceremony.

'You're such a Renaissance man, aren't you?' I wish I could snatch back the wistful tone in my voice, but I can't.

It's nice to find someone whose interests are vast and interesting instead of niche and dull. It's irritatingly sexy.

'Huh?' Helios leans his ear a little closer to me.

'Nothing. Doesn't matter. Just, I guess I'll be off to my grave early as I lack in all departments.'

'That's not what you said.' His lips curl into a smile that I try to avoid looking at, in the same way I avoid looking at the sun.

My phone beeps loudly from my bag and I can feel my cheeks flushing even though no one seems to take any notice.

'I'll put it on silent.' I reach for my bag and pull out my phone. Nancy's name is there, and I can see the start of her message.

Thanks for Anna's number, you didn't say she was Helios's…

The urge to find out the rest quickly takes over and I slip my thumb over the screen to get the whole text.

> . . . sister-in-law. She seems nice. Let me know what you get Helios and I'll put the money in your account. Remember to let me know about Christmas xx

'Nancy said Anna is your sister-in-law.' My eyes stay on the screen in my hand as I re-read the message.

'Nancy is a gossip,' Helios replies bluntly.

'She's really not.' I shake my head at the idea.

It's an unfair statement. If you tell Nancy a secret, she'll keep it, but she was stating it like she thought it was something I might already know.

'You never said you were married.'

'You never asked.' Helios leans away from me and keeps his eyes on the ceremony instead.

That is a true statement, but he could've said when I told him about my divorce.

'Are you still married?' I venture.

'No. We have been divorced for some time now.'

'Good,' I mutter, more to myself than to him. 'I don't think I'd like to be having lunch with a married man who has been hiding a wife from me. That would be less than ideal.'

Helios sways to be nearer to me but keeps his eyes on the square. 'Liking you is less than ideal.'

This part of the proceedings comes to an end, and everyone continues to chatter as they take their seats.

Helios lifts his glass to his lips and says into it, 'Not like that. I didn't mean it like that,' before taking a sip.

The blush over his cheek and the lack of eye contact makes me wonder whether, in fact, he *did* mean just that. That perhaps he likes me more than he'd like to.

Despite all the flags Odina listed, particularly the big red lying one, I think I like him too.

Not that it matters. The only flag that's important today is the Greek one, and before I can question him, we're all standing again for the Greek national anthem.

Chapter 29

As music floods the air, we take to our feet, crossing the square to look down at the street along the shoreline below, where the children begin marching. They're of various ages and all waving Greek flags, while a military speedboat dashes across the waves to mark today's occasion.

As we arrive back at our table, food is there waiting for us. Many people around us are yet to order, probably waiting until after the ceremony. It's only a little after twelve now, as all in all the parade was a short but well put-together event.

I take a mouthful of tangy tzatziki with my crispy slices of salty pork gyros. While we eat, I think about all the local people who were recognised for their contributions to the community during the ceremony.

It was nice to watch people come together and I tell Helios as much. He tells me about the ceremony over in Kos, and how it is much smaller here in Mandraki than the one he was used to.

When I try to ask a question about his move to Nisyros island, all he says is how much he likes the peace here, then slips away from me and back towards his lunch.

When all the food has been consumed and the people around us either leave or begin their meals, I fish my purse out of my handbag and signal for the waiter, mouthing *ton logariasmó parakaló* – bill, please. Helios expressed some level of being impressed when I managed to sort-of order my food in Greek. It's hard going but I'm getting there one new word at a time, usually to then mispronounce it or get the gender of it all wrong.

Helios slumps back in his chair. 'That was delicious, thank you. Or thank you, Nancy.'

'It's fine, I'll get this. If I tell her this is what she paid for, she'll be saying it was a date and asking too many questions next time I see her.'

'At least that won't be at Christmas.'

'True.'

The waiter brings over the *logariasmós*, and I place down a few notes to cover the cost.

'Wait, if this isn't on Nancy, let me pay,' – he pushes the money back towards me – 'for being dishonest about my language skills.'

'Fine. I accept, thank you. But I'll get the next one.'

I take my money and slip it back in my bag. As I look up, I catch the end of a facial expression. The end of a tilted head, perhaps a raised eyebrow.

'What?' I lower my voice a little.

'*The next one.*'

'I know, you hate to spend time with anyone, or perhaps just me. Strange, isn't it? How you're so talkative when we're together, even laughing and joking, but you consistently claim not to want to be my friend.'

'I *don't* want to be your friend. I don't want to do a lot of things I'm good at.' Helios chuckles. A delightful, playful sound.

'You're good at being my friend?'

'I helped you keep Odina safe, didn't I? I could've just ignored you. Plus the wine on the balcony when I thought you would need it, and I always offer you cigarettes.'

'That's positively *unfriendly*. They're like tiny little bullets poking unwanted holes in people's lungs.'

'How poetic of you.'

It's strange to be thought of as poetic. I'm the one who can write a powerful essay to argue any point; it's Odina or Toby who take after Mum creatively, not me. It's nice to know it's in there somewhere, I guess . . . even if I can't write a book the way I thought I might.

'That made you happy, didn't it?' Helios leans his forearms on the table and clasps his hands together as he studies me. I want to wriggle under the light of his gaze, but I'm well trained in staying still in intense situations.

'Yeah, it did. I'm most certainly not the one to look at for poetry in my family. My mother used to write us little notes and poems in cards. Odina and my younger brother, Toby, they do it now. I'm the one people call on when they need a letter or email taking someone down in the most technical way possible, not for the beauty of words, but for their function.'

'As someone who mostly translates fiction, I'm all for a little poetry, but I do also appreciate words when used formally and honestly. I'm sorry about your mum. I couldn't say that before, because I was . . .'

'Playing dumb?' I offer.

'Yeah, I was. I'm sorry for your loss.' There's a softness that falls over his features, one that comes from those who have lost loved ones and truly understand the all-consuming pain it brings with it.

I guess it's impossible to wander through this life without feeling the razor of death shaving off layers of your heart with each dearly loved person it takes away.

'I'd say it's all right, the usual trivial response to the *sorry*, but of course, these things are never all right or OK. But thank you for the acknowledgement.'

Helios throws me one of his signature nods before pushing his chair back.

I do the same, standing alongside him to wave thanks to the waiters and begin the short walk home. It's been an unexpectedly perfect afternoon.

The weather's beginning to turn. The wind whistles along the streets and the kittens all think some invisible hand is trying to stroke them.

Clouds that weren't there a moment ago bunch up over the mountains that encase the Stefanos Crater at the centre of the island. After the previous storms and rain, I now know how quickly things can change.

Without a word between us, we both walk briskly along. The wind throws my hair this way and that. I'm used to having it in a low ponytail or flat bun to wear my barrister's wig comfortably, so I've enjoyed having it loose since being off work. Now, though, it seems to have gone wild and got a mind of its own.

Big, round spots of rain smack against the white stones lining the path, making them look like they've been gifted grey polka dots.

We begin to jog, past cats and people all scurrying for cover before the downpour begins. As we reach my door I snatch a question, not wanting to be alone again quite so soon. 'Coffee?'

'Sounds good.'

We step into my house just in time to avoid the worst of the rain.

Helios follows me into my kitchen.

'How many cats do you have now?'

'Erm . . . all of them?' I shrug and laugh a little at how I seem to be collecting every cat on the island. 'I feed whoever shows up and try to worm and flea and . . . whatever else is needed for as many as I can.'

Five cats join us in the kitchen, including Luna, Cloud and Soleil. I should probably shut the window when I go out to stop it becoming a circus.

'What sort of coffee? Don't say Greek, because I can't make it. But I can do espresso, latte and a bunch of others.'

'Nice piece of equipment.' Helios points at the coffee machine on my counter. 'I'll have espresso, thanks.'

I start moving about the kitchen, picking out cups and pushing buttons.

'I've only ever made drinks for Calliope and she always wants water. Well, she had coffee once, I don't think she was very impressed. Odina's a tea drinker, like my pop, so she didn't want coffee either.'

I'm rarely aware of how I move around a space. I'm confident in all domains. I've had to become thick-skinned to do what I do and live the way I live, yet I'm acutely aware of Helios tracking my every move around the kitchen.

Each time I look at him, his eyes are without exception on me.

I pass him the miniature cup of hot thick liquid and he takes it readily.

'Balcony?' he suggests.

'What about the rain?'

'It's not heavy now. Besides, I like watching the rain. That's how I overheard your whole conversation about Odina.'

He follows behind me, up the creaking stairs, leaving the cats to lollop about the kitchen in peace.

'Nice place,' he says as he scans the living room.

It does look cosy in here, with soft leather sofas, chairs and fluffy brown throws.

'Thanks. The balcony that isn't broken is this way. It leads off the bedroom.'

As we enter the room, I'm glad I bothered to make the bed this morning. The gentle eggshell-blue sheets look calming against the pale stone walls.

The shutters are already open, trickles of rain streaking across the glass outside. Helios opens the door just enough to lean on it and look out towards the glimpse of sea in the distance.

He finishes his drink like it's cool water and puts it down on my bedside cabinet, making sure it finds its way to the coaster I got in one of the shops along the seafront on a shopping trip with Odina. It's made of highly polished volcanic rock.

'Can I smoke?' He turns to look at me as I stand close to his arm, also looking along our road as the rain dies out and the sun peeps through again.

'As long as you blow it outside. Let me get something to use as an ashtray.'

He doesn't ask twice, he lights up the stick and offers me one. As usual, I happily decline.

I take another sip from my cup and place it next to his on the set of drawers. I only have one coaster, so I'll have to hope it doesn't leave a ring.

Downstairs, there was an ashtray under the sink that had been left behind. A heavy glass one. I can't remember whether I kept it or not.

Leaving Helios for a moment, I trot back down to look for it.

It's still there under the sink, only now it's tucked behind surface cleaner and sponges.

I jog back up the stairs and balance it on the ledge of the balcony outside.

Helios's eyes are on me – not the light dusting of rain that's already burning to steam, but me. The intensity of his stare is like being under the glare of a spotlight. It's impossible to ignore.

Something has shifted. Like the energy around him is magnetic and wild.

'I remember seeing you on the balcony for the first time. It was like watching a film.' He sucks in smoke and holds it there for a count.

'Really? Why?'

'You stepped out all wide-eyed, looking out to sea, and you look like *that*.'

He waves his hand at me.

'I'll attempt to take that as a compliment.'

Helios laughs and steps outside now the rain is no more than the occasional spot, leaving only its footprints in the sky.

'You know exactly what you look like.' He takes a step back towards me, biting his bottom lip.

Unlike the moment on the balcony at Calliope's house, I now know that any words that pass my lips will be well understood. I also know he knows exactly how I feel about the way he looks, even if I've kept it to myself ever since.

It's already too late. He knows I'm jealous of the cigarette on his lips, wishing it was me instead.

He lingers over me, making my heart throb.

This man is trouble. I know it.

Chapter 30

'I really wish I didn't like you, Alisha. I wish you still thought I didn't understand you.'

'Even if you didn't speak English, I think there's some things we would both have understood.' My eyes flick over him and the corners of his mouth curl up in a knowing smile.

'True. But I was fine here on my own. Now . . .' He shakes his head and bites his lip again, but doesn't continue with the sentence. 'What would you do if I kissed you?'

The perfect way to gain consent without *actually* asking. Every inch of me pulsates in time with the pounding of my heart.

'Let you.'

Helios flicks away the cigarette in the direction of the ashtray. He draws his fingers over my throat and into the hair at the nape of my neck as his mouth descends on mine.

We meet with no sign of tentative trepidation. This is something we've both wanted for a while and have been doing a dreadful job of hiding from.

I lean back, the hinge of the shutters digging in my back as Helios's solid frame presses into me. Maybe this is my first perfect kiss. Right now, I can't remember any as good as this. He tastes like bonfires and fresh pitta and is just as delicious.

My body presses harder into his as I slip my arms around his neck. I do my best to recall what underwear I put on this morning after my shower. This isn't the way I'd expected today to go, but I'm happy to let it progress further.

Not wanting to let the other go, we shuffle and twist until we fall inside my room, away from prying eyes from the row of houses where anyone might sit on their balcony and see us.

I kick one of the shutters across as best I can as Helios's tongue skims like fire over my neck, setting light to me, leaving me wanting more. The glass doors remain open as I fall down on the bed in front of him.

Leaning back on my elbows, I look up at him, wondering what's going on inside his head.

Scanning my eyes down, I know that at least it's something good.

His chest rises and falls in heavy breaths of desire as he looks down at me. I'm happy to wait for him to decide what happens next. I'm already at home, on my bed. I haven't asked him to leave, but I suppose he could if he wanted to.

'Do you want me to stay?' he says, almost reading my mind.

'Do *you* want to stay?'

'Do you ever answer a question without asking another question?'

'No.'

He rubs a hand over his mouth, covering a frustrated laugh.

He looks from his left to his right, slightly shaking his head in thought before landing his eyes back on me.

'Yeah, I do want to stay.'

Helios leans over me, sliding one arm underneath me and pulling me further up the bed, making room for him to climb on top of me to resume our passionate foreplay.

There's something so 'high school' about it, like it's forbidden to have him here even though it's not. Maybe it's because we both know we won't be telling anyone about this new development.

His lips move over my jawline as my hands move across the smooth skin of his back. I tug at his shirt before half undoing it then pulling it over his head.

Helios's body is taut, smooth and lightly bronzed, with only a smattering of curls over the centre of his chest.

After almost two months of having him as a silent companion and thinking about him more than is probably healthy, I didn't expect anything would *actually* happen in the four months I have left here.

His fingers fumble over my blouse and something shifts as his hand slides inside the cup of my bra. A moan falls from my lips as he grazes my nipple, only for him to retract completely.

His head lowers as he rubs his temples. The only sound is our heavy breathing filling the room.

'What's wrong?' I run my hand over his velvety cheek and down to his chin, tilting it up to force him to look at me, but it doesn't work as he keeps his lashes low.

'I just . . . I haven't done *this* since my divorce. It still feels like cheating. Stupid, I know.'

'I don't think it's stupid.'

He meets my eyeline, but only briefly before snatching his gaze away again. There's a deep sadness there, one that's taken over and now fills the room.

I wriggle away from him and sit on my pillow, tapping the one next to me for him to come and join me.

He doesn't move closer.

He keeps his distance.

'I never expected to like someone else. Ever. And . . . yeah . . . From the moment you smashed that pot out on the balcony and muttered away to yourself, assuming I didn't understand—'

'I didn't assume, you didn't show any signs of understanding.'

'Mmm, guess I didn't.' He tries to hide a smile, dipping his chin again.

'You could be an actor.'

This is enough to make the corners of Helios's eyes crease in gentle laughter.

'Do you want to forget this ever happened?' I ask.

Silence rings in the air and I'm suddenly aware of my state of undress and how much I was looking forward to seeing what Helios looked like without his jeans.

'No. Even if I wanted to walk away, I'm not sure I have the self-discipline to make myself go.'

'Good.' I crawl forward and lie down on the bed to look up at him.

'Would it help if I tell you about my first time after getting divorced?'

'Go on then.' He shifts his weight like he's settling in for a good story.

It's not the best story, but it's a true story.

'It was probably three months after we split up, so the divorce wasn't final, but we were over, Russell and me. I'd had a crappy week at work and I was looking for a distraction. Someone to take me somewhere nice to eat. A reason to get dressed up. It was weird, because Russell and I hadn't gone out together for ages and our sex life was . . . nothing to write home about. That's not a put-down to him, I just don't think there was much spark between us. There was no passion. Or not for me, anyway. It wasn't until I was on a date with this good-looking man that I realised how low my confidence was after only being with Russell with minimal enjoyment. I started to doubt myself and my ability to . . . relax, I guess. It was a little awkward, or it was in my head at least. I asked him back to mine, and he was so intimidated by where I live. I have a private lift to my apartment, and I thought he was going to make a run for it then and there. Not every man likes a woman who earns more than twice what they do. When his eyes went back in his skull, I realised

I didn't have a condom and had to ask if he did, which of course he did, but then he went into this overly practical mode about sharing recent clean doctors' reports. It was like a nervous rambling, which killed the mood somewhat. Better of course to have a regular check, but the way he went on and wanted to show me the results in detail took a lot of the romance out of it all.'

I can't help but think there was an element that reminds me of this moment now, that awkwardness of today's complicated web of factors to consider.

'Anyway, it was all so awkward and depressing I sent him on his way, and I'd barely eaten at dinner with nerves. So I was hungry and grumpy. I chucked on my yoga pants and a big T-shirt and ordered a pizza . . . and had sex with the delivery guy instead.' I cover my face at the memory and begin to laugh.

'That's not how I saw that going.' Helios joins my laughter. 'Please tell me he wasn't some uni student half your age.'

My hands drop to my sides on the bed. 'What a cheek! How old do you think I am?'

'Odina already outed you as in your late thirties, which means they could be half your age.'

'This didn't happen yesterday.' I pick up the pillow next to me and playfully throw it at him. 'No. He was actually the owner of the pizza place, but someone hadn't turned up for work. And now I can never, ever get pizza from there. Such a shame, because it used to be my favourite. Anyway, it got me back out there. I hope my story is helpful.'

'Very. Now I know never to order you a takeaway in case the deliverer, what do you English say? – tickles your fancy.'

He wears a beaming smile like a crown and it's nice that I've knocked the nerves away from him, even if it's only for a moment.

'It's good to see you smile. Look, if it helps, I'm not expecting anything. I don't want a relationship or expect you to be my *new boyfriend.* I'm happier alone. I hate sleeping next to people, I can't do it. They always move about too much and my ex-husband would never respect my night-time routines or give me the space I needed when I needed it. Don't get me wrong, against all my better judgement I *do* like you. But there's less than no expectation here. I'm happy to be your first since your last.' I try to offer an easy smile.

'It does help a bit. I don't have any recent STD test results, though. The last one I took was at university and then I was with my ex, that's where we met, so I hope you're not expecting me to pull out a golden scroll telling you my penis is as clean as a whistle.'

'Whistle? Really?' I lower an eyebrow and roll my lips over my teeth to hold back my nervous laugh.

Helios shrugs and pushes his fingers through his unruly hair, which has already freed itself from any product he put on it earlier. The motion unintentionally shows off the thickness of his arms perfectly.

'People *blow* whistles . . .' I say, trying to spell it out for him.

His right hand whips to his eyes and he falls over on the bed in laughter. 'That was unintentional, I promise.'

Watching him squirm on my bed makes a ripple of lust run through me and laughter spills out of me too. Silly things are always the best things to laugh about and a great way to bring us to where we were before nerves got hold of him.

When eventually our silliness dies down a little, I bring the conversation back.

'Was it a similar thing for you? With your divorce? A realisation that things just weren't working and that's what ended it?'

'No. Not at all.' A frown digs deep into his features like it wants to take root and never leave. It's almost impossible to imagine he was laughing ten seconds ago.

'Then why did you break up?'

Helios stays silent for a moment longer than feels comfortable. He opens his mouth like he might speak, only to shut it again and reopen it like a fish out of water.

'She didn't love me anymore.' His voice isn't much above the sound of the creaking wood as it swells in the changing season, but it rings eerily clearly in my room.

I have no idea how to respond.

My divorce was amicable, easy, sensible. Even though Russell would have continued on like a good soldier if I hadn't broached the subject, I think he was relieved when I told him it was over. He wanted so badly to start a family, and I didn't. He thought I'd change my mind, and I know I never will.

Helios is suggesting he never wanted his marriage to end.

The first question that runs to the front of my mind jumps right out of my mouth. 'Do you still love her?'

'No. Not anymore.'

'Did she cheat?'

'Never.'

'Did you?'

'Never ever. It's not in my nature to cheat. Look, it doesn't matter why it ended. It ended.'

Never? I've seen and heard a lot about the dissolving of marriages. It comes up a lot in my line of work. It makes it hard to believe in true love, even though I believe it of my parents. The main reason for a divorce when one party is still in love is betrayal of some kind.

'Then maybe it's time to move on?' I suggest.

'Maybe you're right. Maybe it *is* time. I *am* very attracted to you.' Helios moves towards me on the bed and my body fills with anticipation all over again.

His fingers reach for mine; they weave together naturally. Our eyes meet and we share a coy smile. He looks good in just jeans.

Firm.

I slide down the bed a touch as Helios reaches across to position himself next to me on one elbow. He looks down at me for a moment with his deep mahogany eyes.

'And anyway,' he begins, 'I feel confident you like me too. Based on the things you said when you thought I couldn't understand you. And the way those ocean eyes of yours scan me when you think I'm not looking.'

Before I can make excuses or a rebuttal of sorts, his lips are on mine and we sink into a deep kiss like the last one. I'd already started to wonder whether it could possibly have been as good as I thought, or whether I imagined it. But I haven't imagined it. He really *is* that good.

I don't want to make any further moves to progress too far from kissing. He needs to dictate the pace, not me.

I haven't had my heart broken before. I've never been so in love that I've been crushed by a break-up. I've often wondered whether I'm even capable of such love. But he has clearly been hurt in the past, and it needs to be up to him what happens next.

It's hard holding back as my fingers run through his thick hair, across the back of his neck and taut shoulders. I want to let my hands wander lower and discover more parts of him, but I do my best to keep them at bay.

Helios rolls me on to my back and begins to kiss down my neck, peeling off my clothes one by one and taking his time to enjoy my body, making me squirm and writhe under his touch.

It's like he wants to know every part of me and learn it by heart. He takes his time and seems to mentally note my reaction to each place he touches. It's as though our time in this room is endless and he is here to enjoy every last second.

I feel like we've been forgotten here and there's no one else in the world. In many ways that's exactly how I feel when I lie on this bed, only now Helios fills it with me, exploring my body like it's a map and he needs to read it all.

Only when he's made my back arch and my fingers have had no choice but to curl up in his hair does he release me from his grasp.

When I catch my breath, I want to reciprocate, but he shakes his head and rests his hand over mine as it attempts to make its descent over his abdomen.

'Another time.' This sounds like a statement, not a question.

Like my exploration of his map is written in stone somewhere, yet it isn't on the agenda for this evening.

I'm more than happy to relive this moment with him and read his body the way he read mine.

He kisses my forehead and lies down next to me, folding his hands behind his head, both of us peaceful in our nakedness. There's no point being bashful now.

However much I'd like to jump on him, I don't. He needs time and space and I don't want a relationship.

I'm here for four more months. It would be nice to pass some of the winter here in Nisyros wrapped around a good-looking Greek before heading back to London, or wherever I end up next.

Chapter 31

'Are you going to sit down?' Helios says from somewhere behind me.

The waves crash against the sea wall. I grip the rough surface and close my eyes to capture the fresh scent of salt and seaweed in the air. It's breezy, but overall the wind has died down a little today.

It's rained again for the past few days, which has meant no silent dates with Helios on the balcony, but the sun has returned today.

Being by the sea means the breeze often brings a chill now it's mid-November, but I love it. The bright-blue sky makes an appearance more often than not and the smack of salty air is the most refreshing way to start any day.

I'm often still found in camisole tops and jeans with only a blouse over the top. Many of the locals sport coats and even scarves. So far, the chill hasn't penetrated that deep, unless the rain starts again. That's the only time I've been forced to opt for something with a little more shelter to it when I go for my daily walks or to the supermarket.

Yesterday, Helios knocked on my door and asked if I'd like to meet for lunch today. I'd started to wonder whether the whole encounter the other day was in fact an elaborate dream from spending too much time alone in my bed.

The look he gave me when asking me to lunch suggested I wasn't dreaming.

I'm most certainly not counting this as a date, though. That would be absurd.

I glance over my shoulder to find Helios pulling out a seat at the table next to where I'm standing. He's correctly deduced it's our table as my handbag is on the back of my chair.

'I'm only sitting down when I have to,' I retort.

Instead of sitting on the seat he's pulled out, he pushes it back in, moves around the table and comes to stand next to me by the wall overlooking the rocks and the sea.

'Have you been swimming in the sea since you've been here?'

'No. Paddling only for me. I'm not the most confident swimmer. I do like looking at it though. The power of it, the way the moon forces all those particles to rise from up there in the sky . . . it's magnificent, and gives such wonderful perspective. Did you know that even listening to the sea for twenty minutes lowers cortisol? Although I'm not sure how wide the studies were or if this was the same for all test subjects, so I wouldn't say it in a court of law, but that's what I read in an article.'

Helios looks at me with a playful intensity, like a cat that wants to play with a mouse before dinner.

'What?'

He bites his lip and leans close to my ear, his breath warm on my cheek. 'You have the same power, you know? To make particles rise and to lower cortisol.'

I twist my face up towards his. 'That was insanely cheesy.'

He pulls away and we both begin to laugh, although my blood has all rushed away from my extremities at our close proximity and the smell of lychee in his cologne and the tone of his voice.

'Seriously, though,' Helios begins, 'I did actually know that. It was in one of the many books I translated. Perhaps they read the same article you did.'

'Perhaps. How many books have you translated?'

Helios exhales hard, turns his back on the sea to lean on the wall and scratches at his head.

'I have no idea. Depending on the size of the book, usually I translate from four to ten a year and I sometimes do final read-throughs of other people's translations. Like a cold read more than a full edit. I freelance for various publishers and work with self-published authors too.'

'What are you translating at the moment?'

'Genre?'

'Yeah, what genre?'

'Guess.'

He folds his arms and looks down at me as I twist to look up at him, one hand still gripping the rough edge of the wall.

I begin to hum in thought as I snatch this moment to openly study him, taking pleasure in the lift of his cheeky-cheekbones at making me guess.

'*Ya sas.*' Calliope walks into the taverna with a big bag on her shoulder and her husband, Nikos, two steps behind her. She smiles at me but continues to address Helios in Greek, with a quizzical look in her eye. He greets her with a reserved smile and throws one to Nikos too before answering her in English.

'I can actually speak English.'

Calliope takes a step back and slaps her hands down by her legs before rapidly talking to him in Greek like it's all one long complex word. I think she might be berating him.

'I cannot believe this.' She waves her hand in Helios's direction and looks from her husband to me. 'He never says. Why you never say this? Why you never say *anything*?'

Before any of us can snatch a breath to answer, Calliope continues in my direction. 'When did you know this? You never tell me either.'

'I found out when Odina was here. Helios actually helped me get a message across to her. That's when he decided to come clean and own up to speaking perfect English. I would've told you, but it's not my place to say.'

'And now you two are lovers.' She shakes her head and twists her face to one side, rolling her eyes at Nikos, who barely speaks any English and instead mumbles something in Greek. I wonder if he even knows what's going on. I'm sure if it isn't clear, Calliope will soon fill him in.

Helios and I splutter and choke by way of denial, but she ignores us completely.

'Enjoy the lunch. You,' – she points right at me – 'you come over on Monday. You bring some honesty and we make the jewellery this time. No more excuse. Bye-bye.' She walks away, waving over her shoulder without so much as looking back at us.

Nikos mumbles a goodbye and an apology before trudging after Calliope.

'How much older do you think he is than her?' Helios whispers in my ear.

'Ten years, give or take?'

'I'd say twenty.'

I don't respond. I don't think it matters or needs a response. Instead, I take my seat and pick up the menu.

'Romance,' I state as I scan the list of drinks.

Helios sits down heavily in his chair, making it moan, but keeps his focus intently on me as he tucks himself in with a loud scraping noise of the chair legs.

'What? You think that he's romantic and that's how they got together?'

I splutter with laughter and cover my mouth. 'No.'

'I'm confused,' he eventually admits.

'That's my guess. I think you translate romance novels.'

At that, he throws his head back in a delightful laugh, enough so that I can't help but chortle along.

'No, no. I don't think I'd be any good at romance.' He shakes his head as his laughter peters out. 'I mostly translate children's books, YA and sometimes sci-fi. A lot of the YA I translate is fantasy. You know, mystical or dragon-themed. No one has ever asked for romance from me. So if that's what you're hoping for, I think you're looking in the wrong place.'

'Oh, don't worry, I'm not expecting romance. Not even a little bit. I don't think I've ever had real romance in my life and it's not something I'm looking for now . . . or ever.'

I turn back to the menu, happy that we are at least on the same page with this friendship of ours.

'Never?' Helios's voice is soft over the sound of the waves sloshing about on the other side of the sea wall.

'Huh?'

'You've *never* had romance, never want romance . . . ?'

'No. I'm more than happy buying my own flowers or taking myself to dinner. I buy the jewellery I know I'll wear and everything.' My tone hints at a sarcastic *wow* at the idea of being able to do all these things for myself.

'Of course you can. But surely someone has at least tried to do these things for you?'

I think back to the relatively short list of actual long-term boyfriends I've had in my twenty years of dating.

'Flowers, yes. But mostly first-date flowers, and that's no more special than a friend popping over for dinner and bringing some with them. It's normal, not romantic. It's not like someone taking note that my favourite flowers are those orange lilies and sending them to me for an anniversary I didn't even know we had, for like, I don't know, a first kiss or something. Nothing like you see on TV or read about in books. I've never had a romantic relationship that metaphorically knocked me off my feet or made me feel like there was someone who I couldn't live without because being apart caused actual pain. I'm too practical for all that.'

Helios's mouth downturns in thought as he casts his eyes over the navy waves all laced with white.

I open my mouth to ask what he's thinking, but I don't really want to know.

Chapter 32

'Coffee on the balcony? I bet you're wishing for a cigarette about now?' I look at my wrist, even though I've forgotten to put a watch on today. Something only a few months ago I would never have forgotten to do.

I glance along the street and hope Calliope isn't lurking about, trying to see whether we go through the same front door or not.

Pushing my heavy key in the door, it opens with a click and, without answering, Helios follows me inside.

'Do you know my entire schedule?'

'No.' I shake my head a little too enthusiastically.

The truth is, even though I don't know the exact times he goes out, I do have some idea of when he is likely to be on his balcony. The walls are thick between our homes, but the windows are thin and I can hear certain things even when I'm not out there myself.

I hope he's not too familiar with my schedule. Looking over and seeing me write my regular emails to Karine, fewer than before but still impossible to stop in hope that they're helping.

'Espresso?' I add to change the subject.

'Great, thanks.'

'You can go up if you want, start opening the shutters.'

I'd like to make it as obvious as possible that he is welcome to stay for more than coffee without making him feel like he *has* to if he doesn't want to. He did say he wanted to have a return visit. It's easy to see the man is a mess of tangled emotions about his divorce, but I think it would do him so much good to start to move on.

I'm more than happy to sacrifice my body to the greater good if it means feeling the weight of Helios between my thighs.

As I take the cups up the stairs, a shot of excitement runs over my spine. It's good to bring back some excitement. It's not something I expected from my time here in Nisyros, but it's very welcome. The whole idea was to leave everything behind and reset my mind so I could get back to work or find something new that I'm good at. So far, I'm not good for much at all, so I'm hoping to feel refreshed and ready to believe in myself again. Being with Helios is very much a welcome therapy.

Helios is standing in my living room, head tilted to one side.

'Here.' I try to pass him his cup.

'What is this?' He points at the canvas leaning against the wall.

'Oh God, don't look at that.'

I step around him, pick up the canvas and turn it around. Another failed attempt to both relax and find a new calling.

'What was it, though?' A laugh is bubbling within him. 'Did you do it?'

'It's dreadful, I'm aware. Apparently, it's harder than I thought to paint people. I can't write books or paint. Do you know, I even tried to knit the other night? It was riddled with holes. How is that relaxing? How is being bad at things ever going to be relaxing? I used to excel at everything I tried and now I can't do anything. The only thing I'm good at is winning in court, and I can't even do that anymore.'

I walk away to the balcony, open the shutters with my mug still in hand and look across toward my fraction of sea view. Helios joins me, standing so close I can smell his coffee as much as I can my own.

'It's such a beautiful day.' I all but sigh out the words.

'Bloody chilly, though,' he says as he faux shivers.

'It's probably ten degrees warmer here than in England.'

We settle into our drinks, both leaning on the balcony as Helios asks me about my life in London, and shares a little about his life at Reading University many years ago.

The most he shares is a funny story about meeting two girls one night, who asked if they could stay in his house because they had locked themselves out after drinking absinth. He couldn't work out if they were genuine or whether it was a pick-up line. It was the same night he started talking to the woman who would become his wife, so he never did find out the truth of it all.

It's hard to get any real information out of him without him quickly deflecting it away. He tells me charming anecdotes about times with friends drinking shots or the silly things he would say in Greek to women giving him too much unwanted attention – *just for being Greek*, he says, forgetting I can see his good looks under his messy hair and intermittently shaven face.

'So what silly things did you say to me when you understood me and I didn't understand you? Were you there being all serious but laughing your socks off at all the crazy things when I turned my back?'

'No, but I don't know why not. I really should have.' He smiles at me, tilting his head for a moment, making me want to run my fingers through the silver strands at his temples as he bites his lip. 'You look cold, come on.'

We both head inside and he closes the doors behind us but leaves the shutters open, letting the afternoon sun stream in and on to my bed like a beacon.

I took our cups away ages ago, I'm not even sure how long we've been outside chatting. One hour? Two? Time seems to pass differently in the presence of Helios. Like he has his own little laid-back rhythm and time isn't part of its structure.

It works differently, clocks tick differently. He is different.

'Are you . . . staying?' I edge in the words, trying to sound casual as my eyes glance from the sunlight on the bed and up to him, standing next to my door like he might be planning to walk right through it and head home.

'Yeah. If that's an invite?'

'It was an invite.' I smile and sit down on the bed, already warm from the sun.

He sits too and I can feel the heaviness of it all, the nervous energy between us. We're two grown adults knowing exactly what we want but not wanting to be the one to make the first move just in case we make it awkward.

That's the problem with living next door to someone you'd quite like to make a move on. If it's the wrong one, you have to live with it.

He moves towards me and I meet him in the middle.

It's nice not to feel rushed or to worry about getting up early for work. In the past few years of being single, there have been times where I've had one eye on the clock, considering how much sleep I'd be able to get depending on how late my date would leave. This often had a correlation to how much fun we were having.

Here, with Helios, time isn't a number. It is barely a construct. It's certainly not something I need to think about or consider.

Our lips and tongues come together to explore once more, and my memory hasn't been exaggerating for the past few days. He really *is* a very good kisser, and his lips *do* instinctively seem to know exactly what I want them to do.

Items of clothing are peeled from our skin and melt away to some unknown corner of the floor, leaving our bodies free to press together as our fingers move across each other.

As we finally slip together, I press my face to his shoulder, gently biting it, something I often do to avoid too much eye contact during intense moments like this. The moment builds and my fingers dig into his flesh as I try to pull him beyond close. Gasps fill our lungs and the whole room becomes clammy until suddenly our eternity ends in sweat and racing hearts.

We pull apart with more resistance than Velcro and flop next to each other.

'Thank you,' Helios whispers, but really I think I should be thanking him.

Chapter 33

Helios lies sleeping in my bed. I don't want to wake him but I'm not very good at sleeping next to someone. I'm not used to it. I can feel the intensity of his heat changing the air in my room.

It's not him, it's me.

Even when I was briefly married, Russell would often sleep in the spare room because *my* tossing and turning would aggravate him. Even though it was *his* tossing and turning and snoring next to me that made me move about, unable to sleep. I never fidget when I'm alone. My mood from constant lack of sleep put him off staying by my side.

I flick open my phone to look across the internet at absolutely nothing in my exhausted state before I click to check my emails.

Yesterday, I emailed Gigi about doing some research for me on mentoring and teaching. Seeing as all my creative outlets have been a bit of a dead end, maybe I could help others in a different way?

I think when I do go back home it might be nice for me to take someone under my wing. Every barrister has to spend a certain amount of time learning from a mentor and this is something I've been avoiding. It's a lot of responsibility to teach someone the practical skills of the trade, but maybe it would be a welcome change to keep me occupied.

Knowing Gigi, she's already sent me more information than I could possibly need and direct quotes from my colleagues who have undertaken the responsibility many times over.

Of course, my emails are saturated with companies offering me something I don't want and a multitude of petitions to sign.

There's one above Gigi's that isn't junk.

There's an unread email from Karine, received earlier today.

I sit up straight in the bed, my heart pounding harder than if a gun had fired next to my ear.

My palms begin to sweat, making the phone slip about between my fingers and spots form in my eyes blurring my vision.

I slide my legs off the bed in the dark and silently glide on tiptoes into the next room to find my laptop.

My fingers act like they're on a slip-'n-slide as I try to open it. It takes three attempts before the room is filled with the glaring light from the screen.

In two clicks, my email is in front of me, and there it is. I didn't imagine it. It's actually her email address, not spam claiming to be her.

I swallow hard and it feels like I'm pushing down a ball of sand that's scraping along my throat as I read and re-read the heading, momentarily unable to open the email itself.

RE: It's not your fault

Chapter 34

My chest heaves in shallow breaths and my mouth's as dry as if I'd put a spoonful of cornflour in there.

As my fingers move across the mouse pad, the arrow on the screen vibrates because I'm shaking like I've got flu.

I take a breath and click on it.

> 24.11.2025
>
> CC: Ines Bernard
>
> RE: It's not your fault
>
> Alisha,
>
> I read your emails. I was very surprised to find them.
>
> We have not wanted to look through Karine's private emails, but we needed to find some information and that is when I saw the emails from you. I had heard that you were not working now and had moved away. I thought I should check

you were OK. It is important with what happened to Karine.

My dear, it was not your fault. You fought for her and she was grateful for you. It is very sad, but nothing would have saved her. She wanted to leave us, and she did.

Karine wanted to see the case to its end. To see you both win. You gave her that gift. She was always proud to call you her friend. You are a strong woman and so was she.

You gave her the strength to look evil in the eye and helped her stand with confidence after all they put her through.

My mother and I are both very grateful to you. You brought her peace, and now you must find your own. She wanted to take her own life, she would be broken at the thought she took yours with her. Please let her death help you to grow, to appreciate life, not pull you to the grave with her.

Karine would not be content with you blaming yourself. It was not you. You didn't do the things to her that kept her up at night. You gave her strength when she felt weak.

You were an ally she needed. You have been the ally many women needed and I hope you will be again. She knew your work is so important and you were the only one good enough to win her case. She would hate to think she were the reason other women didn't benefit from your skill set.

If it helps you to continue writing to Karine, then please carry on. I won't read them anymore. But if you would like, you can email me instead. It's up to you.

I hope you are well. I think Karine would approve of your Helios.

Sincerely

Ines

For your information, I put my email into a translation application, as I was not confident in my written English, but I checked it, and I think it makes sense.

Tears burn across my cheeks and the weight of my head drops to my hands.

My whole body shakes uncontrollably.

Reading over Karine's sister's words can't help me.

I was the last one to see Karine alive. I could've done something, said something . . . anything. We celebrated our win, I thought she would be able to start again. But who could start again after all she'd been through?

I should've seen the signs, I should've realised all was not well.

I was there with her in court telling her story, relaying the details of what happened when she was deep undercover reporting on oil companies and their mistreatment of indigenous people . . . how she was taken as entertainment for greedy white men who wanted to use her up, probably because they had no idea who she was so they thought they could get away with it.

I kept saying how lucky it was she had some proof of what happened before they stripped her of everything.

Lucky.

How could I have used such a word to her? How could I ever have been so insensitive? Why did I pretend to be upbeat when she had been so badly abused? It's not like I hadn't been party to every single vile detail of it all.

I just wanted her back to the woman she was before. We all did.

Sliding the laptop on to the seat next to me, I curl into a ball and try to catch my breath.

I'm so lost.

No matter how much I try to improve this beautiful world, it's never going to be enough. Those fighting to spread the truth get hurt and I can't fix it or save them. I can't protect every woman from the handful of extremely violent men.

Every single day, people hurt people for no good reason.

There's never a good reason. It's ugly, and people do it anyway.

I can't stand by and watch it happen, but I've lost all ability to fight since losing Karine, because even when I win, I lose.

'Alisha? What's wrong?' Helios takes a step towards me in the shadows of the room.

I shrink away from him. For a moment I'd forgotten he was even here, quietly sleeping in the next room.

I do my best to wipe the puddles under my eyes as I twist to sit up, but they just keep refilling.

I try to speak, to let out words, but each time I take a nip of air into my lungs it gets trapped there and nothing comes out.

'What's happened? Is it Odina? Is she OK?' Helios rushes to be by my side, moving the laptop off the seat and on to the floor so he can sit with me, cupping my hand in his, squeezing my fingers desperately tight.

I shake my head and push out a strangled *no*.

'You need air, take time, take time. I'm here with you. In your nose and out your mouth. Slowly, slowly.'

I manage to take a breath but it's small and my whole body still feels like an earthquake. Helios wraps me in his arms and strokes my hair from my face where it's sticking to my tears. He helps me to find my breath and pulls me kicking and screaming from the edge of my emotions.

'What happened?' he eventually asks again when I'm finding some sort of pace to my breathing.

'I got an email . . . long story.'

He squeezes me a little tighter, warming me against the chill in the night air.

'I have a lifetime.' His soft words in my hair are enough to almost release a smile on my face, but memories and heartache come crashing back in without even giving it a chance.

'The reason I came to live here now was because, because . . .' Suddenly, words feel impossible and my chest lurches into convulsive sobs all over again. But only tears this time, not the swirling whirlpool of a panic attack. Snot and tears dive straight into my hands as they cover my face.

Helios coos again and rubs my back, doing his best to calm and reassure me, until my laptop screen fades and we're plunged into pitch-black.

Chapter 35

'I'm sorry,' I eventually manage to whisper to the darkness of the room. Kicking myself for apologising when I've actually done nothing wrong. I've cried in my own home . . . I just wish there had been no witnesses to my meltdown.

I'm not sure how long it's taken me to calm down to the point of being able to speak again.

'There's nothing to be sorry for.'

'Can I please have a tissue?'

'Of course.' Helios jumps up and crashes into what I imagine is the armchair.

He rattles off some Greek words I don't know, or if I do he's saying them too quickly.

'They were next to you on the side table.'

I stretch across and put on a lamp, squinting at the flare of light before getting myself three tissues to dry my damp face and hands.

Helios retreats to sit next to me. He's in his black boxer shorts and I'm in a flimsy cotton nightie. A shiver rolls over my spine, making my whole body jolt again.

Helios grabs the throw off the armchair, puts it over our knees and pulls me in close to his chest.

'You can tell me anything, and I won't judge you.'

'Even if I told you I was an axe murderer?' I snort.

'Nope. I'd just ask *why* you did it.'

'Well, I'll judge me instead then,' I huff into a tissue.

'What for?'

'I don't know, for Karine. Beautiful, strong, kind Karine.' Her name catches in my throat and comes out like a squeak.

'Who is she? Tell me about her.'

I do my best to conjure her in my mind. She was always so elegant, even though she wasn't trying. Her thick onyx hair chopped short and easy to manage and a scarf slung around her neck in most weathers. Her skin glowed with a fresh-faced beauty that needed no effort whatsoever.

She was sharp and to the point without ever coming across as heartless. She didn't smile readily, but when she did, it was impossible not to share in it.

'She was impressive. Feisty. An undercover journalist always hunting for the truth and willing to risk everything to expose the worst people of this world. That's how we got into this mess. She put herself in harm's way to expose some *really* evil people. It wasn't the first time, but this time she got caught out. We'd known each other for years – on and off, because she was always somewhere else in the world working hard undercover. I got an email explaining what had happened to her and how she wanted me to be the barrister to represent her in court. Of course, I said yes. How could I not?'

I vividly remember receiving that email, for a brief moment wondering why she didn't call me herself. Why I was informed by email. But when I next saw her, I knew exactly why.

With most of the women I've represented over the years, I've only known them after. It was hard to imagine them before. Karine had turned into a translucent shadow with hollowed-out cheeks and dark circles around her eyes. She struggled to talk about it. Of course she did.

'We put twelve men in prison. Twelve. It should've been more, but they were the British ones. The ones easiest to find and take down. After we won her case, we went out and had this big celebration. She seemed really happy. I was so relieved, kept saying how *lucky* it was she'd managed to get some videos on the cloud before they stripped her of everything, how she won the case with her detail and brilliant mind . . .'

'Then what happened?' he says as my words trail away.

'She went home and took her own life.' The words come out almost matter-of-fact, because it's hard to imagine it to be real.

It's so real, so dark that it's fallen into the corner of my mind that I can't reach, because I don't want it to be real. It's said in the same way I would read any fact from the hundreds of books I can quote from memory.

'That's dreadful. I'm so sorry. I'm sorry for your loss.'

'It's everyone's loss. The whole world should be filled with strong women like her. It's *my* fault.' My finger beats against my chest. 'I should've been there with her and I wasn't.'

'No. It's not your fault.' Helios's voice is low and frustrated.

'It is. It's why I came here, to escape my shame. Even when I win, I lose. She didn't deserve to be passed around like a common cold, shamed and tortured. No one deserves that. I should've seen what was really happening, how much pain she was still in. How could she not be? She was talking to someone, a professional, about everything she went through. I thought it was helping . . .'

'It's *really* not your fault. You won her case. You gave her justice.'

'That's what this email said, from her sister. Odina said I should send Karine emails to try to help process it all, so I did. Her sister read them all and replied today. So now I'm ashamed, embarrassed and, as Odina would say, *cringe*.'

Helios chuckles at my comment about Odina.

'Feeling responsible for someone else's death is something I understand.' I open my mouth to question this, but he carries on, 'Would you have intentionally hurt your friend?'

'Never.'

'Were you there when she ended it?'

'No, but I was the last person to see her alive. I'm the one that put her in the taxi home. The one smiling and waving goodbye like a fool. I should've gone with her. I should've been there to stop her, to talk to her, to get her help when she needed it.'

'You didn't know. If you had, you *would* have helped.' Helios exhales hard. 'Let's get some fresh air.'

I nod my head but I'm not sure Helios even noticed. Taking the throw with me, I wrap it over my shoulders and follow him towards the balcony door, where we look up at the stars. The night air is crisp and exactly what I need to make me feel something other than the pain numbing my chest and stopping it from working how it should.

'I guess this is why you broke your however many years without smoking?' he says.

'Yeah. Karine smoked, so I had one at her funeral. But she was French and in her thirties so that was almost to be expected. I got myself some of the same brand she smoked, some strange homage, I guess.' I sigh with a smile on my lips but a heart that's pulling it down. 'And maybe a little self-punishment.'

She used to say her smoking was cultural, like wine and cheese and making love. It was a part of her identity. That was all *before*.

'What did you mean when you said you understood feeling responsible for someone else's death?'

Helios takes a cigarette of his own, without offering me one this time. He lights it, making it glow a deep orange as he sucks in the toxic fumes before holding his breath, the way he often does.

'Maybe I'll tell you one day, but right now, I want you to tell me everything you remember about Karine. All the good things and happy days.'

Chapter 36

Hey Odina, I thought you might be interested to know I got an email back from Karine.

I hit pause on the voice note because I can already feel something tighten in my chest, like a thousand elastic bands have been wrapped around my throat and my torso to see how much I can withstand before my head pops off.

Picking up the coffee from my nightstand, I take a sip and try to calm myself again.

I've read the email at least ten times. I read it back to Helios twice last night before falling into a deep, dreamless sleep in the early hours, with him holding me.

I don't remember the point at which I actually fell asleep. I wasn't trying to sleep. I'd been talking about Karine, reciting memories of the few times we met and the emails we shared.

She was one of those people who would pop up when least expected. Once, she came knocking on my door with nowhere to stay but she needed to be in the city for a meeting on a piece she was writing. We stayed up late, even though we both had early starts, because there was always something interesting going on in her world. Something I could learn, something I could collect and store away in my memory of her.

She shouldn't be just a memory, but in the end that's what we all become, if we're lucky to be liked or loved.

I close my eyes and think back to being in the warmth of Helios's arms. His strong frame and velvety skin pressed to me, keeping me safe when I needed him.

It seems impossible that I should feel comfortable there after he was hiding himself from me, but I get this deep sense of his fundamental kindness, even though he would rather shut it behind closed doors.

It only lasted a few hours, but it was the best sleep I've had in ages. Which *never* happens with someone else draped all over me . . . it must have been the relief of getting the email. It let something out. Like I've had something lodged in my throat and finally I've coughed it out and I'm ready to assess what to do next.

Placing down my mug, I press record on my phone once more.

Obviously it wasn't *actually* from Karine, it was from her sister, Ines. She'd had to access Karine's emails. Last I'd heard they hadn't been able to get the right password and didn't have a reason to continue trying. Things changed.

She told me . . .

I try to steady my breath, keep a level tone and consider my words talking to Odina. She is only seventeen, even if she has always been grown-up for her age. I want to protect her still.

. . . she told me not to blame myself. Which I know is true – if I'd known what was going to happen, I would've done something to stop her. It was nice to get a reply, oddly I think it was exactly what I needed. I thought you'd be interested to know I . . .

I stop myself from telling her I've told Helios, like I was going to. It would only incite an inquisition on her part.

> . . . I won't be sending more emails. But it did help me, and I'm grateful that my niece, the future poet-psychiatrist, pushed me into writing things down. Love you so very much.

I hit send on the voice note and shuffle lower on my bed. I've been here since Helios left, other than for practical purposes. The bed is where I'm living today. For what's left of it, anyway.

From here, I can see the sun has been straining to be seen through the clouds all day, occasionally sprinkling the luxury of warmth down on to my windows, but mostly it's been clouds casting shadows across the island.

My bed vibrates, and for an absent-minded moment I think it must be Odina sending back a message, only to realise it's a small tremor from the tectonic plates below me giving me a nudge. It doesn't last long, only seconds, then it's gone. Fleeting, like most things in life.

I close my eyes to sleep, but images from my last night with Karine, exhausted after months in court but wanting to celebrate the win, fill my head.

How I wish I'd invited her back to mine. Maybe I did, maybe she declined, I can't be sure anymore.

Two loud thumps bear down on my front door, making my heart race as I jump out of bed and search the room for some clothes, managing to pull on some leggings and a baggy T-shirt without any knickers on.

Luna and Cloud, my two most loyal cats, are there pacing the floor. They do come upstairs on occasion, but prefer downstairs where they can easily come and go as they please.

I open the door, wishing I'd found a hairbrush to pull through my locks but not having time.

Helios is there, with his fist ready to knock again. He quickly retracts his hand and places it on the tray in his other hand.

'Food delivery. I had a feeling you wouldn't be up to making yourself anything . . . If I'm honest, I've seen what's in your fridge and know there's nothing good in it so . . . heat it in the oven for thirty minutes. The cake can be eaten cold.' He passes it over the threshold. 'If you want to talk, you can pop over whenever you like.'

His eyes flick over me only briefly but I catch it before he continues, 'But I know you might want to be alone or calling Odina or someone.' He shrugs.

'This is incredible, you really didn't have to, I have chips in the freezer.'

Helios raises an eyebrow and makes a *tsk* sound.

'Thank you, this is very thoughtful. I'll maybe see you tomorrow?'

'Maybe.' His lips press gently together into the briefest smile before he walks away from my door. 'And just so you know, I'm not doing this because of the pizza delivery man story.'

A laugh explodes from my chest, something I didn't think I would be capable of right now.

'I should think not!'

Helios looks suitably pleased with himself for making me smile.

'As long as we're clear. See you soon, OK?'

I nod and take one step down before nudging the door closed with my hip.

Maybe I should've asked him in. I'm not used to someone turning up and not seeming to expect something in return. He didn't even look disappointed when I said I'd see him tomorrow.

'Look, you two,' I say to the cats. 'No chips for me.'

I bring the foil-covered tray to my nose and inhale deeply to enjoy the aroma. I have no clue what it is, but it smells like there might be onions and some sort of red wine sauce. A hum of delight escapes me as I walk to the kitchen with a little more bounce in my step than was there before.

I wasn't hungry, but this smells too good to leave. A home-cooked meal and company if I need it, but not demanded of me. Helios is by far the best neighbour I've ever had.

Chapter 37

Each day for five days Helios brings me home-cooked meals, and a variety of cakes also made by his fair hands, knowing I haven't left my house, but not pressuring me to talk or wanting anything in exchange.

I tell him every time that he doesn't need to, to which he always shrugs and says, 'I know.'

He has been the perfect friend, giving me space to decide what happens next with us and our time. He's slipped very easily into the role of provider and carer, something I haven't been used to since I was a child. Helios has continued to say if I want to talk about Karine, he'll listen, but each time I tell him I have nothing much left to say.

When Monday arrived, I thought it was Helios banging on my door earlier than normal but it was Calliope, wondering why I hadn't been to her for coffee, jewellery-making and to talk about Helios's linguistic skills. I pretended to be a little under the weather and promised I'd come over next week to chat.

I needed this time. To re-read the email from Ines and to formulate words in return.

The words there in black and white on my screen feel raw as I cast my eyes over them one last time.

04.12.2025

RE: Thank you

Dear Ines,

Thank you for your reply. I will be honest with you, I found it difficult to read. Karine was a wonderful human who didn't deserve what happened to her.

As you know, I have not taken her decision to end things lightly. Thank you for your kind words and absolving me of blame in this matter. Your words have hung in the air around me for the past few days. Although time cannot heal, I do think it can help with perspective, and you have been the catalyst I've needed to rethink my pain.

I will always feel the weight of Karine's loss in my bones and under my ribs, but I also know that you're right, she would want me to put myself back together and get back to work to give women a voice for justice.

Thank you for reading my emails to Karine. I wrote them under the advice of my niece, as an outlet for the sudden loss.

Your kindness has meant a lot to me. I hope we can stay in touch.

Thank you again,

Alisha

I then run the whole message through a translation system and read it over again. My French is passable, and the email seems to make sense in both languages. I want to send my original words, as well as the translation, for context as Ines has very good English, no matter what she says.

The arrow icon hovers over the word send on my laptop screen.

I click it and close my laptop. I sent the email directly to Ines, not to Karine's address.

Luna purrs loudly on my lap, vibrating my knees. She doesn't have a clue.

It's time to let go and begin to truly move on, instead of hiding away from my feelings and my fear and trying to be someone I'm not.

This is what I'm good at. Helping people.

I just need to heal enough to keep my emotions in check, the way I used to. Hopefully, Ines's words on Karine's behalf will keep me strong.

I've realised, over the past few days, I've been afraid. It's taken Ines's email for me to own up to it as the overriding emotion sitting alongside the sadness of loss.

The fear runs deep and is layered like sediment at the bottom of the sea. The fear that people would blame me, that her family would blame me for not seeing the signs. Fear that this will happen again. That I was so blinded by the joy of beating these people and sending them to prison that I didn't see the open wounds deeply festering in Karine.

It's complicated, and I'm still continually unpicking it, and no matter how often people tell me I should be logical and feel a certain way, just as I might say to someone else, it doesn't dampen down the wild twist of emotions that have been raging for months.

Her mother and sister were there that evening with Karine, supporting her strength and celebrating the success of bringing these men to justice. I remember Ines vocalising how they shouldn't be allowed normal lives again, after all they'd done. Ines and her mother must have left for their hotel only a matter of minutes before we called it a night. Karine was renting a small flat while the trial went ahead. She'd promised to meet them for breakfast in the morning.

Many years ago, I watched a documentary about loss, and how going over it and over it can lessen the pain. I do think something has shifted in my constant contemplation. Memory isn't fixed. The brain can only recall the last time you had the memory. It changes it, twists it up and it only stays as clear as you need it to.

I remember we even had a conversation about it once, late at night in my chambers while discussing the case. How she hoped the memory of what happened would stop being so deafening and would subside over time so she could live some sort of normality again.

I remember that so clearly, as clearly as memory allows, because the word *deafening* rang in my own ears. I'd heard her testimony, knew what had happened to her in more detail than anyone would ever want to know, but there was something about her words in private that had a different kind of intensity.

In my head, I can hear Karine telling me this isn't what she'd want me to be doing. She'd want me back in London.

She told me how my job was important. It's what our friendship was built on, our insistence on helping and educating others in any way we could.

I need to make bigger strides in putting my life back together. I can see that more clearly now.

Today, I thought that, at the very least, I should invite Helios in and provide him with some well-deserved wine with his dinner.

Chapter 38

'Everything that happened with Karine, that's how I ended up here. It was like I couldn't keep myself in one piece anymore. I was called in to speak with a judge, things weren't going in my favour and I thought perhaps I was having an allergic reaction to something because my throat closed up. I was advised to go on sabbatical until I can handle a normal workload.'

The words *burnt out* ring in my ears again, even though I haven't said them.

'It only takes one domino to knock down the whole lot,' Helios begins. 'I often think of the philosopher Pericles, and his words: *What you leave behind is not what is engraved in stone monuments, but what is woven into the lives of others*. I think about those words too often. But I think you can understand them. Karine was a strong thread, and she was pulled away. Life gets hard when those strings are stolen.'

Helios looks down at his plate as my mouth runs dry, hanging open to find words as perfect as his, then he adds, 'But it sounds much better in Greek,' with a smile that lingers under his lowered lashes.

'You're right,' is all I can muster as I do my best to take a grip of my heart from falling apart. The damage to it started when I lost my mum, then with the shock of Karine . . . it's like all the threads have been cut.

'This is delicious, were you a chef in a previous life?' I hover the forkful of freshly caught sea bass in front of my mouth before consuming the delectable olive-oil-covered delight. It's the perfect distraction from talks and thoughts of people who have passed.

'No, no. But my ex-wife is not Greek and I wanted . . . I wanted there to be more Greek food in the house. I like my Greek heritage. I like our food. So did she, once. I did most of the cooking, most recipes are from my *yiayià*.'

'I have no idea how you can go from loving someone one day, and not the next. Having said that, I've never *really* been in love.'

'Then you've never found the right person.'

'Maybe.'

'Definitely. It's different with the right person.'

I open my mouth to push him on this point, because how can someone be the *right* person when they drop you like a dirty sock for no obvious reason. I quickly think it through and know that it's not a kind pathway to tread. I don't want to disrespect him after everything he has done for me.

'What were you going to say?' Helios eyes me carefully as he picks some of the warm pitta out of the bowl between us and begins to pull it apart.

His stare is so intense, almost unblinking, like he's looking into my soul to find answers without me having to speak.

I put more food in my mouth to take a moment to decide on my course of action. Putting down my fork and covering my mouth with my hand is enough to give the impression of being unable to talk, while he keeps his focus entirely on me.

Honesty is the best policy, as ever. I'll just have to tread very carefully.

'Well, I was going to ask you questions about finding the right person, but as you're not together anymore . . . it felt somewhat inappropriate.'

'I don't regret our time together. We were very much in love, but then . . .' He shrugs and says the same as he has before. 'Life.'

'But that's exactly my point.' This time I talk with food in my cheek as I can't help myself, quickly trying to get my words out while also swallowing my final mouthful. 'If you're *so* in love, if love is something *so* real, and someone truly is *the one*, how could it possibly end?'

Helios breaks eye contact, instead choosing to look at the pitta he's pulling apart only to litter his plate with it. 'Because life isn't a straight and simple line. Even where there is love, it doesn't mean things last forever.'

'Like what, an affair? Surely that signifies things aren't right?'

'There can be problems that don't involve others.' Helios fiercely wipes a tiny shred of his pitta around his plate before stuffing it into his mouth, quickly followed by two more pieces. He picks up said plate and takes it the short distance to the kitchen counter.

'I think I should go. Thanks for . . .' His eyes scan my kitchen-diner. We both know he brought all the food. 'Letting me use your plates. And the wine.' He puts one finger up and his face lifts a little at remembering something I did that wasn't just putting plates and cutlery out.

'Wait.' I push back my chair with such a scrape that Cloud scatters away from me. 'Please stay, I wasn't trying to upset you.'

'I'm not upset.' Helios locks his arms into a tight knot about his chest.

I step forwards and clamp my hands on the tops of his arms.

'You are, and that's OK. I really didn't mean to. How can I make it up to you?'

Helios lowers his chin to look down at me. The pale hazel flecks in his otherwise dark-brown eyes look like tiny lightning strikes.

We stay locked in this moment longer than I expect before Helios moves in to kiss me. His arms unlock and he pulls me in, arching my back.

It's only moments before I'm tugging at his clothes, wanting to relive the sensations of pleasure from the other night. The part before everything turned on its head and pushed me back to where I started, in London.

I take a fistful of his black cotton shirt and begin leading him towards the stairs. Our lips barely part as I stumble backwards, occasionally having my toes stepped on as I pull Helios off balance, making us laugh into each other's mouths.

I sit back on the stairs as Helios's lips moves over my neck and my breasts through my blouse.

I begin tugging off his shirt over his head, catching it on his chin in the process and making him look a little like a nun in a bandeau and veil.

'Careful,' he laughs as he unhooks it and discards it over his shoulder. 'Don't break off the buttons.'

I bite back the laughter as he shakes his head, a smile left lingering on his lips. 'Even when you're laughing at me, you're sexy.'

I roll my eyes and stand to continue up the stairs, unbuttoning my fine chiffon blouse as I go, then doing the same as him and throwing it over my shoulder down the stairs.

'Oi!'

The squeaking sound of Helios's feet coming to a halt makes me turn around.

Looking down from the second-to-top step, I find him a few paces behind me, dressed like a cheap Halloween ghost with my shirt on his head.

He pulls it off his face and tries not to laugh as he says, '*Seriously?*'

'Sorry.' I bite my knuckle, as though there was some possibility it *wasn't* me that threw it on his head.

'I forgive you,' he says as he drops it on the stairs by his feet.

Helios closes the gap between us, standing one or two steps below me, making us about the same height.

Although there's still a hint of a smile on his face, making a tiny dimple appear to the left of his lips, he looks me over and lets out a heavy breath before gently skimming his fingers over my collarbone and shoulder to push my hair away.

He continues to trail his fingertips over the curve of my shoulder and along my back to the clasp of my bra, which he undoes with relative ease.

With one simple tug, the bra falls to meet my blouse lower down the stairs.

'That's better.'

Helios's hands cover my breasts like he wants to do the job of my bra.

Our mouths collide again and our tongues begin to explore. As I try to step backwards up the last couple of stairs, I trip and sit down there instead, with Helios on top of me.

We both begin moving urgently, as though we can't wait any longer to make it to my bed. As though it's miles away and we could die from the thirst we feel for each other if we try to make such an arduous journey.

My hands move quickly over Helios's zip to free him and he tugs at my skirt until we manage to get him there inside me, making us both groan as we join.

There, at the top of my stairs, I hold on to him tighter than I've ever held on to anyone. My heart in my chest pounds so hard I can hear it mingling with the sound of our breath.

As I grip the back of Helios's neck like I'm clinging on to a thick rope that could save my life, we look each other in the eye.

It's the catalyst to tip me over the edge.

Chapter 39

'Here's your coffee.' Helios holds a tray that I didn't even know I owned, with two coffee mugs and a strange assortment of biscuits.

Laughter bubbles up as I look him over.

'I really wouldn't hold a tray of hot coffee so close to your . . . sensitive areas like that.'

Helios doesn't respond. He's doing it on purpose, holding it so a mug on the tray partly obscures his manhood as he confidently moves around my home with no clothes.

'If you'd told me when we first met that only a few months down the line you would be strutting around my house naked, making me coffee, I wouldn't have believed it.'

'Neither would I. Not because I didn't want to, of course, but I didn't think I would strut around anyone's house naked. With the exception of my own, of course.'

'Of course.'

Helios places the tray down and carefully retrieves one of the mugs to pass to me across the sheets I'm wrapped up in.

'Do you have to work today?'

'Not today. This week I have to finish translating a book ready for the editor, but then I don't start my next book until the new year. But I'm ahead of my schedule anyway. I always am.'

Helios moves the tray to place it on top of my set of drawers and brings only the plate of biscuits and his mug into the bed with him.

'Any interest in staying in bed all week?'

'I wish I could. Next week I can.'

'Sounds good to me.'

Helios places the plate between us and takes one of the slightly soft biscuits. I know they're soft, because they were soft days ago and they won't have improved.

'You need to buy some real food. Or make some.' Helios holds up half of the chocolate chip biscuit to inspect it for its lack of quality.

I do my best to ignore the comment. Making food has never been a priority for me. We had an au pair when I was young who tried to teach me some Spanish recipes, but I was better with learning the language than the love of food. I'm good at eating it, though.

I suppose I've always believed myself too busy to actually figure out how to make dishes. Why bother when everything is laid out so beautifully by people who are good at such things? If nothing else, my desire to eat out keeps talented people in business and prevents me from giving myself or anyone else food poisoning.

'I mean it,' Helios continues. 'Half of what you bring home in shopping bags should go straight in the bin. We have some wonderful produce here and you ignore it all for soggy biscuits.'

'That's the fun of being an adult, I can do what the hell I like. I can stay skinny by not wanting to eat anything I buy. Better yet, I can burn calories with you by staying in bed for days on end.'

'Best build my strength up then, I guess.' Helios stuffs the rest of the biscuit into his mouth, leaving crumbs to tumble on to his chest.

I pick up a biscuit of my own and inspect it before delicately biting into its floppy exterior. 'Do you want to watch something on my laptop while we eat these?'

'Sounds good. Any suggestions?'

'I'm halfway through watching one of Ali Wong's stand-up sets.'

'Wait, you got halfway through and stopped? How?'

'I was tired.'

Helios shakes his head and tuts before muttering the word, 'Rude.'

I love this reaction on him. On any man. Ali Wong's style of comedy has a strong feminist streak. It's progressive yet silly. It's not for an insecure man.

Helios may be a lot of things underneath his antisocial exterior, but insecure isn't one of them. I bet he laughs in all the right places, all the ones where you hope men will laugh but feel slightly on edge that they won't because they just can't understand the female perspective of 2025.

I place down my drink and watch him stuff another biscuit into his mouth, shaking his head at its inferior quality. More crumbs sprinkle over him, and I've never seen a more delicious plate in my life.

It's hard for me to believe in *the one*, even though I'm sure I saw it in my parents' relationship, but Helios *is* strangely perfect. If I had married someone like Helios, instead of Russell, it might've been a lot more difficult to give him up.

I manoeuvre around the biscuit plate and lick the chocolatey crumbs straight off his chest, forgetting all about my laptop.

Chapter 40

'What's your sister's name?' I wave the photo in Helios's general direction.

'My sister?' Helios hops along on one foot as he tugs on his shoe, too lazy to untie the laces.

After spending the past couple of days in bed, but at least not alone this time, I thought we should do something different. In the brief moments I have found myself alone, I've noticed my mind wandering back to London, and what it might look like to return. Although I think Ines's email has made me want to help people again, I still don't think I have the strength for it. It's still hard to picture yet.

Helios has been the perfect distraction from my pain and my confusion over my future. But more than that, he has been so kind. He's listened to me when I've spoken about Karine, and held me in the dark when I've needed arms around me.

Even with our rocky start, he's single-handedly restoring my faith in people. They can be flawed, but also good-hearted. No one is one thing only and sometimes, in my line of work, it's important to be reminded of that.

'Yes, your sister. What's her name?'

'My sister is called Katerina.'

It'd be nice to find out a little bit more about him and this sister of his. If I can get him to open up about something from before he moved to this little volcanic island, it would be a win.

He knows so much about me and I know very little about him outside of his likes and dislikes in his day-to-day life here. I have his present without much context from his past. There's a gaping gap between his uni life and how he came to be here on his own.

I know he's a translator, is willing to give up what he wants if other people are in greater need and he's willing to look after people even when they don't ask for it. And he's a feeder. Purely based on his 'one person' portion sizes that could feed a family of three or four.

I pick up the larger framed photo of the girl. She's pretty, maybe thirteen or fourteen in this image. Her smile is so wide, she's positively squinting over her braces. She looks like she'd be good fun. There's a glow about her that comes across despite the black-and-white image. Even the frame is shining gold, with embossed flowers climbing over its surface.

I carefully replace the photo to its correct position. 'She's pretty.'

Helios stands just behind my shoulder, looking at the photo I've been examining.

'Yeah.' He takes it in his hand and studies it for himself. 'She was very pretty.' He pauses for a moment, like he's got caught in the girl's eyes, before putting it back down and turning to me. 'So where are we going?'

I twist to face him, suddenly regretting my decision to remove him from his position in my bedroom. Even casually dressed, with unkempt hair, his features come together to something rather alluring, and I know what he can do with his delicious mouth.

'You're objectifying me in your head again, aren't you?' Helios frowns but I don't believe the moody expression for a second.

'At least it's staying in my head now.'

'Hmm. Now tell me where we're going.'

'For a walk and a picnic. Bring your coat.'

◆ ◆ ◆

'I don't know anything more English than a cucumber sandwich.' Helios eyes the thin-cut white bread with even thinner slices of green poking out.

'Battered fish and chips? Roast dinner? Getting too drunk abroad?'

He nods his head as he chews. 'All very English activities.'

We took the dusty path up and out of town, meandering past olive groves and lizards that look like stickers on walls to get to the Palaiokastro Acropolis.

Up here, the air is crisp and fresh. There's something magical about sitting on the edge of the thick fortress walls, what's left of them anyway. All the stones are the colour of an elephant that's been walking in the sun, including the burnt-orange patches they sometimes acquire from dirt and weather.

Everything is square and angular. Great care must have been taken over its construction. I like to sit and daydream about the lives that have passed through here over the ages, adding my footprints to the list.

We chose a prime spot to sit, with our legs dangling over the edge of a wall that looks down at the rows of white and pastel houses in Mandraki, then to the sea beyond. It's deep and dark compared to the icy nature of the sky and the white buildings scattered like dice below us.

I made sandwiches, cucumber and separately feta, and brought a few packets of crisps and homemade fairy cakes. Sponge cakes like these are the only thing I can actually bake, thanks to my mum. She would've taught me more had I been open to listening at the time.

I regret that now, of course.

'Why don't you tell me about your sister? Do you have any other siblings? Or just the one?'

'I have three sisters. I'm the baby. Katerina is closest in age to me. We were very close as children. We still are, but she is busy with her family in Athens. My other two sisters, Maria and Elena, are still in Kos. My eldest, Maria, is a grandmother already. Her granddaughter is beautiful.'

'So are the pictures of all three sisters? Not just Katerina?'

Helios takes a large pinch of crisps and places them in his mouth as he shakes his head.

'Well, she must be beautiful if you and Katerina as kids are anything to go by. I can't believe Katerina looked cute in braces. I hated mine. Did you ever have braces?' I take a bite of my own slightly floppy cucumber sandwich.

'No. My father thought braces were a waste of time. I was lucky to have good teeth. Mine only cross a little at the bottom, see?' He pulls a crazy face at me, jutting out his bottom jaw for me to see the slight higgledy-piggledy nature of his lower teeth.

I shake my head at him, confused and not needing to see his teeth when I've seen them before. I've spent whole hours looking at him, talking to him, taking him in. I'm starting to know his face better than my own in the mirror.

'But Katerina, she had braces?'

'No. Katerina never had braces. I was always so envious of her straight teeth growing up.'

I *know* she had braces in the photo on his sideboard.

'Yes, she did. She does on that photo of yours. The big one in the middle. Unless that's a different sister? But you said your dad thought they were a waste of time? I'm confused.'

Helios looks down at his feet and covers his mouth with a balled fist to clear his throat.

He's blushing. There's a distinct rouge on his cheeks and creeping up his throat under his heavy wool coat.

'It's not your sister, is it? It's not Katerina.'

He doesn't answer. He can't even look at me.

'Why won't you say who she is?' I begin to laugh. It comes out strained and unnatural.

He has a picture of a teenage girl in his home, more than one in fact, and he won't tell me who she is.

The bizarre nature of the situation makes my palms sweat and my sarcastic laughter is accompanied by the crossing of my arms and the narrowing of my eyes, because the memory of him lying to me about his ability to speak English is all too fresh.

What else is he hiding?

Maybe I was too quick to forgive and trust this man when I know so little of who he has been before knowing me. I was tricked by good looks.

'Helios, what aren't you telling me?'

His lips shrink into a thin line and his head gently sways, but his eyes still don't meet mine.

I wait in the sound of the breeze whipping up around us, knocking my crisp packet off my lap. I don't even move to save it.

It's a very simple question.

He fidgets under the weight of my glare before opening his mouth to mumble, 'She's my daughter.'

Chapter 41

'Why have you never said you have a daughter?' I think back to the photos. 'What about the boy? It's not you, is it? He's your son.'

Helios exhales with a hissing noise and looks out towards the sea. It's all navy shapes and a pale sky that only displays specks of light when the clouds momentarily part.

'Yeah. He is.'

'Why didn't you tell me you had kids? It doesn't bother me, if that's the problem. You know I like kids, and it's not like we're dating or anything, they don't need to know about me.'

I'm not sure whether to be offended or understanding. Perhaps he feels he doesn't know me well enough yet to trust me with such information, but my knowledge of them wouldn't have changed our dynamic one bit. Not for me, anyway.

'It doesn't matter. Like you said, we aren't dating, you didn't need to know.'

'But you went to the extent of lying about it being your sister.' An angry bubble swells up in my ribcage, one that's hard to keep in check.

'No, you presumed. I never pointed at a photo and said *that is my sister*, I just didn't correct you. I was actually very careful not to lie.'

I think back across our conversations and it is very plausible that it was me doing the talking, but then I think about the remark about being pretty.

'You said your sister was pretty and held the photo.'

'No, I held a photo and said *she* was very pretty, because she was. I was careful not to lie and say who *she* was.'

'Only to mislead . . .'

We sit in the moment, neither of us knowing what to say or perhaps not having the energy to continue. I shiver as the lively sea breeze thrashes around my hair and neck. The chill is enough to cut through our heated silence.

'Thank you for lunch. I think I should go.' Helios begins to pack himself away ready to go, folding up the tinfoil that had his sandwiches in.

'Running away again, as you always do when you get even slightly uncomfortable.'

Helios stops still and I can see tension in his jaw. I've hit a nerve, but this isn't the first time he's tried to get up and leave when he decides he doesn't want to be open with me.

He's always running.

'Seriously?' I continue. 'Why is this a big deal to you? Is it a secret from all your friends that you have children?' I tuck the wild strands of dark hair behind my ears and study his face, even though he isn't looking at me, as I do my best to piece together the information I have, the way I would when being instructed by a solicitor and getting ready to appear in court.

Then it hits me.

It was always so obvious that I can't believe I didn't see it sooner.

'You said *was* very pretty, about your daughter. Not she *is* very pretty. She can't be much older than that now, not unless you were very young when you had her, so why are you saying *was* like that? When I thought it was your sister, it sort of made sense, like she was a pretty teen, but you're not old enough to have a daughter all that much older than that photo.'

I piece the information together, little by little, but I don't want to finish the puzzle and see how it ends. Fear floods my body from my toes to my suffocating throat and I'm already regretting walking this path.

His hands stop folding the foil into the flat square he's made it into. They're shaking. It could be the cold. He's got a thicker coat on than me, and a scarf. I know it's probably not the cold, but I can't help hoping that's the reason his hands are trembling.

A new thought seeps into my brain, making my heart beat in my chest with a new vigour, a fear that won't relent. When I told Helios about Karine, he said to me that he understood feeling responsible for someone else's death.

I do my best to slide closer to him across the thick wall.

'What happened to your daughter, Helios?'

He closes his eyes and a tear slips over his cheek. He doesn't move to wipe it away, he doesn't even acknowledge it. He keeps his eyes locked, like a portcullis sliding down to close off the entrance to his soul.

'My daughter . . . died in a car accident. It was my fault. I was the one driving the car, I thought I was indicating, I wasn't . . .' His voice gets carried away on the breeze, but I catch it before it passes.

It all makes sense now.

His self-inflicted isolation. That he never stopped loving his wife, but she didn't want to be with him anymore. Smoking his life away with a lack of care for his health. All of it.

It's like he's passed me the final word in a sentence, the keyword that makes the others slot together.

'I'm so sorry,' is all I manage, because what else is there I can say?

Chapter 42

I've had to tell people thousands of times that I'm sorry for things I didn't do, wasn't party to and could never change, but I am still sorry for them. My heart aches for them and there's that part of me that wishes I had magic in the tips of my fingers to take away the pain and the hurt from people's lives.

But nothing could heal the pain of losing a child. Not even magic, I'm sure.

'This is why you said you understand feeling responsible for someone else's death.' I don't phrase it as a question. I know the answer.

'Yeah.' He wipes the tear, but his eyes stay clamped shut harder than before. 'I understand what it is to be responsible for someone else's death.' He opens his eyes and looks right into mine. 'And you, Alisha, are not responsible for a grown woman taking her life. You couldn't have known what she was going to do. I was responsible for keeping my daughter safe. Me.' He pounds his chest. 'It was my fault she isn't here. I was her dad, and it was my fault. It was all my fault. The car behind went into us because I forgot to indicate, maybe braking too hard . . .'

There's a ringing in my ears that won't fade.

It's like Helios has let off a bomb so close to me, everything is out of focus.

I can't let in a panic attack. Not now. I have to deal with this, for him.

I'm never lost for words. I'm not allowed to be. It's been my job to find the right words my whole life, up until the middle of this year when I fell apart.

Now I have to be strong and find words for him, the way he always has for me.

'You didn't do it on purpose.'

'No. Never. She was everything to me. My baby girl. I have my son, Stamatis, too. He is seventeen and lives with his mother. I came to Nisyros to avoid people knowing my past. Knowing what I had done.' He exhales hard. 'Hannah, my wife, doesn't want me anywhere near her or our son. She's too heartbroken to even look at me. I thought moving was the least I could do. I shouldn't have told you. I'm sure you'll make me regret it, like telling you I understand English.' He attempts a laugh at his weak joke, but it comes out strangled and cold.

Helios edges away from me, pulls out a cigarette and lights it behind the shelter of his hands. There's no need to ever ask if losing his daughter was the catalyst for his self-destruction. It's obvious.

I wonder whether the pain inside him is doing him as much damage as the smoke swirling around our heads. Maybe more. The cost of emotional trauma is yet to be so clearly quantified. It's that trauma that brought him to intentionally damage himself with death sticks. It's like his own form of corporal punishment.

'This is why you wanted to isolate yourself, because you blame yourself.'

'Same as you.'

'Same as me,' I confirm. 'Is this why you were upset on your balcony that time?'

Helios nods but doesn't elaborate.

A thousand questions flood my mind, but one won't leave me alone, blinding my thoughts like a lighthouse at sea. It may not be the obvious question to some, but to me, it's the most important.

'Why don't you see your son anymore? I know you said your wife doesn't want you around, but . . . your child? Surely he needs you?'

Helios keeps his eyes on the shadows of the clouds and away from me.

'Hannah doesn't want me near him. Doesn't trust me anymore. Our daughter dying broke us all. She was smart, beautiful and so funny. I miss her laugh so much. I miss my son too, but at least I know he's safe and I get to see him twice a year. It's changed though, like he doesn't even want to see me when I'm there. Hannah emails me updates and photos . . . as long as I don't reply.'

The weight of my barrister wig feels as though it's flown over from England and landed heavy on my head. I have a million questions, but the human in me knows this isn't the time for them, even though I feel that this is an injustice. No good man should be kept from a child just because the mother is angry. I'm for equal rights, a fair ruling. He doesn't deserve this.

Helios can't even look me in the eye. We have both opened up to each other and shared vulnerability we've been running from, and now we can see the broken pieces of us like they've been thrown out over the sea to catch the light and reflect their glare into our eyes. We might be able to run, but we can't hide from the light forever. It's always there, ready to cast a shadow that will forever linger.

He lost a child. The pain is completely unimaginable to me. The shadow it casts can't shrink or diminish my loss of Karine, but it changes it, gives it a new perspective. The idea of losing Odina . . . I couldn't even bear her being in an airport on her own not knowing where to go, and the fact was, she was perfectly safe.

'Oh my God.' I cover my eyes as another stray thought smacks me right between them. 'I said something dreadful to you, about not having a daughter, about Odina and the advice you were giving me. I'm so sorry, what a dreadful thing to say.'

'You did, and it hurt, but you didn't know so I forgave you in the same moment you said it.'

I shake my head at my insensitivity. All I seem to do is put my foot in things left, right and centre lately.

'Thank you for forgiving me, and for trusting me. I'd like to help you to see your son more. You said you should've been indicating? Do you think perhaps you were, and the person didn't see?'

'Please, don't.' Helios throws down his cigarette and rubs it with the toe of his trainer. 'I didn't tell you this for pity or help. It won't change what happened. It won't bring her back. I didn't want to tell you at all. And it is selfish. I came here just like you, to run from it. To shut it out. I thought maybe I would be strong enough to go back to Kos after a year, to face everyone daily who knows, but . . . it's easier here. I exist knowing I will see my son again and that's enough. I put money away for him, I provide for the things he wants to do, I'm glad for that.'

It turns out Helios hasn't just been running from conversations with me. He's been running from everything.

He shrugs as he brushes his hand under his nose and gently sniffs back some of his emotion.

'No one knows what is in someone else's heart. Mine broke almost two years ago and it can never be fixed, but if it helps you to see you were not at fault for Karine, and that you are a good person who has helped so many people . . . that's something. Lyra, my daughter, that was her name . . . she would've liked that. Lyra was . . .' He chokes on his daughter's name and that's when he breaks, pinching the bridge of his nose as though this might stop the torrent of splitting pain ripping right through him.

'I hate saying her name,' he continues. 'It's like she should be there to hear it and she's not. I hate that it will always be *was*.' He sits tall and scrubs one eye with the back of his hand. 'Sorry, I'm fine.'

'No. You're not.'

I shuffle even closer to him, wrapping him in my arms. His cheek presses to my forehead, and his skin feels frozen to the touch where mine seems like it's ablaze.

'It's OK *not* to be fine,' I add. 'When did it happen?'

'Almost two years ago. Not long into the new year . . .'

And with that, his body begins to tremble, and he lets out what he's been trying desperately to hold in. Why he built up a wall, pretended he didn't understand people and why he avoided contact with his neighbours . . . because he really wasn't *fine* at all.

Chapter 43

'Are you getting anything for Helios? Or are you coming all this way to buy nothing?' Calliope sighs at me as I'm yet to purchase anything on our shopping trip to Kos town.

'That's a good question.'

I know the answer is yes. It's the only reason I've hopped on a ferry and come to Kos town with Calliope, to spend a day or two here before heading back to Nisyros to prepare for the strangest Christmas of my life.

It's a fascinating town with parks full of ancient ruins, an assortment of shops and, currently, Christmas decorations lighting up the streets. Sadly, none of it has been enough to stop my mind from coming back to Helios.

After Helios's revelation about his children, and what happened to his daughter, I've been unable to stop thinking about ways I could help him.

I also managed to stay calm and not become overwhelmed with my own emotions. For the first time since Karine, I was able to keep myself under control in the face of trauma.

It was only a few days ago now, but I know I'm stronger than I was and it makes me even more determined to find a way to bring him some sort of peace.

Helios said he wanted to be left alone to finish his translation and I've done my best to respect his wishes. I tried to bring him food, but he politely asked me to stop. It was worth it, though, to see the laughter behind his eyes when he saw my dreadful offering of cooked frozen chips and salad. As I have almost no cooking skills outside of a Victoria sponge, which I made him and he happily accepted, the next day Helios brought food to mine to prevent me bringing more chips to his house. He came in to eat it and talked to me as though I knew nothing of his family situation.

Just as he did for me, I've made myself available to him if he'd like to talk.

We had a couple of quiet evenings on our separate balconies drinking our glasses of red wine, the way we used to. I was making sure I was there if he needed me.

My head has been flooded with questions ever since that picnic. My barrister brain has switched on. I want to ask why his wife doesn't want him near Stamatis? It's so extreme. Does she have a court order? How did the accident happen *exactly*, as Hannah is so convinced Helios is to blame that she's withholding a child from having a father.

I've waited to ask more questions. I've held them back as Helios has retracted from the subject entirely. Last night, he came over to mine and we stayed up late, distracting each other from thoughts we don't want to live with. He even made sure not to fall asleep, instead scurrying off back home, and I couldn't help wondering whether it was so I wouldn't be able to ask any questions.

It's not my responsibility to look after him or pull him back out, but as a friend, and a human, I do want to help him. His suffering is palpable.

I memorise facts for a living and a large part of me is desperate to spew out information to Helios and his ex-wife about why it's so important their son has access to his father.

It's strange to think I could bump right into his ex and Stamatis here in Kos town and have no idea. There's a possibility I would recognise Stamatis from his photos, though. He looks like a mini Helios.

Even if I did see them, I couldn't say anything to them, in part because I have no idea whether they speak English. Helios told me his ex isn't Greek, but that's more or less all I know about her – that, and she's called Hannah.

When I tried to question Helios about what actually happened, it was hard to gain any solid facts that could guide me to a conclusion outside of his opinion: that it was all his fault.

I want to ask Helios if he'd like to spend Christmas Day together. With only fifteen days left until Christmas Day, and an invite from Calliope that I've already declined, I know I'd like to spend the day with him. Even if we sit in bed ignoring the fact it's Christmas and watch comedy shows or documentaries, I'd be content.

It's all different here anyway, and of course each family always picks and chooses their own ways to celebrate the holiday season, but I've heard that gifts are traditionally given around new year in Greece. So rather than force myself to try and make an impossible vision of a traditional British Christmas, I'm giving in to difference. Otherwise, why leave home at all?

'I think as you and Helios are very good friends, you should buy him something.' Calliope says this in a very matter-of-fact sort of way.

'Yes, of course.'

The only other person I really need to buy something for is Calliope herself, but I'm hoping to get some sort of idea from our shopping trip. So far, she's laden with bags of toys, clothes and sweet treats, and I'm walking around empty-handed, wondering what on earth to get the broken man I'm casually sleeping with who is also fast becoming my best friend.

'It's a long time since I dated, so I don't know the answers, but are you and Helios ever going to be more than . . .' Calliope waves a lollipop shaped like Santa at me.

'Having sex?'

'Yes,' she exhales, and rolls her eyes as I follow her to the counter.

She's that bit outside of my generation and from a very different background to mine. So far, I've found her to be modern and forward-thinking in her attitude. She hasn't been judgemental from the moment she guessed, or outed, my slightly-more-than-friends relationship with Helios.

'I hope we'll always be friends. But I'll be moving back to London in three months. There's no point pretending this is more than what it is. Although, I'm keeping the house. Maybe rent it out and come and visit you all when I can.'

Calliope downturns her mouth and nods her head.

'What?'

'Nothing, nothing.' She waves the chocolate Santa at me again and begins to move slowly on to look at something else.

'What?'

'Fine, you drag it from me.'

I do my best to suppress the eye-roll and the laugh that so desperately wants to escape me and let her continue.

'I can't see you in London. I've been in London with all the people, marching, marching here and there, all pressing together with no space for clean air.' She shakes her head. 'It is nice, for a holiday and to see sights, but to live . . .' She pulls another downturned face.

'London was, and will be again, my whole entire life. It's where my friends are, it's close to my family. I miss waving down a taxi to get to museums when I'm at a loose end, or coffee shops on a Sunday. I miss jogging around Hyde Park and late-night cocktails.

I do love it here, though. It's brought out a different side to me, one that I haven't seen much since I was a child.'

'This is good. If the world had the eyes of children, maybe it would be better.'

'That really depends on the child.'

Calliope chuckles to herself as she moves towards the shop counter and places everything down on it. 'True.' She flips into Greek, pointing at everything she's piled up and firing questions at the man behind the till.

It's impossible to know what to get Helios, the man who wants nothing but his child to be alive. The only thing I know I can help with is getting him more access to his son. But so far, Helios has completely clammed up about why his wife is so determined to keep him away.

That's what I should try to get him for Christmas. If I can succeed at this, maybe I can go back to my life as a barrister when my time here comes to a close.

It's going to be tricky to achieve, but I've managed harder feats within my career. I don't like the idea of going behind his back, but I truly believe the reward outweighs the feeling of discomfort.

I can do this. I'm good at this. I deal in evidence every single day, or I did. It would do me some good as well as help him. If I can do this, it's a step back towards who I was.

The start point is obvious, but not necessarily straightforward. I need to find someone who knows someone working for the police in Kos. This would be the quickest and easiest way to find out the details of the accident.

Although Helios blames himself because he thought he was indicating when he wasn't, if the other driver lied, and Helios *had* been indicating, the way Helios thought he had, it could be different. In the UK, sometimes indicators and brake lights are checked to see whether they were hot at the time of impact, therefore determining whether they were in use. Sadly, on many more than one occasion, this can be left out of the final verdict with regards to who is at fault. If any sort of verdict is even required. This is particularly true when someone holds their hands up and claims they are culpable, the way Helios likely did in his fog of guilt.

'Alisha, Alisha.' Calliope all but snaps her fingers in my face. 'I said, where do you want to go next?'

'Oh, I don't mind. Wherever you think is good. Maybe we could grab something to eat soon though.' I follow her out on to the paved street. 'I might head back to the bus after we eat. I'm not very good at finding Christmas gifts, am I?'

'No, you just talk and walk, you no look. How will you buy if you don't look?'

'Good point . . . I don't suppose you have a friend who works for the police force in Kos, do you?'

Calliope screws up her face at this sudden change of subject. 'No. No friend.'

My feet drag a little more across the pavement as we walk with some of the ruins to our left.

They look cold and sad, all grey and lonely, just how I feel as I have no one else to ask.

This isn't a good start.

Walking into a police station when I'm not a native, nor a fluent Greek speaker, and requesting to see case files based on my qualification in England is a bit of a stretch.

Calliope continues, 'Only my husband's brother. I like him like a friend, so maybe a friend.' She shrugs.

I grab her arm, nearly knocking one of her bags to the floor and making her *tsk* loudly at me.

'Can I speak with him?'

'Now? Today?' She looks at me with wild, almost panicked eyes.

'No, no.' I let go of her and regain my composure. 'Maybe later today? Or tomorrow, perhaps?'

'I am staying with them tonight for his daughter's name day. Her name is Annita. Very beautiful name. You can come for dinner.'

'You can't invite me to their house without even asking them first.'

'Yes, yes, you come to dinner.'

'No, thank you. I truly couldn't, but would you please give him my number and ask him to call me?' I stop in my tracks to button up my blazer and tighten my scarf. 'He speaks English, right?'

For a brief moment, I'd forgotten my own limitations living in a country where I can only have conversations in the native language that live as long as a mayfly on a bad day.

'You are very lucky, he is very good with his English. Now, I will only give him the number if you tell me why you want to talk to the police. Have you got problems?'

I look up to the fluffy clouds gliding slowly past us without a care in the world. It's not my place to tell her. It's not fair on Helios.

'I'm sorry, Calliope, I really can't, but I hope that you will trust me and pass on my details to your brother-in-law, to Nikos's brother.'

I wish I could discuss it with her. Usually when I'm faced with a complex legal matter, I have a whole team to discuss it with, and that's something I'm desperately missing right now. I'm used to being instructed, guided by a solicitor. That's not to say I'm not capable, I'm just not used to working in this way.

Her lips purse. 'I trust you.'

'And I'm grateful for your trust and your friendship.'

'Yes, yes, I'm a fool. What is it you say? A soft toucher?'

'A soft touch.' I giggle to myself but don't press the mistake further. I wish my Greek were good enough to make such fun mistakes. 'Thank you, Calliope. For everything. Lunch is on me.'

Hopefully, this brother-in-law of hers will be able to help me to find out what *really* happened to Lyra, and if I'm very lucky, maybe it will bring Helios and his ex-wife a small degree of peace. Maybe enough to open the door to Helios being in his son's life a little more. That's the aim.

My phone chimes from my handbag. I pull it out and see Pop on the screen.

'Hello, it's not Thursday again, is it?'

'No. Where are you, Alisha?' Pop's voice is solid, firm, unwavering. It's not his usual jovial tone.

I stiffen, but carry on walking.

'I'm shopping. Why? Is something wrong?'

'Will you be home soon?' Pop's tone shifts to an irritation I recognise from childhood days of coming home two minutes later than stated.

'Maybe, tomorrow . . . why?'

'Because I'm standing outside your house to surprise you, and you're not here . . .'

Chapter 44

'Helios, I need you to do me a favour,' I coo down the line.

'You want me to let your dad into your house, *nai*?'

'Yes, please.'

'It's too late, I found him on the street and invited him in for coffee. But I can let him in when he wants to get in.'

Relief fills me up. Thank goodness I gave Helios a key to my place. He thought I was crazy to even lock the door, but old habits die hard.

'Do you want me to give him the key?'

'No, no. It's fine. There's another in a drawer he can have, I'm not sure how long he's staying. I can't believe he's here, or there, I mean, with you. I'll come back on the ferry tomorrow morning. I can't believe I've missed his arrival. I've never known him do anything this spontaneous in his whole life.'

'Well, there's a first for everything.'

'Can you keep an eye on him for me? Maybe help to feed him? He has my cooking skills. Even just point him in the direction of one of the tavernas? I'm so sorry to do this.'

'It's fine. He is fine. I am happy to show him around, but he's not a dog or one of your stray cats.'

'Is Alisha telling you I need a babysitter? Don't listen to her. I got here all by myself without any help at all.' Pop's clipped voice is distant but perfectly clear down the line.

'Did you hear that? He said—'

'I heard him.' A smile bubbles into a laugh of excitement that I'll see my pop soon. 'Thanks for doing this for me, Helios. It means a lot.'

'It's nothing. We'll see you tomorrow.'

'Bye.' I hang up the phone with a smile lingering on my face and an extra shot of adrenaline in my chest as I wonder what on earth those two will be talking about over coffee.

◆ ◆ ◆

With Calliope off with her family at the other side of the island, I go to a restaurant in Kardamena. I thought it might be easier to stay here overnight, ready to catch the ferry in the morning, rather than Kos town, which is almost an hour's bus journey away. Less with a direct taxi, of course, but yesterday Calliope insisted we take the bus as it's less than four euros and better for the environment.

I guess I'm used to hailing taxis more than hopping on buses. It was a comfortable coach, not at all what I'd expected for such a small price.

Down a side street, I've found a taverna called Yianni's. A lot of places are closed in the winter, but this one is open. It has vines in an arch running along the alley and plenty of seating inside. The paper mats boast of being here since 1975.

Tonight, with the nights drawing into darkness at an earlier hour and the sea battering the island with a cold salty wind, I'm happy to sit in the comfort of their dining room and consume some delicious prawns in a creamy garlic sauce with both rice *and* something akin to small roast potatoes.

As I chew, I mull over thoughts of Helios. I don't remember the last time I worked on a case to defend a man against a woman.

It's not what I do. I work to protect the human rights of women almost exclusively.

The cases I've prosecuted range from human trafficking, like Karine, to coercive control cases, domestic abuse and more, all with a broken woman, or women, at the centre fighting for her right to have a voice and justice served.

This is different. This is a young man growing up without a father all because of a traffic accident. It's ludicrous for Helios not to have more involvement when he is a good man wanting to play a part in raising his child.

A text message pops up on my phone. I lay down my fork and pick it up. It's not like I have anyone to be polite for.

> This is Christodoulos. Calliope says I must message you tonight and tell you to call me on this number in the morning. I will speak to you then. Kaliníhta, Christodoulos

This *must* be the policeman, Calliope's brother-in-law.

A roll of excitement trickles through my veins. It's that same feeling whenever I'm going to right a wrong or feel like maybe I'll change a small corner of the world for the better.

I had feared I'd lost that feeling forever after what happened with Karine, that even doing good doesn't end well, but knowing I might make Helios's world a little brighter gives me that joy. That feeling of making things right.

Maybe I will be able to return to work anew next year, ready to fight battles for people who need me in the courtroom and give voices to people who can't use theirs.

One step at a time.

◆ ◆ ◆

It's a chilly but beautiful day in Kardamena. The wind has died down and seagulls fly about overhead, calling as they swoop here and there.

I've loosened my cotton scarf and I'm comfortable in my jacket and cashmere jumper, unlike the locals, who look almost ready for snow even though there's not a cloud in the crisp blue sky.

The boat leaves in an hour. Not much is open along the front, so I've placed myself a short distance from the harbour on a bench in the main square. People walk up to put plastic bottle tops in a big red-wire heart. They're collected to raise money for charity.

I want to make my call to Christodoulos in advance of my departure. I'm not sure what the signal is like between the islands and anyway, the sound of the engine and the rushing of the wind and sea as we cut through them would likely drown out our words. I need to be able to hear him, and for him to understand exactly what I need from him.

I would've already called him, but Pop sent me pictures of all the cats, and a rambling message about my coffee machine being different to *his* coffee machine and what should he press. He's only staying a few days. I'm kicking myself for missing him even for a minute, let alone a whole day.

I hit send on my message back to Pop, then go to last night's message from Christodoulos and hit the call button on the number.

He answers within two rings.

'Alisha? Yes?' Christodoulos's voice booms down the line. He sounds jolly and I conjure an image of a soft-looking man in his fifties.

'Yes. Good morning, *kalimera*. Thank you for taking my call. I was wondering whether you can help me. I have a friend who was involved in an accident a couple of years ago – his daughter died in the incident here in Kos. I was wondering whether you would be able to look into some of the details for me, I'm happy to compensate you for your time.'

A grumbling sound rolls around in my ear before he speaks. 'What exactly are you looking for?'

'I want to know whether anyone checked to see if the indicator was active in the car that was slowing down to turn at the time of the collision. The car in which the young girl, Lyra, was crushed. I know sometimes these things are checked to see whether the filament was broken or misshapen . . . if not, perhaps there was an eyewitness who was never called upon, but independently came forward with information? Whose information was ultimately not deemed relevant to the case.'

'OK, OK, I think I understand. Yes, I can look, but only because it's for Calliope. She told me I *had* to help you. So there is no choice.' I can hear the smile in his voice. There's not an ounce of irritation.

'Thank you. I'm grateful to you, and to her for asking this of you.'

'No, I am the one grateful to her. My brother's wife is a very determined woman. She does not understand our word "*óchi*". The *Engliss*, "*No*".' I smile both at his accent and the idea of Calliope ignoring a *no*. That's the woman I've come to know, that's for sure. 'When my wife was told she had cancer, Calliope did so much for us, anything Calliope wants, Calliope, she gets.'

I think of my friend and her willingness to help. She's a generous person with the straight-talking nature of someone who doesn't care, ignoring everyone's *nos*, when the reality is she cares deeper than anyone. Instead of demonstrating it in tender words, she acts on her feelings. She may not say it, but she shows it in her own distinctive way, which, in my opinion, is rather beautiful.

'Now,' Christodoulos continues, 'you tell me everything you know. What are the names of all the people in the accident? What are the cars involved?'

It strikes me how little I know about it all, but I do my best to give him enough information to look into it when he gets a chance. I can only name Helios and Lyra and that it was early in January 2024. Surely there aren't that many teenage girls who die in such a manner on this island? As I give him small details, there's a tone of recognition. He doesn't explicitly say that he remembers it all, but who would forget such an event?

◆ ◆ ◆

On the boat ride from Kos to Nisyros, the sea is calm. Much calmer than when I came across with Odina and we were being hammered by the wind, bouncing along on the waves, having managed to get tickets to one of the only boats to make the crossing that day.

Today I'm at peace.

Today I feel as though I have a little more purpose than I did before.

I watch the waves foam alongside the boat from the upper deck. It's much smaller than the one that came across with my things and then my moped. It probably can't hold more than eighty people comfortably and there's nowhere near that many today, maybe half.

I close my eyes against the sun and feel the sea spray dampen my cheek like tears of joy. I can feel change in the air, and I know things are happening in the way they should.

My phone goes and there's one of Odina's voice notes waiting for me.

> Hey! Grandpop said you weren't there when he arrived. I told him to tell you that he was on his way but you know what he's like when he's made up his mind. Are you with him now?

I quickly reply.

No, I'm on the crossing now. The sea is beautiful today, much nicer than when you came over to Nisyros.

She replies in moments with another voice note.

OK, cool. The boat engine is *so* loud on your voice note, it's crazy. I thought you'd want to know, that me and Guy, that's his name by the way, Guy, are seeing each other again. I've invited him over to meet Mum and Dad, so it's all above board this time. We just get on so well, I can't wait for you to meet him too. Please never tell anyone what I told you. Let's actually never ever talk about it again. OK? He really is a good guy who just misunderstood a situation, and I was being dumb by burying my head in the sand and not talking to him the way I should've. Thank you for getting me to be an adult about it. Love you.

I reply:

I'm glad he'll be meeting your parents, I think that's a very smart idea. I look forward to meeting him when I'm back in London. Love you too.

I keep the message short because Odina is right; even though this crossing is peaceful by comparison, the engine's groaning and echoing in *my* ears, so I'm sure it's worse on her end of the phone.

It's not just that – although I'm glad that she's happy, I can't help but remain cautious of the whole situation. Of this man, *Guy*. At least Nancy and Augustin will have the opportunity to deal with him now.

Chapter 45

'There she is!' Pop opens his arms out wide as soon as I'm off the boat, his silver hair shimmering almost as much as his bright eyes.

'Pop!' I wrap my arms around him and he gives me his trademark squeeze. 'I can't believe you're actually here.'

I hold his soft, wrinkled face between my hands.

The last time I was here with him, there were three of us. Mum in her youth looking like the queen she was, unfailingly elegant in floating clothes and high heels even when they weren't at all appropriate for the uneven roads.

'I miss her too,' Pop says, reading my thoughts before pulling me in for another hug. 'We haven't a second to lose and we've already lost eighty-six thousand four hundred of them because you'd swanned off to Kos without a thought to tell me.'

'I didn't know I was the same age as Odina – fabulous, no concerns of perimenopause for me coming up soon then! Sounds wonderful. Although going back to asking your permission every time I leave the house doesn't seem like so much fun.'

'When did you ever ask me for permission to do anything?' He holds me at arm's length, his grey eyebrows drawn together.

'Good point.' I grin. 'Lunch?'

'Yes, but let's go to Helios for it. You have no food whatsoever and Helios has already kindly offered to host.'

'Host?'

I follow on behind my father in utter bewilderment. Yes, Helios normally cooks for me, but *host? At his house?* That has happened all of once, back when we were waiting for news of Odina when she was stuck in Kos. Ever since then, he has come to mine when we eat together.

Pop bangs on Helios's door with utter abandon and a jaunty melody to go along with it, like *tap-tiddly-tap-tap-tap*.

I begin to count as I wonder how long Pop will wait until he taps out another tune.

Luckily, I don't have to find out, as Helios opens the peeling blue door with a gracious smile. We come in and begin the dance of taking off our shoes as Helios tells us in no uncertain terms that it's completely unnecessary, and we can keep them on if we like, but we both take them off anyway.

As soon as I take a step further into Helios's home, I notice things are very different.

He's moved all the photos of his children off the sideboard.

Where there had previously been a cluster of black-and-white images, now is a cleared, lemony-fresh-smelling void like they were never there at all.

'I have food waiting upstairs, please, come this way,' Helios says.

Pop follows on and starts chatting away to Helios like he's an old friend as I'm left gawping at the empty space.

I run my finger along the shiny veneer of the wood, unable to comprehend why he would take them down. I'm desperate to ask but know that it would be entirely inappropriate in front of my pop.

I don't want to upset Helios, he's my friend and I care deeply for him. I just have this niggling feeling that it's my fault they're gone. That I am in some way the catalyst for this development, which is the last thing I want.

Jogging up the stairs to catch up, the smell of garlic wafts towards me, and when I get to the top, I'm welcomed by an array of food covering almost every inch of the dining table.

'How many more people are coming?' The words drop from my mouth with little thought. 'Are we having a welcome party for my pop?'

'Helios knows I'll need to be well fed because who knows what you might make me tomorrow.' Pop winks at Helios with a twinkle in his eye, knowing my response will be a defensive one.

'You're one to talk. It was you who gifted me with such culinary skills.'

Pops throws back his head and his mouth opens wide in an echoing laugh before he agrees, 'True, true. This really does look delicious, Helios. Thank you again for the invite.'

Helios does one of his slight chin dips of a nod, reminiscent of our first wordless month-and-a-bit of me being here.

I'm glad he owned up to speaking English.

I catch myself looking a little too intently at Helios and glance at Pop, tucking himself into the table. He's watching me watch Helios with what can only be described as a question mark in his eyes. Automatically, I shake my head like I'm trying to shake off the look he's given me, but it's a little too late for that.

'So, I take it you two got to know each other over coffee and dinner yesterday?' I look from Pop to Helios.

They both sent me separate messages after they went for a beer and a meal at a local taverna, saying how much they liked each other. It was really rather sweet.

'Oh yes. Helios here was telling me all about the book he's translating at the moment. Has he told you about it?'

'The one with the little girl and the baby dragon?'

'Yes, sounds like a lot of fun. Maybe one for Odina?'

'Pop, I think she's a little old for that now. She reads dragon books that would make you blush.'

'Please don't say that. To me, she's just a child.'

'She's seventeen. She is and she isn't.'

Helios stays quiet.

It must be hard for him to think about Odina and what she gets up to; she must be about the same age as his daughter would've been if she was still here. He was so good with Odina. He must wonder what his daughter would've been up to, how she would be spending her days, what books she would've been reading.

'What about you, Helios? You're not another one like my daughter, are you? Never wanting children of your own?'

It's as though everything has jarred to a screeching halt. As though my whole body has instantly covered itself with a cold, oily sweat as I stare wide-eyed at my pop, who is completely unaware of the faux pas as he tucks a cloth napkin over his lap.

Helios clears his throat and keeps his eyes on the food as he picks up a bowl of what looks like a tomato stew and offers it to my father.

'I don't think Alisha and I are similar in that way, but I think Alisha has very good reasons for not wanting children. She wants to protect herself from pain, and I understand that.'

'Silly, if you ask me. Having our children was the best thing we ever did. Yes, they're hard work when they're little and they cause endless worry, particularly when they swan off to live in other countries out of the blue, but I wouldn't change it.' Pop takes the ladle from the stew and slops some on to his plate. 'And what do you call this?'

'*Kritharáki*. It's a Greek pasta rice.'

'It all looks delicious. Thank you so much for doing this, Helios.' I put some fried potatoes on my plate and snatch up some pitta. 'So, Pop, how long did you say you're here for?'

'Here's your hat, what's your hurry.' Pop rolls his eyes and chuckles at himself as he brings a forkful of the *kritharáki* halfway to his mouth before answering. 'Only two more nights. I had to see you before Christmas and give you your card and present. Your mum would kill me if I didn't. I wanted to see you anyway, of course.'

I'm proud of him, and warmed by his arrival. This is the furthest he's been since Mum passed away and he travelled for me to a place laden with memories. I'm so grateful to have him as my father.

We continue consuming food and a couple of glasses of wine, and I carefully manage to avoid letting Pop put his foot in it again, thankfully.

'I think we should leave Helios to his work now, Pop.' Lunch has turned out to be a three-hour affair that we'll never possibly be able to reciprocate.

'It was nice to have company, and I'm sure you'll find ways to repay all my kindness.' Helios manages to maintain his straight face, and of course so do I, given all my practice in a courtroom, but inwardly my pulse quickens.

I open my mouth to answer but I'm quickly cut off by my phone ringing from the pocket of my jeans.

It's Christodoulos, Calliope's brother-in-law.

Chapter 46

'I have to take this. Thank you again, Helios.'

I hit answer on the call button and begin a snappy jog down Helios's stairs and towards my shoes.

'Alisha, are you here?' Christodoulos's voice crackles down the line as I press my phone between my ear and my shoulder.

'Hello? Yes, I'm here.' I slip on my trainers, standing on their backs to get out of the house as quickly as possible, not even bothering with the steps up and out, bounding over them in one go.

I can hear Pop making excuses for me and trying to laugh off me running out of the house, but I can't risk Helios overhearing anything that has to be said.

I walk briskly to my front door, which thankfully Pop left unlocked after fetching me from the ferry. I kick my shoes back off before I've even taken the steps down into my living room and dash to the kitchen to be as far away from Helios as possible, in the shortest time.

'You are a very lucky lady, Alisha. I have looked and I have answers. The indicator, it was tested, and it is *yes*. It was on when the accident happens, it was bent not broken. It was your friend, your neighbour, Helios, driving, yes? Well, he *was* indicating, it was the other driver who was lying. It was his fault for hitting the back of Helios and pushing the car into the truck. I think if Helios wasn't so easy to say it was his fault, the other driver would have been arrested for dangerous driving.'

'Could he still? What are the laws in Greece around such matters?'

'I knew you would ask me, so I looked into who it was. He was an elderly man and he passed away over a year ago, so there's not much to pursue.'

'Thank you so much for doing this for me. I don't suppose you could send me some of that information via email, could you? Just about the indicator?'

'If I do, can you promise this will be the last favour?'

'Sadly, I don't make promises I can't one hundred per cent know I'm going to keep.'

Christodoulos groans into my ear. 'Please try not to. Can you promise to keep these for personal use and keep my name away from how you got them?'

'That I *can* do. That I *can* promise.'

'Fine. What is your email?'

Pop comes into the house just as I'm reeling off my email address and thanking Christodoulos for his time and generosity, all of which he said I should credit back to Calliope, which of course I will.

'What was that all about?' Pop pushes up the sleeves of his V-neck jumper and rests his hands on his hips, staring into my soul in a way only parents can.

'Nothing.'

I start to busy my hands with getting out cups to offer Pop some tea or something, to move us away from this conversation.

We move around the kitchen until one tea and a coffee are made. We take them upstairs as Pop chatters about staying here without me last night, and what a nice house it is. How he's proud of me for following my childhood ambitions of living here.

He takes a seat in the armchair and I curl myself into the two-seater sofa, pulling the throw up over my knees.

'Now you can tell me what the call was about, why you didn't want Helios to hear about it, whether I'm wrong in thinking that man next door is in love with you – and whether it's going to be another case of you making men drop like flies at your feet, only to stamp all over them.'

'What do you mean by that?'

Pop sips his tea loudly and the sound alone irritates me, grating against my nerves.

'You never keep a man around for too long. You let them think they're getting settled, if you have them about even that long, then you give them the boot.'

'I was married for a couple of years.'

'Exactly. Russell was a good man.'

'I wasn't in love with him.'

'Maybe so, but you could do a lot worse.'

'You'd have settled for less than what you had with Mum?'

He lowers his eyes towards his tea before shaking his head. 'No. No I wouldn't.'

'So why should I?'

'You shouldn't. Your mother never wanted you to marry him anyway.'

'Didn't she?'

This is news to me. My chin drops towards my chest and my brain opens every drawer of memories to find evidence that matches his statement. Mum never told me she didn't want me to marry Russell. Not once. She was always seemingly supportive.

'No. She said it was you ticking life boxes instead of living them. That woman was always right, wasn't she.'

'I suppose that's where I get it from.'

'I suppose it is.'

'I can't believe she never said anything.'

'She never wanted to play God. We've always been here to give you guidance, but she wouldn't put those sorts of feelings on you. You know that.'

I do. She was the sort of woman to offer advice liberally, but only when it was sought out. She wouldn't poke her nose in where it wasn't wanted. Any comments passed were gentle nudges, not heavy-handed shoves.

We share in a smile, with eyes that glisten in the sadness of feeling the joy that someone built and brought for years, but which they can no longer bask in themselves. It's a strange twist of emotions that coils itself around the jugular if you're not careful.

Mum was correct, I was doing what I thought was right. Something everyone around me was doing. Getting married off, having the big white wedding with blousy roses and lacy dresses. It wasn't because I was *so in love* I had to celebrate it and declare him as my forever man. It was because it was an easy life choice and I didn't want to be left behind. I'm glad I realised that's what it was, even if it took me a couple of years.

'I like how you homed in on the least important part of what I said, Alisha. You barristers are much too good at diverting attention. Now, let me ask again: who called, why didn't you want Helios to hear it, and is he in love with you? More importantly, are you in love with him?'

Chapter 47

'No. I'm not in love with him.'

Pop groans at my reply. 'Shame, he's a good man.'

'He doesn't love me, and I don't love him. Not like that, anyway.'

'Have you asked him whether he loves you?'

'No! How would that even come up? Anyway, it would be absurd to ask, particularly as I don't want to know the answer.'

'And the call? I'm right, aren't I? It's something you didn't want Helios to overhear?'

I take a deep breath and momentarily hold it in my chest, wishing it was filling my veins with nicotine instead of the safe and steady stream of oxygen.

'That's harder to answer.'

'Try me.'

This is my pop. My dad. The man who would protect me and love me no matter what I do. I trust him, but I'm the person who can't understand a jury member telling their husband or wife about a case, because I'm a stickler for fairness and privacy.

'You know I won't tell another soul,' Pop prompts.

My mouth is suddenly dry as I run lists of consequences through my head.

I do trust my dad. He's a doctor, and he understands the importance of privacy. In some ways, maybe I could use him as a sounding board in the same way I might discuss a case with another professional in my chambers.

'I know it goes without saying, but this is strictly between us.'

'Of course.' He nods over his tea.

'Helios does have children. Well, he has a son, and his daughter . . . his daughter was in a car accident.'

Pop lowers his mug instead of taking a sip.

'Oh hell.'

'Don't worry, you're not the only one to put your foot in it.'

Pop rubs his creased forehead.

'The thing is, he blames himself for her death. He was driving, and from what I gather, he was slowing down to turn and the person behind him hit his car at speed, pushing and twisting the car into oncoming traffic. The person behind said Helios wasn't indicating and Helios believed that, and so believed he was to blame.'

'Because he was grief-stricken.'

'Exactly. The wider issue here is, his wife is denying him regular contact with his son and—'

'And you want to step in and fix everything.'

'I've already spoken to the police, and Helios *was* indicating. The filament in the bulb wasn't broken, it was misshapen, thus proving it.'

'Will he thank you for your efforts? You can't go in heavy-handed, meddling just because you're bored being away from your work for so long. If you want to come back, I'm sure you'd be welcomed back early with open arms.'

'I'm not bored and I can't come back unless I'm truly ready. You know that. Anyway, I've been able to read whole books for pleasure again, walk along the beach, relax in the sun, eat feta with complete abandon, paint . . . I even nearly wrote a book.' I leave out the parts about Helios keeping my bed warm through these winter months, the fact my book consisted of one dreadful chapter that had nowhere to go and that when I paint people they all look like deranged thumbs with hair.

'The question is,' he continues, 'are you helping him, or yourself?'

'Him.' I don't even need to think about it. 'If this helps him, then nothing else is important.'

Although we had a rather odd and bumpy start to our friendship, Helios has looked after me and been kinder to me than anyone in a long time. The last time I felt truly looked after was when I was a child at home.

I wrap my fingers a little tighter around my coffee, snuggling down into my cardigan and thinking about what this could all mean and what I need to do with the information.

'But I do think helping him is like proving to myself I can put my feelings to one side again and help people. I feel so strongly that he needs me.'

'Even if you are doing this for him, you need to tread carefully. No matter what the truth is, it'll never bring back his daughter. It won't fix the past.'

'But it could bring him closer to his son. Surely it's worth a try? Even if I piss him off and lose him as a friend, I still think it's worth a shot.'

'I guess it depends how you go about telling him.'

'I'd be happy to discuss ideas.' I smile over my coffee and Pop raises his eyebrows.

'Of course you would. I'm not your assistant or one of your colleagues, you know.'

'You are today.'

I have this feeling he really wanted to say *I'm not Mum*. He's trying to fill her void for us all, and busy himself away from his own pain. I admire him every day.

She was something incredible. I'm sure many people think that about their mums, I'm sure many don't. She was mine and I wish she was here with us now, talking it all through, telling me about her experiences in life.

I'm grateful to have this time with my pop, though, chewing the cud until we have formulated a plan.

Chapter 48

I have vivid memories of being a child and trying desperately to stay awake on Christmas Eve, waiting for Father Christmas to arrive down our chimney. I'd leave out Scotch, homemade cupcakes and a carrot.

Before we were sent off to bed, my mother would read us children's abridged versions of her favourite Christmas stories, such as *A Christmas Carol* and *The Night Before Christmas.*

We would sit cross-legged on the floor. At first it was myself and Augustin, then myself and Toby when he was little . . . and Augustin if we could persuade him to sit with us, being that much older. We'd listen silently, eyes wide at the brightly coloured pictures in the books.

When I was an older teen, I'd go out drinking with friends and pray not to have a hefty hangover that lasted the whole of Christmas. I'd come home and try not to wake Toby, knowing he was probably listening out for my arrival at 2 a.m.

Then there was Odina as a toddler, listening to Mum read those same worn storybooks before being swept off home to sleep in her own bed and wait for Santa, while I was there to stay in our family home, sleeping in my old bed, each year without fail.

This is my first Christmas Eve completely away from home.

I haven't even attempted sleep.

With Pop's help and discussion those weeks back, I decided this would be my Christmas present to Helios. Christmas Day holds little meaning for him.

He isn't much of a churchgoer, but I heard him leave for midnight Mass, the way he said he would. The way he said his family always had, from when he was born.

He hasn't even been away to see his son, Stamatis, or his sisters or anyone.

I want to ask why and when are the allotted times he gets to see him, but I keep it to myself.

I put some red wine to warm on the hob, throwing in some sliced oranges, a cinnamon stick and a little local honey. It reminds me of times loitering in the kitchen at Mum's elbow from before I could have any all the way to the year before she passed, watching and waiting for her to ladle mulled wine into her special clay goblets.

All I have is a coffee cup. I don't even have a ladle here, so I carefully pour some out and take it upstairs to enjoy the night air on the balcony.

As I walk past my bed, I snatch up a blanket and take it with me. The past few days have been mild, almost like a cool spring in London. But when the sun sets and the navy of the sky takes over, it brings a chill and the desire to put on a cosy jumper and a blanket over the knees. It's dry and still enough to sit out late into the night to watch the bats dart about in the dark.

Snuggling down into the chair, I put my feet up on the balcony balustrade and wonder what Helios is up to.

We've spent many days together, ignoring anything that came before us and peacefully watching TV shows, consuming food and wine, or – my favourite relaxing activity – making love throughout my house.

There's not a part of me that hasn't been consumed by him, and I do fear that tomorrow's gift might throw everything off-kilter.

I like what I have here. I know it won't always be this way, but I'm not quite ready to give it up either.

I have no choice. It isn't about me and my feelings, it's about him.

The evening slips away in daydreams of the past, sending messages to friends and family back in London, until I've started mulling another bottle of wine and it's long past midnight.

Footsteps carry along the street as I step out on to my balcony with another mug of steaming wine. I look over the edge and spot Helios with his hands in his coat pockets, trudging home. He's a silhouette under the piercing stars, but one I now know. One I seek out in the dark. From the breadth of his shoulders and chest to his hands in his coat pockets as he walks. I know him.

I lean over just a touch and call down to him, my mug of wine swaying over the edge of the balcony. 'O Romeo, Romeo! Wherefore art thou Romeo? Deny thy father and refuse thy name; Or if thou wilt not, be but sworn my love, And I'll no longer be a Capulet.'

Helios looks up at me, crossing his arms with a tilted stature before calling back.

'I actually think your dad thinks I'm all right.'

'He does, he thinks I should marry you. I told him I'm no longer the marrying kind. Come up if you like.'

Even from a distance like this, I can see Helios's eyes bulge in the moonlight.

I'm struck by my own honest words, and heat prickles my skin under the blanket over my shoulders. Why did I say that? It's true, Pop did say I should marry him, that I seem at peace here and he's never known a man to cook food quite like Helios. Apparently that's what it takes to get me sold off into another marriage.

'I'm sorry,' Helios calls, 'I meant to say: Call me but love, and I'll be new baptized; Henceforth I never will be Romeo . . . sorry about that. I guess if I'm not Romeo, it seems I'm not the marrying kind either.'

'It's a new take on the meaning, but it's fine by me. Now come in, grab a mug and drink some of this mulled wine.'

Helios doesn't respond. Instead, he heads straight for my front door. He kept the key to my house from when I asked him to feed all the cats while I was over in Kos with Calliope.

We have that comfort now, at least in my home, that he can walk in, grab a drink and meet me upstairs, either in my cosy living room or out on the balcony.

I listen to his movements in the kitchen, his chatter to whichever cat is prowling around, and then the creaking of the stairs as he comes up and meets me on the balcony.

'Fun at church?'

'Who doesn't enjoy a birthday party?' he chuckles.

'Good point.'

We clink mugs and carefully sip the sticky sweet liquid.

'Why are you out here so late?' Helios places his mug down on the edge of the balcony and leans his back against it to face me.

'I've been messaging some friends, enjoying the wine, thinking about the past.'

'About Karine?'

'No, actually, my mum. You never talk about your parents.'

'I do see them, when I go over to Kos, and I call them twice a week on pain of death.'

'And yet you haven't mentioned them and you're not spending Christmas with them?'

'They're not the ones banished from seeing my son. I left everyone I loved in Kos. It's better that way. You look beautiful tonight, by the way, even wrapped in a blanket.'

I'm not sure whether the compliment holds truth, but what I do know is that Helios couldn't have changed the subject any quicker than he did.

'There's plenty of space, if you're cold. I see you left your coat downstairs.'

'I did. I should've known better. It'll be covered in cat fur in five minutes.'

Placing my mug on the chair, I step towards him, open up the blanket and wrap my arms around his neck to shroud him in warmth. I press myself against him, my head resting on his shoulder.

Pop was right, I am at peace here.

The embrace continues and our breathing shifts slightly to be in time with each other in the quiet of the night.

A small curl of anxiety pierces the space under my heart like a corkscrew. It's different from the panic attacks or my fear of never being good enough to head home and practise law again. This is a new sadness. One that feels like the corkscrew may have given me a slow puncture in one of my lungs. It won't be long until all of this is part of my past.

'You know,' Helios whispers in my ear, 'however much I love this cuddle, I am a little disappointed.'

'Oh?'

'I thought perhaps you were going to be naked under there and you were about to flash me.' His chest rumbles with laughter and it's impossible to stop myself from joining in.

'When have I *ever* flashed you?'

'Never, but there's a first time for everything. I thought perhaps it was my Christmas present.'

'I suppose it *is* Christmas Day now, isn't it.' I look up into his eyes, darker than the night and just as mysterious.

My mouth presses to his in a brief kiss, the sort shared by people in a relationship, not friends with benefits.

I've been denying the idea, pushing all my feelings away, but I know we act more like a couple now than friends.

It doesn't matter, of course, this can never be more than it is right now. We only have three more months of this. He said it himself, he isn't Romeo. He isn't here to marry me or sweep me off my feet. I don't believe in romance like that.

The slow puncture in my lung feels a little like it might steal my breath for good.

Gripping the blanket behind his neck with one hand, I begin to kiss and lick the rough stubble of his neck as my hand travels down to undo the belt of his jeans.

I can feel the weight of him, trapped and needing to escape. I help him out and he lets out a low groan as I take hold of him.

This is what we are. Pleasure, not forever.

Our lips meet and we begin to kiss deeply as Helios's fingers find their way between my thighs, making me moan.

Here, on Nisyros island, I arrived lost, and Helios found me, took my hand and now we're lost together.

My heart throbs in my chest, pushing air faster from my lungs . . . I have no idea how I'm ever going to find my way back to London.

Chapter 49

Twilight begins to crawl up to my balcony window and we're still locked together, my legs wrapped around him, calling his name into his ear.

When both relent, unable to continue, we eventually fall slack on my bed.

Kissing Helios's stubbled cheek, I tap him on his bare bottom to stop him from drifting off.

'I need to go to the bathroom.'

He kisses my mouth, holding my chin and looking at me for a moment longer before letting me go. I take my blanket, wrapping it over my shoulders to stay warm. As I get to the doorway, I turn back.

'Helios?'

'Um?'

I open the blanket to flash him. 'There, to make up for earlier.'

He chuckles as he slides his arms behind his head.

'Careful, I could go again with that sort of incentive.'

I laugh to myself as I turn to walk to the bathroom. There's an A4 envelope waiting for Helios on the side table in my living room. I know how important this information is to his life. Later today, everything will change.

After a perfect night tangled together, I think it's time to give him his real Christmas gift, and hope that our night together isn't the last.

After nipping into the bathroom, I wrap myself back up and scuttle out to grab the envelope.

Before I've even entered my bedroom, I'm explaining, 'I know it's early, but I'd like to give you your main gift now . . .' My words fall away as I step inside and find him fast asleep.

I walk around to the left side of the bed, where he is lying, and place the envelope next to him on the nightstand.

Climbing in carefully next to him, I pull the blanket over us both and lay my head down on his chest. He stirs only to pull me tighter into him before falling straight back into a light snore.

I close my eyes and listen to his heartbeat. I wonder if it sounded different before it was broken by the loss of Lyra, the girl with a smile as bright as the sun even in a black-and-white photo.

It's strange, if his daughter hadn't been killed, he would still be happily married, and we would never have met. I don't know who would've lived next door to me in his place. I don't know how broken I still might be if he hadn't been here to talk to me and help me heal.

Yet, if I could, I'd give him his daughter back even if it meant losing him.

The thought feels like the burn of ice in my veins; a chill crawls over my spine with it. I would readily sacrifice my happiness for him. I never truly thought that with Russell. I wouldn't even shift the time of my exercise class to suit him better, even though I could easily have done so.

I met Helios over three months ago and being with him is the best part of my days.

A solid lump forms in my throat at the idea of being without him. It's probably all the hormones released from intercourse, but the puncture deep under my ribcage knows it's more. Tears run along my cheeks and on to his chest.

I keep my eyes shut, and think of the three months we have left to spend together . . . that's assuming he's happy with my Christmas present and doesn't see it as a violation of his trust.

Maybe that's what I'm most afraid of.

◆ ◆ ◆

'What's this . . . ? Alisha? What's this?'

I groan and stretch, wondering how long I've been dreaming about being a child on Christmas Day.

I roll over to find a topless, perhaps still naked under the blanket, Helios, sitting up with the envelope on his lap and papers everywhere.

'What is this?' A deep frown zips together his eyebrows.

I tug the blanket to cover myself as I move to sit facing him.

My barrister voice automatically comes in. 'It's proof that you were not at fault when Lyra died. You were indicating *and* braking. I've also put together some documents, referencing Greek laws. You might want to use the information to get further access to your son. I paid for a Greek solicitor to help me out here and there with some details and . . . I believe her contact details are in there too.' A deafening silence fills the air as Helios looks from one page to the next. 'Merry Christmas.'

The air in my bedroom is thick enough to be choked on. Even if he hates me, I care about him enough to hope this will help him either way.

'I didn't ask you to do this,' he mumbles.

'I know you didn't. I want to help you, like you helped me.'

'I didn't ask for help.'

I clear my throat and sit a little straighter. 'Again, I know. But I didn't ask for help either, yet you have been here for me, and I wanted to repay you somehow.'

'But I haven't done anything.'

'Yes, you have. You let me talk when I needed to be heard, you were compassionate, brought me food so I didn't have to cook . . .'

'You *can't* cook,' he mutters under his breath.

'True, but I didn't ask you to look after me, yet you still did. Look, you don't have to do anything with this information. I thought knowing you were not at all at fault might make your ex-wife forgive you enough to give you more access to Stamatis, and he might see you differently too. Even if you hate me forever for doing this, it was worth a try.'

'I don't hate you.' His voice is as sharp and hard as a shard of glass. 'I . . .' He hesitates before eventually saying, 'Thank you.'

There's a look in his eyes that I've never seen before. A glistening light. A small part of me wants to ask what he was going to say before *thank you*; the other part of me never wants to know, just in case it was something I don't know what to do with.

My heart feels both crushed and as light as a feather. I can help people again. And I helped the most important person of all.

Chapter 50

'Merry Christmas!' Odina frantically waves and grins at me on the phone screen.

It must be about eight in the morning there and she's in berry-red pyjamas with gingerbread men all over them. I'm already dressed, showered and alone again while Helios has gone home to shower and ready himself . . . apparently.

He couldn't get away from me and my *gift* fast enough. Helios may have said thank you, but actions speak louder than words.

'Merry Christmas, everyone.' I wave back as she holds the phone towards everyone else in their pyjamas, all surrounded in torn wrapping paper.

'Have you opened your gifts yet, Alisha?' Toby shouts out of the crowd of faces.

When we were growing up, it was a bit of a running joke: *who can open their presents the fastest, Alisha or Toby.*

'Nope. But I am washed and dressed. So I'm ahead of you in that at least.'

'Maybe this is what I'm wearing today, you don't know,' Toby retorts with a grin that consumes his face.

There's so much hubbub blaring out of the phone, it echoes in my empty room. The cold blade of regret cuts deep. Why have I kept myself away from all these loving people?

It's not *them*, though. It's all of it. It's like every night I went to sleep in my bed in London, I couldn't stop dreaming about Karine. It still happens here, waking up in a cold sweat wishing I'd done something differently, but it's a lot less. Having daily reminders was making life in England too hard. Daily reminders of my failure and inability to help anyone else.

Things have shifted. I'm stronger now, but I'm not sure I'm up to the reminders being so strong yet. I guess I won't know until I'm home.

'Are you seeing Helios today?' Odina puts the phone close to her face again and gives me a certain type of look, a raised eyebrow that twitches like it's desperate to wiggle.

'Yes, we're having dinner together.'

The whole family makes an elongated *ooh*-ing sound then explodes in laughter and chatter, layering sound in a deafening crescendo.

'Please stop, you crazy lot.'

The phone gets handed around and I have a little chat with everyone present. They say thank you for the gifts I sent them and I promise to open my gifts a little later on.

I don't like to tell them that I'm so deflated by my gift to Helios dropping like a lead balloon that it would hurt to open presents and smile.

To their credit, no one pushes me to open them or asks why I haven't.

Pop is last to take the phone. He quickly walks away from everyone else.

'Pop, are you hiding in the coat closet under the stairs?'

A light as hard as a shard of glass cuts over his face and it looks as though he's been engulfed by wool, leather and fake fur.

'I'm not *hiding*, but yes, I'm in the closet.'

'What *are* you doing then?'

'I wanted to ask you whether you gave Helios his gift yet?'

I exhale hard at the memory of the morning.

'Yes, I did.'

'And?'

'And he went home pretty quickly, with very few words shared between us. He did say thank you, but he left the papers here. So it wasn't like he rushed off with them so he could look over it all.'

'Give him time. We all need some time when there's a big loss outside of our control. If someone came to you with proof it wasn't your fault Karine did what she did, remembering you already know in your heart you ultimately couldn't have changed it, even with this proof, would you feel any differently about it all?'

'No,' I whisper.

It wouldn't change my feeling of responsibility. My logical mind can't save me from it. If someone laid out what happened that night to me as if they were in my place, I would tell them there was nothing they could've done. It doesn't help replaying it over and over with the black shadow of regret.

Then there's Helios.

To be a parent is to wholeheartedly assume responsibility for someone else until they reach adult years. Of course, this is at times ludicrous. No one is able to protect anyone else absolutely, we all get hurt. Then on top of that he was the one behind the wheel, the one that couldn't change what happened after their car was hit. The one to walk away without even a scar.

'Give him time. I think this information will ultimately be something he's glad of. I'm proud of you, Alisha. Your mum would be very proud of you too. She always was.'

'Please don't be nice to me, you'll make me cry.'

'Then I'll stop.'

'You know, whenever I said that to Mum, she'd call me a silly name and we'd laugh.'

'Stop being a ninny. Is that better?'

'Yeah. Thanks, Pop.'

I gently sniff and nod my head. Mum used to call me a cow or a silly beggar, or some random animal that popped into her head, which would always break the tension of whatever situation I was in. Pop gave it a good go, and picked something right for him.

'Grandpop, can I please have my phone back now?' Odina extends the *please* to last longer than the rest of the sentence put together. She must be somewhere on the other side of the door and behind the phone screen.

After a last goodbye to my family, I'm alone again and silence echoes between the stone walls.

I've always been perfectly happy alone. The quiet of my own mind has always given me security. I can't explain why things are different now, but they are.

Is it because of Karine? Or Helios?

Chapter 51

Helios potters.

Pottering can be fine, but he silently moves around my house, occasionally stopping to stare at the papers I've given him while I open a bottle of champagne. He's only been in here all of five minutes and I get the distinct feeling he's readying himself to leave.

He hasn't even taken off his trainers.

Helios said he would bring some food, but I haven't asked when we're planning on eating it. Or cooking it. Or bringing it over.

I'm not chasing.

I opened all the gifts from my family when I got off the phone to them. Pop left them here when he was visiting. There's a Chocolate Orange and biscuits and all sorts in there, so I won't starve anytime soon if Helios has changed his mind about making dinner.

I also took the time to give all the cats their Christmas toys, including a cat tree that I put together while they rubbed around my legs as we waited for Helios's return.

I knew today would be strange. It's Christmas Day and it feels like a day of forced proximity to a man who can no longer speak.

This is far beyond the measure of strange I expected. I thought perhaps the worst-case scenario was him telling me I'd crossed a line, broken his trust, gone behind his back, and he would leave me here all alone to eat a bag of nuts and whatever is in my freezer drawer before consuming all the sweet treats from my family that I predicted they would send me.

Instead, I'm left feeling haunted by a new ghost in the shape of Helios.

Standing in my kitchen, he picks up the papers and puts them down again for the hundredth time.

'They're not going to bite you if you look at them for too long,' I eventually comment.

'I know that. You know I know that.'

'Do I?' Everything I've been bottling up brims to the surface as I tug on the cork of the champagne that just won't pop.

'Yes. I'm just surprised someone as smart as you would give this to me *today*.'

'Really? It's a gift. Where I come from, Christmas Day, the twenty-fifth of December, is the biggest day for gift-giving all year round. Yes, it's not chocolate or clothes or whatever else money can buy, but it had thought. And yes, I'm *smart*. I'm book-read, not a robot, not someone who's inherently smart at every subject. I can't even write a book or paint a picture, and I can't read how everyone feels at any given moment . . . I make mistakes, I don't always understand things even though I might be able to quote them exactly. I'm good at learning facts and dates. For example, did you know a man could legally rape his wife in England before the law was amended in 1991? Nineteen ninety-one! Or that it was only in 2019 that the law in Greece was amended so rape could include non-consensual sex that wasn't violent? Before that, if a woman froze, it was considered consensual. Even if she had said no! No wasn't enough to have its own meaning. Can you imagine that? I can quote from the European Convention on Human Rights without even thinking about it – which are important laws, by the way, ones I personally believe your ex-wife is in violation of by withholding access to your son. Some very misguided and truly unbelievable individuals want us to get rid of the Human Rights Act in England, all because it had the name tag of *European* even though we Brits all but wrote the bloody thing ourselves—'

The cork pops and flies across the room, rebounding twice before making Helios duck behind his arms.

'OK, OK, take a breath, calm down, you don't have to shoot me.'

'No. I can't *take a breath*. I can't *calm down*, and frankly I find it irritating to be asked to curb my reactions for your comfort in my own home. You have no understanding of how deeply I feel things, just as I have no understanding of your feelings on any given matter. I have to wear an invisible mask all too often to protect others, that and a heavy wig to hide under in court. This sabbatical wasn't my choice. I was forced to leave because I couldn't handle my emotions any longer. They *suggested* I take a year away, so for six months of it I'm here. You know, sometimes I think other barristers, not all, but some, have no feelings at all. They can stand there and defend anyone, because everyone has a right to a fair trial. Do you know how impossible I find that? How impossible I find looking at you and wishing I could take away your pain because I'm overwhelmed by it myself? If I could've given you back your daughter, I would. But this was the best I could do, and I know nothing will ever be enough.'

I've said too much. Gone too far. Found the line, jumped over it and run another mile.

I shake my head and redirect myself away from everything I'm intentionally holding back. 'Anyway, I understand that perhaps this isn't information you thought you wanted or needed, and perhaps you don't. Perhaps you will live out your days wondering *what if I'd used those papers Alisha prepped for me*. When I'm long gone in three months from now and living back in London and you're here speaking to no one every single day – sorry, let me correct myself, calling only your parents twice a week for a five-minute update – perhaps you'll consider *why* I think you should utilise these papers. Ultimately, I did it to give you a door. It's up to you whether or not you walk through it.'

Helios opens his mouth to say something, only to think twice before then deciding the action is worth his time after all.

'I *am* grateful to know it wasn't my fault. Nothing will ever ease the loss in my heart. Wishing that when I pulled my steering wheel away, she hadn't been exposed to the truck coming towards us.' Helios's face looks tinged in grey and hard as stone. 'But knowing there was nothing I could've done more than I did to prevent it . . . it's something. It could mean something to Stamatis and Hannah.'

'Good,' I say quietly, mildly ashamed of my outburst. 'Now, would you like a glass of champagne?'

One side of Helios's face slides into a smile. 'Sure.'

I begin to carefully pour the glittering liquid into two specially purchased glasses.

'You're very impressive, you know that?'

'I do.' I don't look at him, I keep my eyes on pouring.

The sound of him chuckling releases the tension that's been squeezing under my ribs.

'Yeah, I bet you do. You should. You're incredible.'

Ignoring him again, I pass him a glass of bubbles.

'Can we take this to my place?' Helios says before I can raise my glass in a Christmas toast.

He indicates towards the door and starts moving before I can say no.

Picking up the bottle, I follow on behind him. It's another bright-blue day outside, but one that still needs a fire to sit in front of as there's no cloud to act as blankets to tuck us into warmth. I walk behind Helios barefoot on my toes as they're nipped by the cold slabs of stone underfoot.

'Actually, you take this and I'll go get the shoes I wanted to wear—'

'No, please?'

He holds the door for me to come into his home before he dashes around me and scuttles away behind the grass-green curtain and up the stairs. Before following on, I hold my hands up to the warm glow of the fire he's lit in his entrance-cum-living room. It's so cosy and Christmassy to have a fire. I wish I'd made mine up.

Turning away from the glow, I notice he's put all the photos back in their place. I never had the courage to ask him why he had taken them away, but it's good to see them where they belong.

'Helios?'

He doesn't answer, so I begin moving towards the stairs.

'Helios?'

The house smells like roast potatoes and pitta bread, making my stomach rumble and groan as I haven't even bothered with breakfast, saving myself for any feast Helios said he would bring to mine later.

'Did you hear me?'

As I reach the top of the stairs, there's Helios standing on the other side of his dining table, waiting with a gentle smile on his lips.

Everything has been laid out perfectly for a Merry Christmas Day.

There's a small plastic tree in the corner, flashing with multicoloured lights. A red paper cloth on the table with a big red candle in the centre, circled by seasonal leaves and berries. There's even gold tinsel here and there around the room.

He's gone all out to try and make it Christmassy . . . for me.

He steps towards me, takes the bottle out of my hand and places it on the table.

'Merry Christmas, Alisha. I didn't know what to get you, so I thought I would bring you Christmas instead. To you, Alisha.'

He taps our glasses together, the ting of crystal ringing through the room.

‘I . . . thank you,’ Helios says, before dipping his head and kissing the corner of my mouth.

This gift of mine hasn’t pushed him away. He’s still my friend. Mine.

One I want to keep forever.

Chapter 52

'How long has Helios gone for? Did he tell you?' Calliope stops threading lava stones for a moment and tilts her head.

'Two weeks.'

'And you know where and why?'

'Yes.'

'And you're not going to tell me?'

'It's not my place.'

'I know, I know. At least now I know if I have secrets, I can trust you to keep them.'

'You can.'

Across Calliope's table lie small round volcanic rocks of various colours and shades, along with metal clasps, earring hooks, pillars and many other jewellery-making items. We discovered about a month ago this isn't something I'm gifted or quick at, but it is something I can do. Just.

I pick up a pink stone for the bracelet I'm making. I've been invited to sit with Calliope and her mother to make jewellery today. It's not the first time I've been invited but only the second time with her mother present. Calliope's mother doesn't speak much English, only what might be helpful in a shopping situation, but Calliope translates the bulk of what's said.

'How do you get the stones to be such pretty colours?' I ask Vasiliki.

I've been meaning to ask this so many times but the conversation, due to interpretations, is often at a pace that makes me forget what I was going to ask next.

'It is a big secret. I won't translate, my mother will never tell. We have special flowers here on the island that we collect in the spring, that's all I can say. We dye them and shape them together in the spring months. Maybe you can join us this time?'

'I'd love that, but I'll be back in London by then.'

I nod and note she really won't be translating any of that for Vasiliki as she picks out beads they made together last year.

For a week after Christmas, it was as if nothing had changed and shifted between Helios and me, and yet, at the same time, it had.

He invited me over to his house instead of always coming to mine. We even made love in *his* bed, on *his* floor and *his* couch, not only at mine. It's like he wanted to show me how much it all meant to him by letting me in.

All the while, I had this strange nagging feeling in my stomach that felt like a goodbye.

I knew it would happen, but this was sooner than I'd hoped. I wanted to stay in this bubble until it was so thin I couldn't even see I was in a bubble anymore and only then let it pop, just as I was ready to emerge from it.

I'm sure I would've got there eventually.

Although I *think* I know where he is, that's not exactly true. I made a point of not asking where he was going. It was casual, the way he told me.

I'll be going to Kos for a couple of weeks, I'll see you when I'm back, nai?

That's all that was said on the subject.

We have no obligation to each other. We're friends, and friends generally don't keep tabs on the other, or know every single thing that happens blow-by-blow the way a partner might. So I said yes and didn't question him. There was no need.

I might've added *have fun* as he departed. I can't remember now, something incidental that felt completely misplaced.

There was an overriding feeling in the air that if I did ask him questions, it would quickly come across as though I were pushing him towards something, instead of letting him decide on his own.

Now I have a handful of days left until he comes home and I'll find out whether my good deed had a positive outcome . . . assuming that's why he's there.

'Who is your bracelet for? Odina again?'

'No, actually. This one is for my assistant, Gigi. I'm going to make some for the barristers in my chambers too. We're all pretty close, all things considered.'

'That is lovely.'

'I think so too. What's the news on the meditation retreat for next summer?'

'It is bad news. I would need to buy so many things. I don't think I can, what is the word . . . invest it, in myself. Not now.'

'Like what?' I can't think people would need to bring much more than themselves and the right attitude.

'The yoga mat, the cushions, the little music speakers. I know where, I know how, but . . .' She shrugs. 'Maybe another time.'

I huff out through my nose, thinking it all over. 'I'm sure it'll happen soon.'

'Maybe.'

I hesitate for a second as I consider asking Calliope something while I thread another rough little bead. 'Calliope, do you think you could teach me how to cook?'

'I don't know, how bad are you? Is this why you never ask me to your house for food? Why we have to always go to the tavernas?'

'I can put a simple salad together—'

'A baby can put some onions, cucumbers, feta and olives and oil in a bowl and make it nice.' She thrusts her mop of hair off her face, tucks her glasses back up her nose and rolls her eyes behind them.

'Exactly. I'd like to make something else. I can make a Victoria sponge cake too, so plain fairy cakes and cupcakes . . . but I'd like to make something Greek. Not too difficult, but tasty. Something that I can easily make back in London and pretend I'm here.'

'Or you stay here? No need to learn to cook when you live here.' Her shoulder rubs her ear as her hands are full of beads again.

I make a noise of acknowledgement in the back of my throat.

'Even if I stayed, I'd like to make myself something other than oven chips.'

Calliope looks horrified at the idea of me only eating oven chips, halting her shoulder ear-scratching dance altogether.

'Fine. I teach you something easy, but you have to listen, *nai*? You are good at secrets, but can you listen?'

'I can.'

Calliope makes a humming noise as she eyes me. 'This we wait and see. You come back tomorrow, you can make my Nikos some dinner.'

'Not yours?'

'Maybe. I'll see when you make it.'

She might be serious, yet I can't help but beam at the idea of being taught to cook something Greek. Even if she is already concerned about eating it.

If I can cook something for Calliope, maybe I can repay Helios for the many meals he's made for me.

Chapter 53

Five knocks strike my front door. Five. All with great abandon, like someone's fist is tap-dancing across it.

My stomach flips as I wonder who it could be. Both Helios and Calliope knock in completely random styles. That, and ever since my father's surprise visit back in December I've wondered whether he might do it again, or whether someone else might.

In some ways, it's good. Now I know I'm not so disconnected. It's one of the layers that helps me to know I could step back into my old life because everything is running along as it always has, only without me there to oversee it.

Abandoning my coffee and tripping over four cats on my way, I head to the door.

I unlock and step down again to open the door, letting the grey tint of diffused late-January sunlight form a halo around Helios as he darkens my doorstep.

'Good morning, Alisha. It feels like I haven't seen you in a month. Can I come in?'

'Of course. It's good to see you. Welcome back.' I take another step back as he comes down and kisses my cheek. He lingers there for a moment longer than someone who is just a friend, but doesn't attempt to kiss my lips. There's even an edge of formality that wasn't there before.

Perhaps my work did the trick and I've fixed his family so well, he has no need for me anymore. He's likely back with Hannah and here to thank me and tell me as much.

We really have tied ourselves into a confusing knot.

'I'm here to thank you,' he says.

I knew it. I brace for impact, having to turn away towards the kitchen so he can't see my face.

'Coffee?' I call over my shoulder.

'Yes, please.'

'Espresso?'

'Please.' He clears his throat and repeats himself like I haven't heard him. 'I'm here to thank you.'

I busy myself for a moment at the coffee machine and pull out an espresso cup from the cupboard on the wall before turning to face him.

'I've been over in Kos,' he continues as though I didn't know that much already. 'It was all planned for me to spend time with Stamatis and my parents over the new year, it's one of the only holidays I get with him. Hannah gets Easter, Christmas, name day, birthday . . . I get *my* birthday and new year's. Anyway, I showed her everything you gave me. I didn't want to jump to legal action, I wanted to keep things sensible, amicable, but you're right, I want to see my son. We've already lost so much. I will never get my daughter back, but my son . . .'

'Helios?'

'Yes.'

'Are you getting back with your wife?'

Helios splutters and covers his freshly shaved face with his hand, trying to hold in what seems like a laugh.

'No, no. I want to be with . . . I want to . . . You know. I'm happy here.' He clears his throat.

The relief I feel is like jumping in the sea on a hot summer's day. Joyous and calming with an edge of *too cold for comfort.*

It's what I wanted him to think and feel on the one hand, but on the other . . . we have less than two months until I'm back in London. This has nowhere to go.

'Hannah listened. She will let me see Stamatis more than twice a year. I told him too, everything. I could see a change in him already. I am in debt to you for the rest of my life.'

'No, you're really not.'

I pass him his coffee and he takes it, our fingers glancing past each other naturally as he does so.

'Would you tell me about her? About Lyra? Maybe a story you remember?'

Helios's jaw goes a little slack and he freezes like a waxwork.

He always freezes when I ask about his past. My question will likely have a similar outcome and he'll make an excuse to run, the way he always does. But I want to know more about her than her ending.

There's a shift in his posture, standing taller, his face lifted. He even looks like he went to a barber while he was in Kos, instead of giving the impression of possibly cutting his own hair with kitchen scissors.

'Sure,' he croaks, before taking a seat with me at my kitchen table.

Helios thinks for a moment, looking down into his cup before he begins.

'Like you, she had a thing for cats. All animals, but very much kittens and cats. She would volunteer to help out at the animal shelter in Kos. They sometimes have this stall to raise money and she would donate things or practise her English, talking to all the people on their vacations as they went through the town. She helped raise good money for them. She was very hard to say no to. A lot like you. I think she would have liked you very much.'

A heat rolls over my cheeks as I reach across the table and squeeze his hand.

'You must all miss her so much. Thank you for sharing a part of her with me. Now would you tell me something about Stamatis? How was he when you saw him?'

'Unsure, at first. But then I showed him the proof that I *was* indicating and that my brakes were all working. That it was all the fault of the old man behind going too fast, not looking.' Helios's fingers contract away from me, making his forearms ripple with tension.

He lets out a breath through tight lips before continuing. 'It changed something. Stamatis opened up to me a little. We have a long way to go, it's been two years now since it all happened. Two years eight days ago.' He pauses, and I can hear him swallow back his pain. 'Stamatis even asked me why I left him to look after his mother alone.' Helios shakes his head and his eyes lose focus.

'But you can help now, you can be there for him, right? Hannah agreed?'

'She has agreed once a month.'

'That's fantastic news. I'm so happy for you.'

'It's because of you, Alisha.' Helios reaches across the smooth veneer of my table to take my hand once more. I've been holding my cup, and he has to slide his fingers over my wrist to free my grasp from it before holding my hand in his. 'I'm starting to get my son back.'

'I'm so happy for you. You deserve it after all you've been through.'

'I want to take you somewhere, to thank you.'

'How about we go for a walk?'

'I thought maybe something more than a walk?'

'Maybe, but for now, I think I need to stretch my legs.'

'Oh yes, of course, this is your normal walking hour.'

I hate to admit to being so predictable, but in London, I'd be tied to my desk reading through case files miles high, standing in court, or walking from place to place to stay fit. Walking is one of my hobbies, my latest being jewellery-making with Calliope, of course. Which I'd like to continue doing when I'm home, as my own kind of therapy. That, and secretly learning to cook . . . slowly.

Helios watches me patiently as I slip on some trainers and grab a jacket. His coat is thicker than mine, but I still find it mild compared to England. I don't know how long it would take me to feel how the Greeks do about the changing seasons here. Much longer than I have left on this beautiful island.

We step out under the dusty blue sky, with its thin layer of white making it look almost grey. A mischievous breeze makes my hair swirl enough that I look forward to getting back to London so I can get it trimmed. The air around us runs along the streets and through the brightly painted shutters to make its own shhing music.

'What have you been up to while I was gone?'

'Well, I've made another bunch of bracelets and necklaces with Calliope, named a few more cats and given them any necessary medicine.'

'Maybe we should call you Taylor Swift. Doesn't she have a lot of cats? Lyra always liked Swift, that's why I know that, before you ask.'

'I believe you.' It's nice to hear him say Lyra's name and bring her gently into conversation instead of denying she ever lived. 'I always wanted pets, but it wasn't practical before now.'

'What will you do with them when you go back to London?' Helios's voice shifts; his tone lowers a little, making him hard to hear under the noise of the wind and the loud squealing of children playing a road or two over.

'I've decided not to think about it. I'll still have my place here. If I leave the window open forever and ask someone to dump food in once a week, they might not even notice I'm gone.'

'Of course they would. It would be impossible not to miss you.'

I catch his eye and the glitter of bronze flecks that dig into the dark brown shimmers even on a quiet January day.

'Watch out!' Helios catches my hand and pulls me into his chest as a kid on an electric scooter whizzes past us, calling something – I think *sorry* – in Greek.

'Are you OK?' Helios holds my face with his free hand, searching it as though it might have an injury.

His eyes bulge like I've never seen and his forehead creases in what can only be fear.

'I'm fine. I should've been looking where I was going. It's always so quiet, I forget myself sometimes. There's always a scooter or bike, I should've known.'

I turn to walk away but Helios keeps hold of my hand as he walks by my side.

It's the first time we've held hands like this. My heart is still racing from the minor close encounter. The comfort of his touch makes me feel a little less wobbly, but doesn't help with the speed with which my blood races around my head.

I should slip my hand away. Pretend I need something from my pocket . . . but I don't. I want to hold him there, close by my side.

I don't need something from my pocket. I need my hand in his.

Chapter 54

A loud thumping sound rouses me from my sleep. Helios stayed until late last night, but went home as he hadn't unpacked from his trip over to Kos.

The hammering gets louder. My room is pitch-black. The shutters do a good job of keeping the light out, but even so, it must still be dark outside.

I sit up, my legs pinned by the weight of Cloud still sleeping, gluing me in place.

The banging continues.

'Is that someone knocking on the door?'

Cloud doesn't answer, so I slide my legs out, take my phone off charge to use it as a guide, and head towards the stairs, creeping along in the light of the torch.

The hammering continues as I stand at the bottom of the steps, my heart pounding in time with it.

'Who is it?'

'Helios.'

'Helios?' I mutter as I step up to the door. 'Why are you here, waking me up?'

Helios steps inside without an invite.

'Because I'm here to take you out.'

'You know what the time is, right?'

'Yes. Just past six thirty. I am often up at this time, unless I have stayed here awake all night with you.' He leans in and intimately kisses the top of my head as his hand rests on my lower back with complete ease.

It's getting harder to say we're *just friends* to Odina when she sends voice notes asking.

'OK, well, if we're going out, give me half an hour. I need a shower and to get dressed.' I trudge back towards the stairs as Cloud and Luna stretch and rub around each other, right in the way.

'No need. All you need to do is put on a swimsuit and grab a towel.'

I jar to a stop and slowly turn back to face Helios. He's standing proud with a cheeky grin hanging on his face like a forgotten Christmas decoration that's seeing how long it can hang about unnoticed, desperate to make it into February.

It's only now I catch sight of the towel casually slung over his shoulder. I rub my eyes and check that it is in fact a towel.

It is. An autumn-orange towel.

'You're not kidding, are you?'

'Nope.'

'It must be about six or seven degrees out there. It's been really cold for the past few days. It's not even February, for God's sake.'

'Yep.'

His grin doesn't relent. It makes me want to smile right back. After all the sitting next to the lonely man on the balcony, broken and frustrated, at first not even free enough to have sex with someone he wanted because he was glued to his past and unable to fully move on, not even wanting to speak to someone . . . this is beautiful. His smile is beautiful.

I didn't mean to come here and help heal another person, but it is the one thing I wanted to do in life, heal people, find them resolution and justice. It's all I'm good at. That's something this trip has taught me, if nothing else.

Seeing him now makes me feel like a light has been set in my chest and it's shining on him like a spotlight, making him flourish.

His light does the same for me. Without him, I don't know where I'd be right now.

'You're crazy,' I say through a smile.

'No, what is it Odina says? I'm *delulu*. The question is, are you?'

Maybe I *am* delusional. I take a deep breath in through my nose and huff it out. 'Wait here,' I demand, before continuing to edge around my cats and back up the stairs with a laugh caught in my throat.

◆ ◆ ◆

The sun begins to rise behind me, making my shadow stretch across the coarse sand so it looks like the sea is licking the top of my head.

When I arrived in September, and even in October, the water was quite fine. The days were getting shorter but they were warm, often hot. I'd walk along and paddle in the sea. Tourists were here, particularly in September, filling spaces, but few to sunbathe and swim. This would be the place for a walking day trip, so that's what I did too as I thought back to my time here with Mum and Pop.

I didn't feel up to swimming then.

I like going in the sea well enough, feeling the salt make my skin clean and tight. Sadly, my emotional state forbade me from coming here to have fun. I hadn't broken down the barriers required for that. Karine had all her fun snatched away from her, and it felt inappropriate to enjoy myself too much, like dancing on her grave. I was being silly. Letting myself fall into my very own quicksand, dragging myself under with my own emotions.

Karine would never have seen it that way, like I was celebrating in spite of her, but *I* did. It was irrational, but emotions often are.

Being here on the volcanic island of Nisyros has brought me healing. Perhaps Calliope and her friend she told me about, Dimitri, are right. Perhaps this island and the volcano that made it do have healing powers. I've found clarity and a man I adore.

Helios drops his coat on the sand, then pulls off his jumper and his T-shirt and drops them both on top of the coat.

'You know, in many countries they do *real* cold-water swimming. Here, the water is probably still at least seventeen degrees C. It's nice. Refreshing.'

'How often do you do this?'

'Twice a week. Maybe more. It's the best way to stay in shape.'

I have a vague memory of Calliope mentioning that Helios liked to swim, but I guess I haven't been awake to see it and assumed that was an activity saved for the delicious summer months, not in winter.

'Well, I personally disagree. My recent exercise activity has been . . . very satisfying.' I arch an eyebrow in Helios's direction, and he catches the look.

He bites his lower lip and looks me up and down.

'I'm glad to hear it. It's also why I haven't been going most days like I used to.'

'Are you sure those aren't the mornings you're going? To cool yourself off?' I bridge the gap between us as he drops his jeans to reveal actual Speedos. It might be the first time outside of watching the Olympics I've seen a man wear fitted swim pants that *actually* look good on them. All too often, it's larger men with bellies that fall in a way to make them look naked as they parade around the beach or pool.

'My eyes are up here.' He curls his index finger around my chin and lifts it to meet his eyes.

His lips touch mine. Out in public. Not right before we fall into bed, but out in the real world, his warm lips press against my frozen skin.

Helios puts his hands inside my coat and slides it off me as his tongue slips in my mouth. I don't stop him from undressing me; having him so close to me is enough to keep me warm. There's no one about. This cove is secluded, and surely no one else is mad enough to be down by the water this early in the morning.

Leaving my jumper on, he unzips my trousers. With only a wiggle, they slide easily to the ground for me to step out of. In doing so, I press myself closer to him and feel that undressing me alone has been enough to get his full body attention. With a little more intent, I push my hips forward, making him moan into my mouth.

He takes two steps towards the sea, bringing me closer to it.

My fingers trail over his chest and his hard nipples as the waves lap up to our feet, making me shiver. I continue down to feel him through the thin Lycra.

'Why did you *really* bring me here, Helios?'

'To swim.' He closes his eyes before sucking air in through his teeth while I kiss his neck.

'Are you sure?'

'Scout's honour. But feel free to carry on. I brought you out here to enjoy yourself. I wouldn't want anything to get in the way of that.'

My hand stops and I do my best to hold the laughter in my chest.

'Well, in that case I best get in the freezing water.' My voice is thick with sarcasm.

I step back and pull my roll-neck jumper over my head, throwing it towards the pile of clothes, and shiver in a navy bikini that's more like a crop top and cheeky shorts.

This wasn't how I originally imagined I'd spend beach days on Nisyros. I had thought about reading books and warming my soul until I felt up to giving myself back to my work, not shaking half naked by the sea in January.

The sun keeps rising into the sky behind me in a failing attempt to keep me warm. Helios, of course, is already up and holds the promise of a lot more warmth.

If having sex in the sand means I don't have to go swimming in the sea, I'm open to the idea. It's never been there on my bucket list – sand can be a bit of a pain – but at least I know with Helios it would be worth it.

He grabs one of my hands; his other hand wraps itself like a snake around my middle and pulls me forwards.

'Well, come on then. I'm more than happy to get in the water,' he says.

Damn. My sarcastic plan didn't work.

His lips crash into me like the waves as he attempts walking backwards as we kiss.

My feet all but scream as they hit the water. My toes recoil and try to hide under my feet for warmth, but Helios keeps moving, pulling me into the sea and into him.

'If you think I'm having sex with you in the sea, that's a big no. Do you know how many bacteria there are in there? I don't fancy having a urinary infection for the next week.'

'I've never expected anything from you, Alisha.' Helios pulls me into his chest as the water slaps over my knees. He pushes a loose strand of hair off my face like I've seen done in a thousand cheesy romcoms, but never experienced in real life.

Instead of laughing about it, Helios looks into my eyes with complete seriousness and says, 'But you keep surprising me anyway.'

'It's easy to surprise someone when there's no expectation.'

Helios rolls his eyes as his soft lips descend on mine. It isn't with the normal raw passion I feel throbbing between us. It's a slow, soft kiss, like being touched by the fingertips of a dream or a cloud.

When he pulls away, we lock eyes for a moment more and it feels like the words on a thousand pages of a book pass between us unsaid, but I can't understand any of it. Or I don't want to.

'No more waiting about,' Helios says by my cheek. 'It's time to swim.'

Chapter 55

'How about we do something different tonight?' I say as I pop the cork on a bottle of red.

For days we have shared one balcony for wine. Often I sit and read a book and Helios cooks dinner. Every single night.

Even when I was married, we didn't spend *every* night together. Rarely, in fact.

I'm always surprised that Helios and I still find things to talk about. We share stories from our past, as well as family anecdotes and updates.

Tomorrow, he's heading back to Kos to spend a few days with Stamatis and his parents. He's been positively pinging off the walls about it.

I'm happy for him, but with only thirty-three days left on the island, all I want to do is spend them with him. I know that can't always be the case.

Even though I feel ready to return to work, I don't feel ready to leave here. A sensation I still can't believe has happened along the way.

'Wait, you want to change this beautiful thing we have going? I'm not sure I'm ready for change.' Helios shakes his hands and backs away, but the lack of creases at the corners of his eyes reveal he isn't really smiling and joking. Maybe he is thinking the same as me, that part of him wishes we could continue how we are.

'You sit upstairs on the balcony under a blanket, next to a candle, and I'll make us dinner?'

'Salad sounds lovely.' He kisses the top of my head and irritation squeezes my fingers together.

Although patronising, I know he isn't wrong, based on his experience of me thus far. But I can stay smug in the fact that today he *will* be wrong.

'Something like that,' I say as I turn away.

Wine glugs delightfully into each glass and I pass one to him. We do a brief *yámas* and he picks up his current book, a twisty thriller, and heads up my stairs.

As soon as he's out of sight, I take a sip of wine and get to work peeling and crushing garlic until my fingers are ingrained with the stuff.

Over the last couple of weeks, Calliope has taught me how to make pythia, a chickpea fritter, and the last lot I made were actually really good. I've already made some almond and garlic sauce to go with them, plus a sponge cake, which I've hidden in a cupboard, so now I've only got to put this together. And the salad to start, to throw him off.

I'm halfway through cutting an onion when my phone starts ringing from the kitchen table. I dash about to wash my hands and half dry them in time to answer a call from Gigi, my assistant in London.

Since I got myself settled here, we haven't had much reason to speak. Occasionally, I've asked her to sort things out for me, like putting together the gifts I ordered and getting them wrapped at Christmastime, or looking at mentoring opportunities. I do still pay towards her presence in the office. A good assistant is hard to come by, and she's the very best. There's no way I'd want to lose her.

'Hi, Gigi. How are you?'

'Hi, Alisha. I know you wanted to be left alone for a full six months, but there's something that I think you need to hear about. Someone who *specifically* wants you to look at a case.' Gigi's not exactly whispering, but her Welsh accent is clipped and lower than normal. She's under strict instructions to leave me alone unless *I* contact her. They were the instructions I gave her too, I suppose.

'Mmm.'

I pick up my wine glass and lean against the counter. It must be big for her to go against my wishes like this.

'I know I shouldn't be asking, but my gut told me you'd be so angry if someone else interfered. Can I email you the information?'

A distant sound echoes in my ear on the phone. I can see Gigi in my mind's eye tapping the desk frantically, the way she does if we've got a particularly heavy day or she needs to be the bearer of bad news. She's probably chewing her gel nails right off too, knowing her.

I don't even think about the words that come out of my mouth.

'Gigi, I trust you. You can email me further details. If you think I should take a look, I'll take a look. Send me what you can and I'll be in touch. Is there anything else?'

'Yes, I'm so sorry for phoning and we all miss you. I'm sorry for bringing this to you. I really am.'

I've missed the comfort of my team of women too.

'Thank you, Gigi. I've missed you all too. And don't worry, I'm happy to take a look. Speak soon.'

I press my screen to end the call, putting the mobile back on the kitchen counter, but I keep my glass of wine close to my chest.

Going back to London. Now. London.

It's hard to imagine. Thirty-three days. Even a moment ago it was something I could pretend wasn't really going to happen right away. Now . . .

Closing my eyes, I can see it, the lights at midnight, the traffic, the buzz of bars and something different to see at every step. The shiny red buses, boxes of noodles and dumplings when I'm feeling lazy or the delights of getting dressed for the theatre or the Victoria and Albert Museum . . .

But I'm not ready to let go of Helios and what we have here.

I know it's temporary, it always has been temporary.

I open my eyes and decide it's more important to focus on the here and now than the *what if.*

Turning back to my onion, I can at least pretend the sting in my eyes isn't the emotion of not wanting to leave Helios behind, but knowing I have no choice in the matter. We have separate lives to live, after all.

'Hey, you. Do you need a hand?' Helios's voice suddenly shifts. 'What's all this? I thought it was taking a little more time than a salad does. Wow!' His eyes light up at the various foodstuffs spread around my kitchen as I do my best to form the balls ready to be fried.

'No, I can do it all. You relax.'

'Can I relax here? I was missing being near you.'

'I thought you were reading?'

'I was, but down here I can see you every time I look up from the pages.'

Helios brushes my hair off the back of my neck and presses kisses on the curve of my shoulder as I move my hands the way Calliope has shown me.

'Don't distract me. When I pick up my knife, I could lose a finger.'

'Good point.'

He pulls out a chair, slides down his reading glasses from the top of his head and opens his book to continue within my sphere of movement.

We don't need to talk. There's something calming about his energy that feels comforting to be around. Even the cats seem to think so as Luna jumps up on to his lap and snuggles into him, her grey paws padding into his knees.

I wonder whether friends can be soulmates.

I wonder whether soulmates can live miles and miles apart and still find time to be together.

Chapter 56

The day after seeing Helios off to Kos, I open the email from Gigi.

If I was back in the office, and agreed to the case, I can quite imagine rooms being piled high with heavy folders of information to be processed. This is purely the barest of bones that she has sent me. The things Gigi could get away with sending me via email.

The file is named Crown vs Mellor. My heart plummets to my feet and my body flushes hot then cold.

Mellor?

Is this why Gigi thought I needed so badly to see this? Is this why the client was asking for me to be involved and contacting Gigi, requesting my attention even while away?

I put my laptop in my backpack and ride off to the middle of nowhere to sit among the olive trees before reading a word more.

The trees haven't lost many of their silvery leaves through winter. They still shimmer like a make-up artist has been over them with highlighter. Their beauty is a welcome distraction as my head feels light and yet heavy with questions.

Closer to Stephanos Crater, the land is arid and the earth rises up out of the ground in harsh lines. But under the trees, there's a softness, even with their pointed leaves. The thick gnarled trunks are like comforting beings all of their own, who can listen to me think without ears or questions of their own.

I open up the files and there it is, in black and white: Jett Mellor. A celebrity who often features heavily in Nancy's charity events. He gives time and money to women in need *all* the time. He's one of the good guys . . . or so I thought.

I speed-read the files. Gigi knows well enough that I know this man.

My eyes skim over the information provided. There's a lot of women who have been brave enough to come forward. Twenty-five-year-olds claiming some of these acts were performed nine or ten years ago, some saying they thought they were being scouted for modelling jobs in music videos as they left school. Some girls are only turning eighteen now.

Sickness rolls through me in waves like in the sea, creeping up on me then crashing against my stomach.

I've kissed this man's cheek, laughed with him over dinner. He's an actor, fifteen or twenty years my senior and well known. Well respected.

A lot of this took place in areas I know in London. Schools in locations I know well. Even a school I once attended.

I have the same response I always do when I know I'm going to take on a case. A hardening in my stomach, like a fist is forming ready to punch down the accused.

This man is guilty, but he'll have some of the best representation money can buy to belittle these women and make them out to be liars, even though they have nothing to gain from all this. Cases like this are impossibly hard to win, but I have a reputation second to none at winning them.

The insult of turning up and pretending to sympathise with victims at charity events, all while doing *this*.

I close my laptop and place it next to me on the dirt.

The sky is as white as clean linen. It's as blinding as if the sun were glaring right at me, even though it's nowhere to be seen behind the thin veil of cloud.

I left a fire crackling in my wood burner at home, and this case has set light to me.

I close my eyes and tilt my chin towards the sky. This needs more thought. But I know I'm strong enough now. I didn't read the files and choke on them in a swirl of panic. I felt the way I used to feel.

Opening my eyes, I pick up my laptop and get back on my bike to clear my head.

◆ ◆ ◆

There's something about the crystal-clear nature of the sea here that promotes mental clarity too. Not only does it offer a reflection of everything you see and feel, but it shows you how fluid it all is. Everything is ever changing.

I always used to sit on high sea walls looking down at the waves. My mum hated it. She'd sometimes stand behind me, her fingers biting at my T-shirt or coat, anything she could get hold of, *just in case.*

I don't have her here to protect me anymore. I wish I did. I wish I could call her up now and tell her about Helios and the fractures I've caused in my life by living here. How half of me needs to go to London and win a case against a man I trusted to sit at a table and chat with Odina, while the other half wants to hide from it all in the arms of Helios in Nisyros.

The white sheet of cloud cracks and breaks. The sun doesn't reach the peaks of summer, instead keeping its reflections along the surface of the sea low and glittering, like a million sequin-clad showgirls dancing without a care on the ripples.

This is where it all began.

This is where I rolled imaginary dice as a child and laid out some big ideas for my life, without realising just what a toll such decisions would take on me personally. I can't claim to be born here on this beautiful Greek island, but everything I've done since being here was born in among these volcanic rocks and olive trees, while looking out to sea.

It set me off on a journey, and now it's come full circle. I made it back here after all those years. Now I have to make a decision about what to do next.

People need me back in England. I'm not needed here, not anymore. Helios doesn't *need* me. Even if he maybe wants me. I've done all I can to help him. He's happy he can see Stamatis again. He can start rebuilding his life now.

I wanted to live here, and I have. I wanted to save women from feeling afraid in their own homes, which I can't do, but I've helped many to have a voice when they couldn't speak for themselves. I've brought them the justice they deserved, pushed for better standards . . . but I've barely made a dent in the face of the inequalities women still contend with each day.

Even now, so many young women are brought up to be treated so very differently to their male counterparts, they don't even see the issues when they look in the mirror. The lack of equal health care, self-care and their sexualisation isn't just normalised, it goes unnoticed like clouds in winter. It can be the breeding ground for all the ugly behaviours and troubles that end up opposite me in court.

I can't say no to this case.

I still have so much work to do to help future generations of women.

Gigi knew that. She's been with me for a long time now and has spent her time acting like a shadow, there to support me and learn my every need before I know it myself. She knows I'm the one to win this case, and I know it too.

I close my eyes to the glittering showgirls on the sea and take in the clean salty air and hold it in my lungs.

This is my purpose in life. To help those who can't use their voices to fight back. I'll email Gigi and tell her I accept. I'll return to London once Helios returns from Kos.

I nibble my cheeks as a scratching sensation crawls under my ribs. It's as though my heart has grown hands and my ribs are the prison bars holding it in place, preventing it from getting in my head and stopping me from heading back to London.

I've never felt this way about saying goodbye to someone.

It won't be a goodbye. It can't be. It'll be a *see you again* . . . I just don't know when.

I wish I could take him with me, but he isn't going to want to leave here, not now he's getting his son back in his life. It wouldn't be fair of me to ask that of him. I wouldn't.

We will stay friends. I hope he wants to stay friends.

Either way, this beautiful romance is coming to an end, like it or not.

Chapter 57

'These are for you.' Helios passes me a large bunch of orange lilies, my absolute favourite flowers. I love their smell and their tropical look that feels like sunshine even in the rain.

I stand motionless for a split second before taking them. 'You remembered.'

No lover has ever intentionally got me orange lilies, known how much I love them. One man brought some with him on a first date. At first I thought it was kismet, but I soon realised as I took them out of the wrapping that they were discounted in the shop. Those flowers well outlived the relationship. If you could even call one date a relationship.

'They're beautiful, I love them. Thank you.' I inhale their sweet scent deeply, all but pressing my nose to them.

'Not as beautiful as you.' He leans down and kisses me softly on the mouth, like it's normal to greet me like this. I suppose it has become normal for us.

There are no more kissed cheeks or coy looks. We've become an *us* and now I have to pick us apart and hope we can stitch back what's left into a long-distance friendship. Maybe one that reconvenes once a year when I visit on holiday. Depending on trials and work, of course . . .

'I'm making you dinner again. A different dinner this time.'

'A farewell meal *and* a welcome home. I could get used to this.'

I stop sniffing the flowers and turn to him. 'What do you mean, *farewell*?'

'Before I left, you made me dinner, and now a welcome home meal too. Have you been spending a lot of time with Calliope while I was away?'

'Oh, yes. A bit.'

'What did you think I meant?'

'Nothing.'

I don't want to spoil tonight with the truth. I want to hear about his time in Kos, how Stamatis is doing, see the photos he took of him, and later feel Helios's mouth and the weight of his body on mine again.

'What's wrong?' Helios sits down with his elbows on the kitchen table and leans his chin on his fists. He looks like a concerned psychiatrist.

'Nothing, why?'

'I know there's something wrong.'

'How do you *know*?'

'Well, I've spent the past few months watching you.'

'That doesn't sound creepy at all.'

'Let's think back to the creepy things you've said to me . . . *It's a shame I won't be kissing you with lips like that* or *your cigarette is so lucky* . . .'

'That was different, my inner monologue fell out because I thought I was speaking to a brick wall. You can't use things against me that I said before you told me you understood me.'

'Fine. Tell me what's wrong then.'

'Nothing's wrong. Let me finish making dinner. How about you tell me everything about Stamatis while I cook?'

Helios tells me how much his son has grown, how he's started to open up to him a little after being quiet for so long.

There's still a lot of work to be done, but things are progressing well. Stamatis lost his sister; they've all had a part of their hearts ripped out of their chests and the bleeding will never stop, but it can be managed. At least now Helios is there for his son when he needs him.

'His English is really coming along nicely too. I think you should meet him. I told him you helped me, you were the one to prove it wasn't entirely my fault, that you are a big reason his mother let me see him properly again. He's really interested in practising his English with you.'

'I really would love to meet him.' I'm glad I'm not facing him as I chop.

'But . . . ?'

How does he already know me so well? Only my mum could pick out the words I wasn't saying. Even Pop can rarely get that right.

'*But* what?'

'You wanted to say, *but*. In your head you were saying *but*. I could hear the space where it wanted to go.'

I pick up the wine bottle and lighten its load by pouring some into our glasses. 'How do you do that?'

'Do what?'

'Know me so well?'

'I told you, I'm the creep watching you and actually listening when you speak.'

I can hold the attention of judge and jury and bring them into my narrative, make them see the truth the way I can see it so clearly in my head until they all agree with me enough to sentence people to live behind bars, yet in my personal life I haven't felt this same magnitude of attention . . . ever. I've never felt as seen as I do with Helios.

I slip into the seat opposite him at the table. His forehead is wrinkled up and his eyes stay completely fixed on me.

'I can't keep anything from you, can I?'

'Nope.'

I exhale hard, knowing that there's no point even trying to keep this in any longer.

'I got a phone call from Gigi, the night you left for Kos. She wanted to tell me about a high-profile case. They want me to prosecute and Gigi thought I should at least hear out the details.' I shake my head. 'It's more than that. I know him. The defendant. The perpetrator. I know him. I can't ignore this one. I don't trust anyone else with it. And . . . I'm ready.'

'When are you leaving?' Helios reaches across the table and takes my hand in his.

'Three days. I was hoping to have a week with you, but it hasn't worked out that way.'

He nods his head and keeps his eyes on our hands. 'I guess I knew this wasn't forever . . . I just . . . I just wish we had longer.'

'Me too.'

'Do you think you'll come back?'

A silence lingers around us as I try to find words that have lodged in my throat.

'I'm not selling the house or renting it out. The cats need a place to stay so . . .' I shrug, wishing I could say something that wasn't so distant and oddly practical. I'm not used to feeling this way, like my insides have scrunched up into a ball.

We share a smile but it's not enough to bring light back to Helios's eyes.

'Can I keep you for three days? Lock you in your room?'

'Told you you were a creep.'

'I am what you have made me.' Helios chews his lip for a moment. 'It's true, you know? You've given me hope again. Nothing could ever fix what happened to my girl, but I have hope that I can be there for my son. You've given me a life again.'

'And you've helped me too. You looked after me, let me talk about Karine without judgement or pressure. I could open up about the strain of my job, the panic attacks, the hate mail and threats, the long hours, the soul-destroying nature of dealing with certain types of people . . . all of it.'

'So . . . does that mean I can lock you in your room for three days or . . . ?' Helios bites back a smile and his dark eyes shine again as he looks at me.

'Maybe.' He always brings a smile to my face and a light to my chest.

Helios snatches his hand back and slaps his palms down on the table – 'I totally forgot' – and with that he disappears towards the front door and out of the house.

I strain, leaning half off my chair to look towards the front door from the vantage of the kitchen.

Luna saunters through the open doorway Helios left when he disappeared.

'Do you think he's coming back?' I ask her.

Luna only gives me the briefest acknowledgement but doesn't seem to know or care as she plonks herself down to lick between her claws.

After less than a minute, Helios can be heard slamming his front door shut and heading back over to mine.

He comes into the house holding a box of chocolates.

'I was too excited about the flowers and I forgot the chocolates.'

'I really *am* going to miss you when I'm gone.'

Helios's arms sag by his sides.

'I'm going to miss you too.'

I've never felt my chest squeeze as tightly as it does right now.

It's like a small death of the cells in my heart and I can't make peace with it. My closest experience of this sensation is when my mum passed away. That constriction squeezes every cell in my body and I feel as though I'm spiralling out of control.

Nothing truly bad is happening here, so why does it hurt so much?

Chapter 58

The air is electric.

I've heard people say that many times. I've said it myself. Felt it in court. I've felt it other times too, for one reason or another. That tension coming off others, silent yet perfectly audible in its vibrations. As though an individual, or group, aura has extended out and is touching the others around it. The hairs on arms rise and spines tingle.

We are electric beings.

Our atoms generate huge amounts of it and we pass messages through our bodies using this electricity. Is it so strange to believe that in heightened moments this sensation can be felt on our skin, in our veins, perhaps in our souls?

I feel it on Helios, an electric charge as he silently holds my hand.

A voice sounds from speakers in Greek, then in heavily accented English. People mill about waiting to check bags and have their passports stamped in the stretching rectangle of Kos Airport.

Our feet come to a halt not far from the line I need to join. There's an information board and I spot my flight back to Athens before my onward one to London. It's going to be a long day.

'You should go.' I release my hand from his, hoping this will be enough to break the electric wire between us.

It doesn't help. Instead, that same invisible wire wraps itself around my chest, making it hard to breathe.

'I could go with you to check your bag? It's heavy.'

'It has wheels.'

'But you'll need to lift it on to the belt.'

'And I'll have to lift it back off the other end without you.'

'True.' Helios lowers his eyes and bites his lip.

He is barely able to tear himself away from me, and my feet are unable to walk away from him.

Helios keeps his eyes low.

'I nearly forgot to say . . .'

His eyes reach mine with a light of hope that makes me regret starting this sentence in this way.

'. . . there's going to be a delivery. Can you give it to Calliope, please? It's ten yoga mats and a speaker. Tell her I believe in her and I'll be back for some classes in the summer . . . if I have time to get back.'

'OK . . .' He smiles just a touch, showing the smallest glimpse of the dimples at the corners of his mouth before they fade away just as quickly. 'I . . .' He clears his throat. I've seen this many times in court as a delaying tactic to give space for thought. 'I've loved this winter with you . . . you've made me young again. I thought my life was over. That my only purpose was to pay for my son until he goes to university and then smoke myself to death. I . . .' He takes a breath, and I get the sense he's choosing his words carefully or reciting a practised speech. 'I'm eternally grateful for your friendship. I'm going to miss you. Everything about you.'

The last part is said under his breath, like it slipped out of its own accord, and it cuts like broken crystal, digging deep into my skin.

'I feel the same.' My voice is raspy and alien. 'The past few months have been the best of my life.' My voice sounds so unnatural and strained, it's hard to keep it all in check as I'm suddenly questioning every decision I've ever made. 'I'll always be grateful you owned up to speaking English.' We share a laugh to hold back tears. 'But we knew this would end here, saying goodbye. Well, maybe not with you following me all the way to the airport.'

'I didn't expect any of this. Spending my winter with a woman like you. When you're home, I wish you happiness.'

'You too. I hope you get more time with Stamatis. Right, I can't delay anymore, I need to join this queue. You've already made me late enough this morning.' I nudge into his ribs a little and get a glowing smile returned to me.

Our morning together was worth missing the whole flight for, but people need me in England, and I can't escape my responsibilities any longer.

'I know, I know.' The smile lingers on his lips before it drifts away. 'Promise to message me when you're home safe.'

'I will.'

'If you ever need me, I'll be there. You know that, right? I owe you everything.'

'You owe me nothing.'

He shakes his head. 'Maybe I was wrong, maybe you don't know how incredible you are.' He tuts before continuing. 'Anyway, you have to come back, you need to meet Stamatis.'

'You know I will.'

Our lips come together one last time and I try to remember every kiss we've ever had, from the first right up to this one. It's an impossible task but one I'm happy to take on.

He no longer tastes like bonfires, not since he decided to cut back on cigarettes, now he has something to live for. Now he tastes like delicious bittersweet regret.

Our fingers stay knotted, tangled together like seaweed, until eventually there's no choice but to step away and break the bond.

I smile and mouth goodbye, leaving the lump in my throat to sink into my chest, where it sits like an anchor dragging me down.

I can't look back to see if he's there as I wind through the taped-off area where I have to wait to hand over my case.

As I get to the front, I give my passport, my suitcase, my life here in Greece.

I have to do this, I know that.

I know that we only really worked because here I was recovering and had time for personal freedom. But that isn't a long-term life. I'm too young to retire or spend my whole life sitting about. I was not born to sit indoors for the next forty or fifty years without a job or a role. And clearly I can't do anything other than be a barrister.

My heart pounds, throbbing in my ears. I'm being ripped in two in a way I never imagined possible.

With my passport back in hand, I head to the right to go straight through passport control and to find my gate.

Before rounding the corner to head to the next phase of my journey, I look back to the space where we said goodbye. There's a family there now, discussing what needs to be done and what line they need to join, I suspect. A man with long dark hair and a blonde woman linking his arm stare up at the screen as their two young children bury their noses in books.

He's gone. Helios is gone.

As I turn away, I catch sight of him, standing near the exit. He gives me one last signature nod goodbye and I swear I can hear the high-pitched scream of my heart fracturing behind my ribs.

Chapter 59

Alisha Harding is written in thick black letters on a handheld whiteboard. The plane was delayed, but at least my bag was first off the belt. It's such a relief to see my name there waiting for me. I'm exhausted. Thank goodness for Gigi organising everything for me.

I spent both flights, Kos to Athens then Athens to England due to it being out of season, flitting between regret for not owning up about my feelings for Helios and feeling anxious about the case ahead of me.

I already have a meeting booked with the solicitor. Gigi informed them of my return and organised a meeting for tomorrow morning.

'Ms Harding?' A tall man with thick golden hair in a topknot looks down at me as I approach him and the board with my name. He's smartly dressed in black jeans and a shirt.

'That's me.'

'I can take that for you.' He expertly takes my suitcase, wheeling it along between us as we walk. 'Did you have a nice trip?'

'Yes, very nice, thank you. Although it's colder here than in Greece. I wish I had a thicker coat with me.' I pull the tailored tweed blazer a little more closed.

'I can imagine.'

I think back to Nisyros with its marshmallow-white buildings with their perfect blue doors, one with Helios behind it. *Nice* doesn't seem the right word for the trip.

Helios told me he intends to sand his door down and give it a well overdue paint job at last. I hope to see it in its new state soon.

Just saying his name in my mind is enough to draw a longing from me like heat drawing out a splinter, only this is much more painful.

'This way.' We walk quite some distance away from the airport as the driver makes small talk. Gatwick is a reasonably large airport and just over an hour from my home in Kensington. I can't wait to get in the car and fall right asleep after the exhaustion of travel and my swirling mind.

'Here we are.' The man indicates a smart-looking black Mercedes people carrier with blacked-out windows.

'All this for little old me? Surely that's for a group of at *least* ten.'

'I had to drop off a hen party before picking you up. You will have your pick of seats.' He shoots me a warm smile before sliding the door open and letting me in.

Automatically, I go straight to the seat at the window with the table. The one facing backwards. Most people would avoid such a seat, but ever since I was a child, I've quite liked the sensation of travelling back to front. My grandparents had a banged-up Austin Montego seven-seater. Toby and I would always sit in the boot, staring at the drivers behind us. Toby would moan he felt sick within minutes, but I rather liked it.

I pull my phone from my Saint Laurent bag and write out a message to Helios.

> I'm now in the cab, although today it's more of a van! Say hello to Stamatis for me.

I want to say I miss him already, but I don't want to do anything that might draw him away from his son. It's not fair of me to give him that dilemma.

I add some kisses and hit send.

The driver jumps in the front seat and we head out of the airport at long last.

'Just to keep you informed, Ms Harding, there have been a few accidents on the motorway, so we're going to have to take some diversions to avoid getting in a standstill.'

'That's fine, I'm in no rush.'

It's not like there will be anyone there waiting for me.

Only Helios and Gigi know I'm on my way home. If I'd told Odina, I know Nancy would've organised a big fancy surprise party in my apartment that I just don't want to face.

A message pings on my phone. Of course it's Helios. We begin a little back and forth as I tell him about the people I was sitting near to on the plane, and he tells me about Stamatis.

It's dark out of the window as we turn into country lanes to avoid traffic.

It's hard to keep the smile off my face as I message Helios. He likes to say things he knows will make me laugh.

The van comes to a slow stop. I look up and over my shoulder to see if we're at any lights or traffic, but there's nothing. Only pine trees and hedges.

The side door slides open. A man in a ski mask jumps inside the vehicle, pulls my phone straight from my hands and throws it out of the door into the distance before snatching my handbag and ditching that too.

'Wha—?' is all I manage before the man and three others bundle into the van. It speeds away, leaving a dust cloud and my phone long behind us.

Chapter 60

I stay calm.

Outwardly. Which is, in fact, all that is important.

That's something I can be proud of, no matter how this ends.

Only a matter of months ago, I don't think I could have managed to keep my composure in a situation like this.

On the inside, it's a different story. It's taking all my strength not to shake and quiver like an autumn leaf about to drop, and my throat feels so dry that I could choke every time I attempt to swallow.

But I can't let them see any of that. I can't show them I feel weak. If they hadn't thrown my phone out, I'd have had some small hope of someone seeing where I was, but that's why they dumped it. I even have a tracker in my case, but it can only be tracked by my phone, and the one person who has the ability to see where I am has no reason to check on me.

My hands are strapped together with cable ties behind my back, painfully digging into my bony wrists with their stranglehold.

The man opposite me has placed a gun on the table but is yet to speak.

No one has spoken, me included.

All my concentration is going on my breath. It has to be steady. Calm. When I do choose to speak, I need to sound just right. I can't show the fear that's stamping down on my throat and making it want to close.

It's too dark to see where we might be going and it's hard to keep track of the left and right turns.

I wish I'd been facing the front. If I escape this, I will never ever face the back again. Not ever.

There are a million things I would do differently.

I do my best to collect my thoughts. I talk to people for a living, twist their words and change people's minds. I need to do something. Anything. If these are to be my final moments, I may as well try to understand why.

'May I ask, do you know who I am?' I begin.

The man opposite me begins to laugh before arrogantly tugging off his ski mask.

'Do you think we would be so stupid as to put this much effort into abducting someone random? I thought you were meant to be smart. You seem fucking stupid to me.' He laughs and wipes an imagined tear from his eye. 'I do, Alisha. I do know you. Do you know me?'

In all honestly, I'm not sure.

It's hard to concentrate properly with my heart pounding in my ears. There is something familiar in his square jaw and tight lips. His skin is clear and pale, much like his eyes, but his hair is as black as coal, shaved to a millimetre in length all around his head.

'You look familiar.'

A sneer wrinkles his nose as he scoffs.

'I should. You put my twin in prison last year. He was stabbed in jail and died a month later. And all for what? Sleeping with some prostitute?' he snarls.

He has to be talking about Karine's case. It's the only one I worked on last year. I can see it now. His brother was tanned, and his hair was longer. He was particularly strange. I couldn't stand having his gaze on me for even a moment. He took pleasure in people's discomfort and he struggled to hide it. He came from money and therefore thought he was exempt from trial, until he was put away for his crimes.

He wasn't like the others. He was the ringleader.

My eyes flick to the silver metal on the table, lit up in a ghoulish blue from the lights inside the Mercedes. I have to stay calm, even though I can feel the dripping of adrenaline and anxiety like raindrops crawling down my spine.

I tilt my chin up to give the air of confidence that I'm not feeling. At best, I'm feeling queasy. 'Thomas. Your brother was Thomas McConnel.'

His eyes turn to pinpricks. 'Don't say his name, bitch. It's not yours to say. Gag her.' He tosses his head towards one of the other men still masked. 'I don't want to hear another word until she's begging for her life, right before I end it.'

He picks up the gun and presses it to my forehead as another man rips off duct tape and slaps it hard against my lips.

I can't keep it all contained; my heart is beating so fast I'm sure they can all hear it trying desperately to make its own escape. I look into the darkness of rural roads and fill up with the concrete regret of leaving Helios for this.

In all the years of death threats and hate mail, I've never taken any of it all that seriously. I had one issue with threats from a stalker once before, but it was quickly shut down. I knew the risks of my job. That not everyone wants to find justice, but still, with all the possible futures I've been imagining for my life, I never once imagined it falling into this.

◆ ◆ ◆

Time passes in silence as the brother watches me like every blink costs him money he doesn't want to spend. Now and then he picks up the gun, checks it over, checks it's loaded, aims it at me with a smirk and mouths words at me like *soon* and *not yet*.

If I hadn't had Helios's example of a good man over the past few months, this would be the moment where I could so easily doubt them all. Enough anger burns in my gut that I'm sure if I do by some miracle survive this, I'll have an ulcer at the end of it.

Being gagged makes me truly defenceless. My words are my power and they've taken that from me.

I keep replaying videos I've watched demonstrating how to get out of cable ties but in none of them were people being watched with a gun at the ready. Even if I did manage to get them off, I've got nowhere to go. My only hope of escape is running when the vehicle stops.

But no one can outrun a bullet.

I close my eyes and all I see is Helios. I shouldn't be here. I should be there, with him.

Hours pass by as they avoid any major roads. They probably have it all carefully mapped out to avoid cameras and to take me to somewhere I'll never to be found. No body. No crime.

Thomas was calculating, so I shouldn't be surprised by any of this from his twin. He was trafficking women for years and getting away with it. If it wasn't for Karine, he'd still be doing it now.

I try to swallow but my throat is thick, and my body quakes a little harder with each passing second. I can't stop it anymore. It's not cold in here, they've got the heat on, but my hands are cold and numb from the ties and it's impossible not to shiver like I'm naked in the snow.

The van draws to a stop, and I fear my life is about to draw to a close.

I think of my mum, of Karine, of my family not even knowing I'm back in England because I was too selfish to tell them. Then there's Helios. Regret fills me like an overflowing cup. I'll never be able to tell him now that I love him. I've known it for too long and pressed it down, not wanting to admit it. Every time I close my eyes, it's him that I see.

I hold on to thoughts of him to comfort me, not knowing what will come next.

They pull me from the people carrier by my shoulders, out into the frozen night air. I do my best to resist, but with my hands behind my back and adult males versus my comparatively small frame, it's easy work for them.

It looks like an abandoned farm of sorts and smells like it too, with the stench of manure stinging my nostrils.

The headlights illuminate a derelict barn. Everything's overgrown, encasing us in a central driveway of mud and slop. My shoes stick one moment and I skid along the next, as they pull me in front of the van.

They leave me standing in the headlights, making me squint, unable to see what might happen next as they all plunge themselves into the shadows, moving around me like wolves.

The main man, Thomas's twin, begins to laugh from somewhere I can't see. My breathing spikes, it's hard to contain it. I want to run, but where would I go? They're everywhere, there's nothing I can do. My brain scrambles as I try to think my way out of this, but there's nothing.

This is it.

He begins to mock me, degrade me, etching out ugly pictures and even detailing things about Karine's case before getting angry and shouting his mouth off about his brother and what happened to him and how it's my fault. Wanting me to know exactly what he thinks of me.

He details what he will do as tears begin to fall from my cheeks and on to the tape over my lips.

My life doesn't flash before my eyes in the lights of the people carrier, only my times in Nisyros. Firstly with my mum and dad thirty years ago, then with Helios. Mostly with Helios.

It's the place where I've been the happiest in my life.

The times shared between our balconies sipping wine, then the feel of his skin and his lips touching mine.

I close my eyes and try to block out the voices hyping themselves up for the kill. This is either going to be his first murder, and he's mustering up the courage to go through with it, or he's like an orca toying with its prey before pulling it to pieces. Maybe both.

Even the sound of a helicopter overhead doesn't make him flinch. He laughs at my shaking, at my fear and my closed eyes as he tells me what he's going to do next, that he'll enjoy hurting me and where he'll bury me.

But I'm not here. I'm in Nisyros, holding a bunch of orange lilies, and Helios is smiling so much I can see those little dimples at the corners of his lips.

The voices change. The wind shifts. They all start shouting, calling. Not just *him*.

Maybe this is it? I do my best to go over and over my time with Helios but I can't shut the voices out.

It's not at me. Their shouts are not at me.

I squint open my eyes to see what's changed.

Another light beam floods the muddy drive.

Not from another car, but from the helicopter. Something is said over a speaker about *under arrest* and in the distance sirens begin to wail.

I raise my arms behind my back, chop them down and towards me as hard as I can to snap the cable ties, then drop to my knees in the mud, cover my head and curl into a ball of relief as the men scatter like marbles away from the light.

Chapter 61

'It was all because of Helios. If it wasn't for him . . .' Odina shrugs, unable to – or not wanting to – fill in the blank.

My entire family encases me in my hospital bed, filling the private room to the brim.

Although I'm outwardly fine, they wanted to keep me in for a few hours for observation after I gave my statement to the police. 'Helios might've been the catalyst, but without you having Auntie Alisha's location on your phone and knowing she had those tracker things in her suitcase, they would never have found her in time. Don't sell yourself short, kid. We could make a detective out of you yet!' Toby wraps his arm around his young niece and squeezes her.

Apparently, when I stopped midway through our texts, Helios was concerned, but gave me space to reply in case I'd fallen asleep or something. It was twenty minutes later, when he got a message from a local florist, who was apparently meant to hand-deliver some of my favourite lilies, informing him no one was home yet, that he decided he didn't want to *wait and see* if I was OK.

From what I gather, Odina and Nancy did the rest. Firstly contacting Gigi, who broke down saying they should call the police, then looking at where my phone was and getting the local police to look for it. I hadn't even considered the suitcase tracker to be useful in finding me. It can only be tracked using the app on my phone. Luckily for me, Odina even knows the passcode for my phone and remembered me buying the tracker. Without our close relationship, I don't think I'd have been saved in time.

'It was a team effort,' Odina deflects, leaning her head on her uncle, who is still in his flannel pyjamas under his coat. 'If Mum and Dad didn't know half of London, then the police might not have responded as quickly as they did.'

It's true that I've seen the chief of police at more than one of Nancy's charity events and between them, they know all the right people.

'Is Gigi still in for questioning?' Pop asks no one in particular from the worn blue leather chair to my left.

'It's not her fault,' I pipe up from under the hospital sheet before anyone else has the chance to answer. 'If they were threatening her, it's not her fault. She has children. She was scared.'

'Do you know whether she made up those files about Jett, or did they?' Augustin folds his arms over his broad chest. He's used to being up at silly hours for work, so this late hour doesn't seem to be an issue for him in the least. He's assumed the sensible big brother role, in the way he always has.

Poor Jett, the whole thing was fabricated to lure me back from Greece. They knew the shock of someone who was such a supporter of women's rights grooming young girls would be a strong and likely catalyst to get me back in London.

'I don't know. It doesn't matter who falsified the papers Gigi sent to me. I don't blame her. She must've been terrified. She wouldn't have done this otherwise.'

'*You* must've been terrified. I bet your whole life flashed before your eyes,' Odina says with a haunting intensity.

'I was,' I whisper, and look down at my fiddling fingers pinching at the thin cotton sheet resting over my lap. 'But more than anything, I'm just really, really angry. Angry for me, angry for Gigi . . . angry I fell for it, angry I came home early. Angry about all of it.'

I don't want to open up to any other emotion. Not yet. I can't.

I don't want to vocalise the tidal wave of terror that was flowing at an alarming rate through my veins. If it wasn't for my lifetime of training to have a calm exterior in court, I don't know what I'd have been like.

The police had to scrape me up off the dirt in a puddle of my own tears when I allowed myself to let some of it out. Too weak to stand, too deep in shock to think straight. Now I can only feel the tingling pins and needles of pure anger.

In many ways I was lucky. Very lucky.

They could've done anything to me, and they didn't. My only wounds are on my wrists, minor cuts from the cable ties, that's all.

Although they wanted to wreak some sort of vengeance on me, in the time they had hold of me they could have done a lot worse than they did. I think they thought they had all the time in the world to take me to the middle of nowhere and get rid of me.

I do my best to push away the thoughts of what happened and let the seething, volcanic anger settle into my bones for the fight that will one day send them to prison.

It's strange, though. I *was* terrified. Adrenaline coursed around my veins, but my life didn't flash before my eyes in a normal sense.

All I kept coming back to was what I *hadn't* done in life, not all the things I had. My time in Nisyros was all my mind wanted to show me, and all that did was wrap me up in regret.

I should never have left.

'Miss Harding?' A doctor pops her head around the door of my room with the detective inspector in charge of my case just behind her shoulder. 'Can we come in?'

'Of course.' I shuffle a little higher in the bed and my family splits in two to allow them the space to step into the mint-green room.

I recognise the detective, but not just from today. From a case in the past, perhaps? She's sleek, smart and doesn't take anything from anyone. Layla, I'm sure her name is Layla.

'From our perspective,' the doctor begins, 'we're happy to discharge you, but we don't think you should be alone.'

'She's coming home with us,' Odina announces.

'Good,' the inspector joins in. 'For our part, we will be in touch soon. We've got your mobile number and your statement. We only ask that you don't leave the country, certainly not without informing us. We want to make sure this is not an ongoing threat. You said you've had death threats before?'

'It's a hazard of the job. I don't know many barristers or solicitors who haven't had some sort of threat or hate mail. One or two have been attacked or had dreadful things sent in the post. I've never taken many all that seriously. But I didn't know I was under threat this time.'

'And you're sure there was no warning or threat leading up to the abduction?'

'No, but I haven't been home in almost six months. I assume that's why they had to threaten Gigi, because they couldn't find me.'

The detective nods. 'We would like to take the opportunity to have a look through your post, in case we can find anything relevant to the case. If you're happy with that, Ms Harding?'

'Of course. But Gigi was the one in charge of checking my mailbox at home. She would be the one to speak to.'

The detective's lips form a thin line and her brows knit together a little more.

'In that case, I'll speak to her about it too.'

Sliding her hand into the front pocket of her tailored trousers, she pulls out a card and passes it to me. 'Thank you, Ms Harding. If you need me, this is my direct number. If you need *anything*, call it. Day or night. If you see anything suspicious, anything. If not, I'll be in touch very soon to follow up.' She snatches a breath. 'I've followed your work for many years, Ms Harding. We need more women like you in the world.'

'Thank you, that's very kind of you to say.'

I glance down at the card in my fingers. I was right. Her name *is* Layla.

'You can leave when you're ready. Would you like a police escort?'

'No, no. I'm sure it'll be fine. Thank you for your time. Both of you.'

They nod as my family chimes in with thanks before the two women exit the room.

'Time to go home,' I announce with a grin that doesn't feel like it belongs.

'Time to come to *our* home.' Nancy folds her arms over her chest, knowing me all too well. God, I wish I knew how that woman's hair always looks like a flowing dream, even in the middle of the night. I must look utterly crumpled.

I lower my voice with a steely determination. 'I'm not putting Odina or you at risk. I can go home.'

'No, you are not! Weren't you listening? *You're not allowed*,' Odina all but squeaks, stamping her heel to the floor.

'She can stay with me,' Pop announces. 'You *are* coming home. To the family home with me.'

'Fine.'

I don't have the energy for another fight tonight.

◆ ◆ ◆

'Pop, can we nip to mine, please? I just want to check on things and grab some clothes. You know, seeing as all my things from my suitcase were taken as evidence. Is that OK?'

Pop glances over at me from the driver's seat. It's almost 3 a.m. but I'm still wide awake after everything that's happened.

'I'm not sure that's a good idea?'

'Come on, my building is safe. You know it is. I have alarms, cameras, everything. They took me to the middle of nowhere for a reason. My apartment is the opposite of the middle of nowhere.'

Pop hesitates, tapping his fingers on the wheel as he thinks it over. 'All right, but I'm coming up with you.'

'Pop . . . no. Let me have five minutes. That's all I'm asking.'

I can see the tension in his jaw in the lights of London, even though it's the middle of the night. His grey hair looks a mess, which is never the case. Poor Pop, he didn't need this.

I reach over and squeeze his arm gently. 'I'm fine, I promise.'

It's not entirely factual, but I could be a whole lot worse.

It's only five minutes before Pop is pulling into the parking for my building. There's no allocated space for him, as I only pay for one, so he'll have to linger in limbo while he waits for me.

'I'll be quick, I swear.'

Before he can protest, my seat belt is undone and I'm out of the car and running for my elevator.

In the small lobby are some flowers. I scoop them up off the floor.

Orange lilies with a note:

> *Welcome back to London, Alisha. I would say welcome home, but I'll save that for when you're back in Nisyros. H*

For the first time since hearing police sirens and seeing the light from the helicopter like an angel shooting a beam of hope down at me, I let everything in.

Tears burn my cheeks as I fall into my elevator and scan my pass to get to my home.

The doors close to the lift, but the floodgates open inside me and I collapse to the floor in a heap, wishing Helios was here to hold me together.

Chapter 62

With trembling hands I open my junk drawer in the kitchen and rake about for my old phone, the one I forgot to give away for recycling.

Batteries, instructions to appliances I don't own anymore, cookie cutters, odd stamps, all fill the drawer. I push them from one side to the other until I find the phone and turn it on. I know I left it with at least fifty per cent battery to preserve the phone.

It only takes a moment to be ready.

Insert Sim Card is there on the screen in bold. How could I not have thought of that?

I throw it at my sofa all the way from the kitchen and screech. I just wanted to call Helios in peace, without anyone else there to hear me. Odina kindly wrote his number on a scrap of paper for me, but I have no way of calling him.

'Wait,' I say to no one.

Marching over to my central living area, I pick up the phone, which is luckily unscathed from my outburst.

Clearing the screen of the Insert Sim Card warning, I go to WhatsApp. It's still installed and linked to an old phone number. I can call him with my Wi-Fi.

Pulling the scrap of paper from the pocket of my jacket, I quickly add Helios's number and begin to call.

The droning tone seems to go forever. It's the middle of the night there too. Maybe he's sleeping.

'Hello? Who is this?'

'Helios?'

'Alisha? Thank God. Are you all right? I've been so worried. Odina said you might call me. I've been sitting up waiting for you, just in case. What actually happened?' His voice is laced with the tones of fear. I know them all too well.

'I, I was abducted. The whole case was just a ruse to get me home. If you hadn't told Odina to look where I was . . .' The shiny metal gun flashes behind my eyes. I swallow back the lump in my throat. 'Who knows what would've happened. You saved my life.'

I begin to sob, pinching the bridge of my nose to hold it back, but it doesn't work.

'I wish I was there to hold you.' Helios's voice is like gravel in my ear.

'Me too.' I swallow, but my voice is thick and trembling. 'Helios, when I was there with a gun pointing at me, all I had was regret.'

'You're safe now, that's all that matters.'

'I need to say this.' I lightly sniff, wiping away tears with my sleeve. 'It didn't matter, all the things I had done, because there was one thing I *hadn't* done and the reason I hadn't is the right reason but . . . I don't want to lie to you anymore.'

'OK . . .'

'I think, I . . .'

As I say *I love you*, he says *I love you* too.

We both laugh and cry into our phones.

A loud ringing makes my chest feel like I've been electrocuted. Peeling myself up off the floor, I scuttle towards the elevator monitor and the person buzzing in.

'Pop is buzzing to come up,' I splutter. 'Can we talk properly tomorrow? I just had to tell you the truth.'

'We will talk more than tomorrow. I love you too, Alisha. I didn't want you to feel like you had to stay here—'

'And I didn't want to get between you and Stamatis.'

'I wouldn't have Stamatis in my life if it wasn't for you. I'm glad your pop is there. Are you staying with him tonight?'

'Yes, there was no way I was allowed to be alone.'

'Good. Please message me. I love you.'

'I will. I love you too.'

I hang up the phone and go to the monitor to let my pop up. He's pacing and looks distraught that I've already taken longer than my allocated five minutes.

I push the talk button. 'I'm fine, come up or I'll be down in a minute.'

'Thank God. I'll wait here then. Please, hurry up.'

I cover my face with both my hands. I have no idea what's going to happen next, but what I do know is, life can change in a second, and I'm going to do everything I can to spend more time with those I love.

That's what's *really* important, after all.

Chapter 63

July 2026

My heart races and my hands tingle with sweat. It's not just the heatwave throbbing over the boat burning my back. It's the anticipation of him.

My nerves seem almost childish. It's not like we haven't spoken. He knows I'm on my way to him.

My suitcase is smaller than the last time I was here. My house in Nisyros is still full of things I left behind. Full of memories I didn't want to displace. The past few months have felt more like two years.

I told Helios not to come and get me at the airport. This will be the first time since the last time I got off an aeroplane. After everything that happened, I needed to take a taxi and have it end normally. I'm sure Odina is tracking my every move still. Quietly knowing that is enough to make me feel safe.

I knew Helios wouldn't listen, though, so I kept my flight information to myself, just telling him I'd be arriving this week. He won't be there at the harbour waiting, like he wasn't at the airport. He'll be . . . somewhere. Somewhere on this beautiful island I called home for a short time in my life.

The landscape looks unchanged, like I've been away fifteen minutes. Nisyros protrudes out of the sea; volcanic slopes grow out in striations with puffy, shimmering olive trees rising up with it. At the bottom, it's edged in pure-white houses that look like lace sewn on, decorating its edge. The biggest difference is the weather. Even in the shade, it's baking hot in July. I'm not sure how I'll cope without air conditioning now.

The boat vibrates and groans as we slow down, ready to come into port. There are a few people lingering here and there on the shore. The boat is full, so we'll be the ones to overcrowd the port of Mandraki, not the local population, who are smart enough to stay out of this heat or are busy working.

I didn't see this side of things when I arrived in September last year. People still came across, and there were busy days, but this boat has very little space left on it, if any.

The sea air whips around and I close my eyes to remember those long walks up to the fort to look out to sea, or on the beaches, and the nights sitting with Helios quietly on the balcony or wrapped in my arms.

I've missed him more than I thought I could miss anyone.

I take in a deep lungful of fresh salty air and hold it for a beat before slowly releasing it through my teeth. A lot has changed since my time here last year. I've changed. I've gained a new perspective.

When I arrived here last time, I was so broken up about Karine I thought I wouldn't be able to function as a barrister again, that my whole life had been wasted on an unrealistic idea. Now, with Nancy's help, I've set up a fund in Karine's name. It's for up-and-coming female journalists to follow stories they can't always get funding for, and another fund for all undercover journalists in trouble after trauma experienced at work. Nancy was more than happy to hold some rather beautiful events in

Karine's name, and a lot of money has already been raised. We've already started helping people.

I've been focusing on that while the case against my abductors is being brought forward. I've only dared to come away for two weeks now, before proceedings start. The idiots have tried to plead not guilty. Their last act of defiance, which means I'll have to be up in court as a witness, a victim. It'll be strange, but I'm strong enough now. Thanks to Helios and my family.

As the boat comes into port, people quickly push forwards to disembark, not wanting to miss a moment of their handful of hours visiting this magical place.

I let them push.

I step back, waiting on the boat. I already knowing my way through the winding streets lined with perfect cobalt doors and dotted with trees and brightly coloured flowers. Most of these people will come here once in their life. For a while there, I thought perhaps it would be the same for me. As I grew up, I wondered when I'd make time to return.

Dragging my suitcase alongside me at the back of the crowd, I'm grateful when a Greek man working on the boat steps forward and takes it off me, placing it safely on the concrete of the port.

'You're not for the volcano? I've seen you before?'

'Correct. I have a home here.'

'You're back for good?'

'Sadly not.'

'Maybe one day.' He smiles with his weathered eyes and goes to help someone else, who's asking which coach they need to get on for their journey to Stefanos Crater, deep in the heart of the island.

I take a step to the left, away from the crowd edging towards the coaches on the right or the taverna at the front of the harbour.

There he is.

Under one of the brightly coloured parasols, holding, but not drinking, an espresso. Helios. He's said to me that losing his daughter aged him, then the fear of losing me aged him again, giving him more grey at the temples.

To me, he looks magnificent. I want to be close enough to see those dimples in the corners of his lips when he's trying to hide a smile, and the flecks of light in his dark eyes.

He freezes for a moment before putting his drink on the table and abruptly pushing his chair back.

It feels impossible for him to be here in the flesh, and yet totally natural.

I make out his words from a distance – 'At last' – as the tension falls away from his bones.

He all but jogs towards me.

'How did you know I'd arrive today?' I call out to him.

'I didn't. I've been sitting here every day this week waiting for the ferry, hoping you'd be on it. Typical you to string me along and arrive on a Thursday. Always making me wait.'

'I'm so sorry,' I laugh, and leave my suitcase behind, taking steps to split the difference between us.

As we reach each other, we collide with abandon. It's so simple and yet so very complex. It's not the kiss of two friends who have missed one another, it's the sort of kiss people give when they truly believed they were never going to see their love again, and they've found them at long last. Helios pulls me to his chest and I take fistfuls of his cotton shirt to know that he's real.

Our foreheads rest together as Helios's mouth slips into a contented smile and he says at long last, 'Welcome home, Alisha.'

Chapter 64

'I want to say thank you, for helping my father.' Stamatis speaks slowly but well.

He looks like a younger version of Helios, only with very curly hair, skin a shade or two cooler, a thicker Greek accent and round glasses sitting pride of place on the bridge of his nose at all times.

'He helped me first and then saved my life. I assume he told you about Odina and his big rescue operation with her, too?'

Stamatis looks from me to his dad. Helios's back is to us as he carries on cooking in my kitchen. Nothing changes.

'No? I knew about the story with the men, but no rescue?'

'Really?' I launch into the story of how Helios had to own up to speaking English to get me in contact with my niece.

Stamatis looks genuinely surprised, although mostly at his father for hiding his linguistic prowess, and laughs in all the right places as I tell the tale. Helios joins in here and there but lets me take the lead.

When the food is ready, we all sit together, still chattering away. This is my very first time meeting Stamatis, and it's going better than I could've hoped. I've been here a week already, monopolising Helios's time.

I have caught up with Calliope too, of course. I surprised her by coming along to one of her meditation sessions. I even got to meet her friend Dimitri with his healing hands, and he really *was* very interesting. The session was so popular, there wasn't even a yoga mat spare for me to sit on! Which meant Calliope insisting I sit on hers. It was nice to play a very small part in her success as a thank-you for all those cooking lessons.

'And what about you, Stamatis? I know you have an aptitude for languages like your dad, but is that something you want to use?'

Stamatis looks at his hands on the table, splaying out his fingers in thought.

Helios smiles at me. Every time he does, warmth spreads through my body and a tingly feeling tickles my skin.

Stamatis looks up at me through his glasses with a similar intensity I've seen on Helios. 'I want to do something to honour my sister.'

'She would want you to live your life for *you*, not for her,' Helios says in a slightly lowered voice.

'I know, but . . . she wanted to go to university and see the world . . . She always has so much energy.'

'Had,' Helios quietly corrects. 'She *had* so much energy.'

'She was like you, helping people and animals.'

Almost on cue, one of the many cats rubs around my legs. It's been nice seeing them again over the past week.

'So you think you might want to help people? Or animals?'

'Maybe. I'm going to start by studying English, if I get all the grades I need. After that, maybe I can decide what to do with it. I'm good at English, Baba has helped me.'

'Pfft.' Helios rolls his eyes.

'You have.' Stamatis looks a little put out by his father's reaction. 'I just do not know what will come after.'

'You'll figure it out.' I want to ask what his mum thinks, but I'm not sure where the line is so I keep the question to myself. 'You're still young. It will all fall into place, if and when it's meant to.'

Helios slides out of the chair next to Stamatis, but his eyes linger on me. I can't make out his expression. One of his eyebrows is perhaps a touch lowered . . . there's something there.

Then he mouths the words, 'Thank you.'

'And you? I think Baba wants you to live on Nisyros again. Do you think you will?'

I lean my chin on my hands and look up at Helios. 'Maybe. Maybe one day I'll be lucky enough for this to be my real life.'

'Alisha *mou*, every moment is your *real life*. You can't escape it.'

'Good. I don't think I'd want to.'

I *do* want to be with him though. With Helios. But we both know it's not on the cards just yet. Not full time. Not waking up next to each other and drinking wine on balconies.

We've had to live apart, and we've spoken every day and made it through. I don't know how long it'll have to continue like this, but for now, it's just the way it is. I can't take him away from his son, not after everything. We have our roles to play, for now at least, but maybe one day it'll be different.

I've lived a life without romantic love, and now I'm lucky enough to believe in *the one*. Which is something I never saw for myself. But now I see it, I know it, I feel it and it doesn't matter where we are in the world, I know it won't change how we feel about one another.

Chapter 65

28 October 2026

When I close my eyes, I'm always there in Nisyros, walking along the path by the olive groves up to the fortified walls to have a picnic with Helios under the warmth of the sun. The last few times I've done a bit better than the cucumber sandwiches of our first picnic, at least.

I've been away from the warmth of Nisyros for two months and it feels like a lifetime. But the countdown is on now. Helios will arrive in London in a week and I can't wait to have him with me.

I've stayed in London for the trial. It's strange to be the victim, not the barrister in a wig. But I wanted to see this through. I've also started supporting other people's cases. I'm still not ready to get back in court quite yet, though.

When I eventually arrive home, there's a bunch of orange lilies waiting for me next to the lift. I pick them up, knowing who they're from, but not knowing today's reason.

The card reads, *For the first anniversary of a perfect first kiss. H*

I hate how much I miss him.

I send him a text:

Happy Oxi Day

What are you up to? H

Not much, I'm going out to meet Odina soon.

Sounds like a good Friday. H

Exactly

I went to visit Stamatis at his university halls today

You kept that quiet! So you're in Athens, right?

I run about my apartment, putting on the outfit I'd left out, knowing it was going to be a quick change this evening after work.

I grab my keys off the counter and drop them in my handbag before heading back over to my lift. I'm already running two minutes behind and I hate to be late, particularly for Odina. I don't like leaving her waiting around on the street for me.

She asked me to meet her at a bar not far from mine. She leaves for a gap year travelling around Greece with Guy in a week and this is our goodbye meal before her farewell party. I'll miss them both. Guy's actually a decent sort. Enough to make me believe we can all make mistakes and redeem ourselves. Much like Helios and his acting dumb around speaking English, only to be my perfect man.

As I slip into my lift, I check my phone. No message back yet, only the ellipses of a message soon to arrive from Helios. It doesn't usually take him twenty minutes to reply, but if he is in Athens, I suppose he's distracted.

I drop my phone in the pocket of my backless dress and check my watch for the fourth time.

Two minutes past eight.

In my heels, I march down the street. I've always said to Odina, never wear shoes you can't run in. I could run in these, at a push, but I really don't want to have to.

I still find it strange to meet her in a bar since she turned eighteen. After all the fuss she made about wanting to have a drink with me, she's already decided she doesn't drink and hates to lose control. I respect her for it and know she's a cheap date, sticking to mocktails instead.

My road is reasonably quiet, but it's not long before I'm on a busy thoroughfare, weaving past women and men in suits or joggers with AirPods and handbag dogs keeping to heel as we all make our way around the grey streets of London.

'Your building looks like a hotel,' booms a voice behind me.

It's enough to make my feet stutter like mistimed notes on a piano. I turn on my heels and see him there, smug as anything.

'It looks like you live in a hotel.' Helios repeats his idea now I'm facing him.

He looks out of place here, like a lost teddy waiting to be found. Everyone else moves with purpose while he looks at me like I'm the only one here, like a rock in a river of people. I've never seen him in such a smart shirt before, slim cut and the palest marine blue, paired with his good jeans and a smart jacket.

I don't ask him why he's here or even say hello. I tilt my head and begin like this is the middle, because maybe it is.

'Yeah, it does. But you've got the holiday location. You know you've said that before, right? About my place.'

'Have I?' Helios takes a step towards me as people flow by us like the cold sea in winter.

'Twice, on FaceTime.'

'Must be true then.'

'Must be.'

'You look good. You smell good too.' Helios's hands slip round my waist, under my jacket, and find my bare back to rest on.

'How are you here? I can't believe you're real.' My fingers run along his freshly shaved cheek as I search his dark eyes for answers. 'You said you were with Stamatis?'

'I was. Now I'd like to take you to dinner.'

'I don't understand, and I'm late to meet Odina.' I take a step away from him and grab his hand to pull him along. 'Come with me. I know she'd love to see you.'

'You're not late. She isn't there.'

'What? Where is she?'

'I don't know, maybe at home? I asked her to get you out of the house. How do you surprise someone who lives in an apartment in London with a video telecom and a private lift? You can't just knock on the door. This was the best I could do.'

I shake my head in disbelief.

We haven't seen each other in the flesh since July. Helios was doing his best to support his son around his translation work, and I've been prepping for court and setting up the charitable funds.

I didn't want to push Helios to visit me. All his money goes towards anything Stamatis or Hannah need and I didn't want to put pressure on him when I have no idea about his financial situation.

To have him here, in my home city, for the very first time, seems like I've slipped into another dimension.

We begin walking along slowly, hand in hand. I do my best to keep my eyes on him to check he is real and stop him from vanishing.

'You said you were with Stamatis?'

'I was. What I didn't mention was his first choice was to come to England to study English, like his old man. He's settled in and I'm here to visit him.'

I shake his hand a little.

'You lied to me about Athens.'

'No, I let you assume.'

I narrow my eyes on him and squeeze his hand, knowing this was his way of surprising me but still annoyed about his fibbing.

'This is so exciting, does that mean you'll be visiting more?' I feel like a teenager, giddy, wishing I could control myself and seem cool but completely unable to hide how I feel all of a sudden. 'Where are you staying tonight?'

Helios presses his lips together and shrugs. 'Might check into somewhere but I was hoping . . .'

I begin to laugh and nudge into him. We both know he'll be staying with me.

'Yes, you're staying with me.' I grin up at him.

'With Stamatis here, I have no reason to rush back to Nisyros. Even with Brexit I can stay here for six months, more with a visa . . .'

I stop in the street, making a tall man in high-tops nearly trip over us.

I step round to stand in front of Helios and look into those beautiful ebony eyes of his, with the little flecks of light I love to fall into.

'You're staying?'

'*Can* I stay?'

'Of course you can. I want you to. I'd love that so much.'

'Well, that's lucky, because I love *you* so much. Life is too short and there's only two people on this earth I want to spend all my time with. And you're one of them. I know that this might sometimes have to be long distance, but if the last year has taught me anything, it's that we could make that work, if we had to. But I'd rather be near you.'

His words swirl around me.

I've never felt the weight of this feeling before, how my chest feels like it's been filled with water when he's gone and bright light when he's near, and now he's here with me and I don't want that to change. Ever.

'I love you too. And I was going to tell you, since 2024, UK lawyers have been able to practise UK law in Greece again. I might be able to either work remotely there or give advice to people who need to know about UK laws and legislation. It means I could take months away at a time and still be helping people.'

Helios begins to chuckle. 'So hopefully we don't have to do long distance after all.'

I grab his shirt and pull him into a deeply passionate kiss, only to quickly pull away.

'What about the cats?'

A half-smile lifts Helios's face. 'Don't worry, I hadn't forgotten the cats. I thought we could send for Cloud, Luna and Soleil to come and live here? Calliope has agreed to put food outside your door for any of the other strays that need it. She did roll her eyes and tut at least seven times though.'

'Thank you. I love you so much.'

I slide my hand over his clean-shaven cheek, nothing like the stubbled wreck I met last year. We were both so broken back then.

Our lips meet and I never want to stop kissing him. Someone in the street says *get a room* and some teenagers pass comments as they weave around us.

I fell in love with my best friend, and at last we can be together in both of our worlds.

ACKNOWLEDGEMENTS

To write an acknowledgement is always a strangely stressful thing. I'm always worried I've forgotten someone, all while already being nervous about the book itself. I often remember an idea I had for it the day it's published (typical). Anyway, cross those fingers I remember all the lovely people involved!!

Thank you to Victoria and Lindsey, our trio in edits has been such a comfortable and lovely thing. I know I had a mild five-minute meltdown at the start of this one, but as usual you were both bang on with your comments and I'm glad I made those shifts and switches to make the novel stronger. I still can't believe it's the last one for us as a three, but Victoria, I wish you luck in your new job (not so new by the time this is out!!).

Thank you to my new editor, Bekah, who pitched me eight titles for this book during our very first meeting. (At that point, the book was nicknamed only 'Balconies'.) I loved them all but *Between Greek Balconies* is so perfect and I'm grateful for your insight!

Thank you to Jenni, my copy editor, who always comes in and cleans up any mess as she goes and gives those all-important last details.

Thank you to all the proofreaders, cold readers and Greek native readers who look over my manuscripts for that authenticity and detail. It's such an important part of the process!

Thank you to everyone working hard on my books!! Designers and typesetters, marketing teams – everyone!! I love my job and without everyone getting it right at each step of the way, I wouldn't be lucky enough to call this my job!

ABOUT THE AUTHOR

Photo © 2023 by Samuel Thomas

Francesca Catlow writes bestselling fiction filled with passionate love stories that feature flawed, and sometimes broken, characters as they face a crossroads in their life. She often explores heartbreaking themes while also whisking readers off to beautiful locations.

Francesca loves to travel. Born and raised in the heart of Suffolk, England, she has travelled extensively in Europe with her French husband and, more recently, their two children. In 2024 she relocated to France where she spends her days dreaming up stories and her evenings sitting in her garden relaxing with her family.

In 2023 Francesca was a finalist for the prestigious Kindle Storyteller Award, and was nominated for an Innovation Award for her work with libraries in Suffolk.

Francesca loves to hear from her readers – if you would like to contact her, you can do so on her social pages, or subscribe to her newsletter.

To stay up to date, and for free content, please visit https://francescacatlow.co.uk/subscribe

Facebook: @francescacatlowofficial

Instagram: @francescacatlowofficial

X: @francescacatlow

TikTok: @francescacatlow

For trigger warnings, visit: francescacatlow.co.uk/trigger-warnings/

Follow the Author on Amazon

If you enjoyed this book, follow Francesca Catlow on Amazon to be notified when the author releases a new book!

To do this, please follow these instructions:

Desktop:

1) Search for the author's name on Amazon or in the Amazon App.
2) Click on the author's name to arrive on their Amazon page.
3) Click the 'Follow' button.

Mobile and Tablet:

1) Search for the author's name on Amazon or in the Amazon App.
2) Click on one of the author's books.
3) Click on the author's name to arrive on their Amazon page.
4) Click the 'Follow' button.

Kindle eReader and Kindle App:

If you enjoyed this book on a Kindle eReader or in the Kindle App, you will find the author's 'Follow' button after the last page.